Amos Ferguson

Bible poem or Versified Scripture in Rhyme

Amos Ferguson

Bible poem or Versified Scripture in Rhyme

ISBN/EAN: 9783337270292

Printed in Europe, USA, Canada, Australia, Japan

Cover: Foto ©Andreas Hilbeck / pixelio.de

More available books at **www.hansebooks.com**

BIBLE POEM,

OR

VERSIFIED SCRIPTURE IN RHYME,

CONTAINING THE BOOKS OF

Genesis, Solomon's Songs, Matthew, and some others.

BY

AMOS J. FERGUSON.

ALSO, POEMS ON THE

PIONEER AND HIS DAUGHTER,

OR, THE LADY OF THE FOREST ;

ELRIC AND EARL, an Allegory; and the LOST BOY.

BY

MRS. A. J. FERGUSON.

JAMESTOWN, N. Y.:
JOURNAL PRINTING ESTABLISHMENT
1883.

PREFACE.

In presenting this work for the perusal and consideration of the public, a respect for the inquiries of men requires that I render my reasons for so doing. Seeing that a vast amount of poetry (as they call it) is brought before the public view, founded on mere earthly trifles and things only of a day exciting thoughtless levity, I felt impressed to make a Bible Poem, as I thought that Book to be the most valuable revelation in the world. I feel that its immortal and most holy sentiments ought to be embalmed in holy song in the minds and hearts of mankind forever. This is my object in presenting these stanzas to the public. I have read a verse of scripture at a time, prayerfully waiting till it should be formed in my mind in metre and rhyme and after this manner I have written these lines as they came to me. I do not claim that they are faultless. Pope says,

" Who e'er expects a faultless piece to see,
Expects what never was, and what will never be."

I have halted many times in this work, but as many times have I been encouraged to proceed with it. And taking it up again, the passages which seemed most difficult have become clear and easy of composition. Its aim is to aid the mind in retaining a firm hold upon the Holy Scriptures, and I offer it for the cheer and consolation of every Christian household whose members shall delight in making melody in their hearts and in singing aloud the Holy Word of God.

AMOS J. FERGUSON.

Jamestown, N. Y., July, 1883.

GENESIS.

1 O, Spirit, Eternal, Divine, ever pure,
Which prompteth mankind in all good to endure,
Inspire Thou my heart with Thy most holy flame,
To sing to God's glory, His Word, Works and Fame.

2 God in the beginning made heaven and earth.
The earth had no form and was void at the first,
When darkness upon the great deep did behoove
The Spirit of God on the waters to move.

3 Then God said, "let light be," which instantly came,
Through Earth's nightly region it flashed o'er the main.
God maketh the darkness, and light he creates,
And doeth his pleasure in all things he makes.

4 God said, "light is good," for its radiance adorns
All works of creation with brilliance and morn.
He called the light "day," and the darkness called "night,"
And evening and morn were the first day and right.

5 God said, "let a firmament be amid Heaven,
To raise vaporous waters from Earth be it given;
To form them in clouds and divide from the main,
And waft round Earth's region, to shower it with rain."

6 Then God made a firmament, which did divide
The waters above from the floods of the tide.
So God called the firmament "Heaven," and did say,
The evening and morning make the second day.

7 Then God said, "let waters be gathered in one,
Let dry land appear," and behold it was done—
As Earth's cooling shrinkage pressed fires from their sleep,
They lifted vast continents up from the deep.

8 Whose waters retiring, left realms of dry land
For subsequent Edens, for beast, bird and man.
Then cold north-west hurricanes swept earth's domain
And frosted her regions and bound in ice chains.

9   Then thundering glaciers plowed down mountain's side,
And huge floundering ice-bergs sowed rocks in the tide ;
Then isles were uplifted by earth's inward throes,
And tall mounts were reared to perpetual snows.

10   Then God said "let Earth bring forth grass, herb and seed,
And trees yielding fruit of its kind," as was need.
So Earth brought forth grass, herb and seed of its kind,
And trees yielded fruit, as the Maker designed.

11   God called dry land " earth," and the waters called " seas,"
Thus far things were made, and they did him well please.
He said all was good, and the eve and the morn
Dispersed the third day of the Creation's dawn.

12   Then God said, "let lights in the firmament shine,
Dividing the day from the night, and for signs,
For seasons, for days and for years, let them be,
For lights from the heavens, on earth and on sea."

13   God made two great lights, ruling Earth's day and night,
The stars he set also, in heaven so bright.
To part light from darkness, bright radiant they stood,
And evening and morn were the fourth day and good.

14   God said, " let the waters bring creatures that move,
And fowls that may fly in the heavens above."
He made the great whales and all creatures of flood,
Winged fowls of each kind, and He said " it was good."

15   So God made all creatures, each after their kind,
That each to its own sort should only incline,
And blest them to increase in sea and on earth,
When came the fifth day of the Creation's birth.

16   When God had made cattle and beasts of each kind,
And all things that creep on the earth that we find.
He said, " Let us make a new being called man,
Of will power and knowledge to keep a command.

17   For I will make man in My image, the best,
With high God-like powers to obey or transgress.
But I will be mindful of man as My child,
And give him My Spirit, to lead him from guile.

18   No power can subdue, or confine or control,
Or force 'gainst its will, the will-power of man's soul,
For which I will call him to judgment to come,
For deeds good or bad in the flesh he hath done.

19   If man cannot sin, then he cannot obey;
      Nor could I regard, though he curse or should pray,
      Who cannot be false, they can never be true.
      Nor can I reward them for aught they should do.

20   No sin can defile, or obedienc keep clean,
      A soul with no power to be good or be mean.
      No blame can exist where no choice doth abide,
      Nor righteousness be, where no free will decides."

21   So God made mankind in His image of love,
      And said, " multiply, and subdue and improve,
      And keep my commands, since none else can I bless
      With joys of My love and eternity's rest.

22   Lest man fall in sin, and his guilt ever stain,
      I ordain a lamb for his sacrifice slain,
      That all who repent and shall do My command,
      May wash their robes white in the blood of that lamb."

23   Thus Heavens, Earth and Hosts were all finished and made,
      And called very good, when God rested and said,
      I give man and beast herb and fruit for their meat,
      When sixth day, and age, made creation complete.

CHAPTER II.

1   Blest Heaven inspire, and my spirit incline,
      To sing of God's glory and works most divine ;
      How He on the great seventh day made a rest,
      And ending His work, made that day ever blest,

2   O, ever blest rest, sanctified from above,
      In which all shall enter who seek for God's love,
      Let not unbelief rob thy soul of that rest,
      And hinder thee entering to be ever blest.

3   My song now begins back to third day of earth,
      When things were first made at the Creation's birth.
      When God had not caused it to rain on the ground—
      To till and subdue Earth no man was yet found.

4   The Lord God formed man of the mould and the dust,
      And breathed in his nostrils his soul's life at first;
      And man then became as a God-living soul,
      With high powers of will, which man only controls.

5   God planted a garden in Eden's domain,
He there put the man in that garden to reign.
From grounds of that garden the Lord caused to grow,
Trees pleasant to sight and for good food also.

6   The fair tree of Life mid that garden was placed,
To make man immortal—from death ever safe;
And the tree of Knowledge, of good and evil—
Thou shalt not eat of it, thy soul it will kill.

7   A mist then arose, which did water the earth,
Then herbs, plants and flowers, bloomed in Eden's first birth.
To water the garden a river was found,
Which parted at Eden with four heads around.

8   The first river, Pison, girds Havilah's land
Of onyx-stone, bdellium, and gold bearing sand.
The second is Gihon, which compasseth around
The warm Ethiopia, where topaz abounds.

9   The third river Hiddekel, long having ceased,
Once rolled toward lands of Assyria east.
The fourth is Euphrates as history relates,
It ran through the city of Babylon the great.

10   Then God placed the man in the garden to dress
And keep it an Eden of undisturbed rest.
Then God did command the new man, and repeat,
Of every tree here, thou mayest freely eat;

11   But that tree of knowledge, of good and evil,
Thou shalt not eat of it, lest thee it should kill;
Thy power to obey is thy power to transgress,
Thine act of that power then must curse thee or bless.

12   Accountable man to be blest must obey
The God who hath formed him of mould and of clay;
If thou touch the tree which I bid thee deny,
Then surely all guilty, thou dying shalt die.

13   The man then surveyed both the fowl and the beasts,
And gave them all names, from the great to the least,
He wondered to see none like him, walk upright,
But all bent to earth with no knowledge or light.

14   He found none among them with whom he could mate,
Not one to speak to him, his soul to elate,
He saw loving consorts 'mong birds and 'mong beasts,
With whom they were sporting in amorous feasts.

15   Dove mates sweetly cooing, while building their nests,
      Male birds fondly wooing in songs of caress ;
      The stag with proud antlers, the doe with her fawns,
      Were prancing and bounding o'er woodland and lawn.

16   The man feeling lonely, for love he did sigh,
      And said, " where's my mate ?" as a tear dimmed his eye.
      " No consort to love me, or speak a kind word,
      I am not contented as beast, fish or bird.

17   It seems my dear Maker ought give me a love,
      That I might live joyful with her as the dove.
      A kind one and constant, to cheer me and bless,
      And meet my affections and fondest caress."

18   God said, " 'tis not good the young man be alone,
      He shall have a consort, a dear loving one.
      I'll place her before him in angelic form,
      His love, pride and glory, and bride to adorn."

19   So God caused deep sleep on the young man to press,
      And took from his side, and then closed up the flesh.
      From that which was taken, He built a fair maid
      And gave to the young man, who smiled as he said,

20   " Most fair in creation, most dear to my heart,
      It seems that from thee I could never depart.
      Thou first formed in man, then from man built a maid,
      Divinely, twice wrought, is this love of my aid.

21   Thy temples pomegranite, 'neath golden locks hid,
      Thy cheeks are fine damask, thy lips rosy red,
      Thy form wondrous graceful, thy step like the roe,
      Thine eyes with the love of my Maker doth glow.

22   Dear bone of my bone, dear flesh of my flesh,
      All beauteous, fair woman, created to bless ;
      Since thou hast been taken and built from my side,
      Please tell me lov'd maiden wilt thou be my bride."

23   She spake as the rose of first love flushed her cheeks,
      " O gallant young man, since my love you do seek,
      Your pleasure, dear sir, I incline to respect,
      Since man was created to love and protect.

24   At this sweet reply her fond swain ceased to speak,
      The thoughts of her love filled his soul, flushed his cheek,
      He took her fine hand with first love's genial air,
      And touched holy kiss on the lips of his fair.

25   This first young man bowed, in first love to caress
      The first bride which Eden, or Earth ever blest;
      And left all things else for her sake 'neath the sun,
      His choice, pride and glory, and most lovely one.

26   For this cause shall men leave their parents so kind,
      And cleave to their wives with fond hearts so inclined;
      To be no more twain, but forever one flesh,
      To people the earth and their Maker to bless.

27   Our first parents then, had no sin to cause shame,
      Like young, harmless children, had never known blame;
      With hearts pure and holy, no sin to forgive,
      In that blest condition God taught them to live.

28   If man doeth not sin, endless life doeth him bless,
      But if man doth sin, sin shall bring him to death.
      Who serves Me shall eat of My fair Tree of Life,
      Who sins against Me shall feel guilt, death and night.

CHAPTER III.

1   The serpent means Satan, fallen angel, or devil,
     Or one who doth turn from known good to do evil;
     Who made impious war once, 'mong angels in heaven,
     And for his rebellion was out to earth driven.

2   When God bade all angels to worship his son,
     Through whom man's redemption from sin was to come,
     Then Satan opposed the salvation of man,
     Refusing to worship God's son at command.

3   He drew on the rough edge of battle his band
     Of rebel-armed angels, the good to withstand;
     With fire-flashing swords and with adamant shields,
     They charged Michael's angels on Heaven's fair fields.

4   Then Michael and angels, they fought and prevailed
     'Gainst Satan the serpent, and forced him to quail.
     A loud voice in Heaven was heard at that hour,
     " Now is man's salvation God's kingdom, Christ's power."

5   Who knows to do good, if he then doeth evil,
     He transforms himself, by that act, to a devil;
     Those who obey God, they are saints, of God born,
     Those who yield to Satan, to devils transform.

6　The serpent, called Satan, was more subtle far
　　Than all things living on earth that there are,
　　He said to the woman " Yea, God said that ye,
　　Shall not eat all fruit of this garden's fair trees."

7　She said, "God permits us to eat of all trees
　　Within this fair garden, as oft as we please,
　　Except of one tree which he bade us deny,
　　For if we eat of it we shall surely die."

8　Then Satan declared, "thou shalt not surely die,
　　For what hath been told thee is not but a lie.
　　For, sure God doth know, in the day that ye eat,
　　Your eyes shall be opened and ye be complete.

9　As gods, having wisdom, to know good and ill,
　　That pleasures of knowledge, your spirits may thrill."
　　When she thought the tree would yield fruit and make wise,
　　So beauteous and pleasant attracting the eyes.

10　She then ate the fruit from thereof, seeming sweet,
　　And gave to her husband, who also did eat.
　　Their eyes were then opened, they felt guilt and pain,
　　"God said, " they must die, or my son must be slain,"

11　The voice of the Lord in the garden they heard,
　　Then, for the first moments, all guilty, they feared.
　　Then God called to Adam, who answered and said,
　　"I hid from Thy presence, for I was afraid."

12　God said, " hast thou ate of that tree which brings death?"
　　" My consort gave to me, I ate, I confess."
　　God said to the woman, "hath sin been thy fate?"
　　" The serpent beguiled me," she said, " and I ate."

13　God said to the Serpent, " for this thou hast done,
　　A worse curse be on thee, than all that hath come,
　　Cast down on thy belly, with chains shalt thou strive,
　　And grind, and bite dust, all the days of thy life.

14　'Tween thee and the woman, is enmity bred,
　　'Tween thy seed and hers, and it shall bruise thy head,
　　Thou demon, who dost no compassion reveal,
　　If man shall repent, thou shalt but bruise his heel."

15　God said to the woman, " this sin must increase
　　Thy sorrow, and bondage, disturbing thy peace,
　　And Adam, because thou my law didst transgress,
　　And eat of that tree which I told thee brought death.

16 Now cursed is the ground for thy sake : thou in strife,
And sorrow, shalt eat all the days of thy life,
The thistle and thorn, both, shall damage thy field,
In toil and in sweat shalt thou **live**, till thou yield.

17 And turn to the ground from whence taken at first,
Of dust thou art made and thou shalt go to dust."
Here man was first subject to vanity made,
By reason of hope God subjected and said,

18 I now subject man to this vanity dire,
" For such I charged Adam that sin did require,"
Then God made for Adam and wife, coats of skins,
And clothed them and said, " man is guilty in sin.

19 Now lest he should eat of life's fair tree at hand,
And never taste death as I told in command,
I drive out the man to repent and gain grace,
And Cherub's swords flaming round life's tree I place."

20 Then God taught young Adam and wife by his word,
To bring him sin offerings, atoning with blood.
Then Adam did call his fair consort's name Eve,
Because she was mother of all that did live.

CHAPTER IV.

1 Now Adam and Eve's first-born son was called Cain,
Eve said, " I a man from the Lord have obtained."
Their next son was Abel, a shepherd most kind,
While Cain to the tilling of ground did incline.

2 Then God and his angels taught mankind and blest,
Requiring of them pure sin offerings of peace,
All typical of the pure lamb that was slain,
When earth was first founded, man's life to sustain.

3 For God had ordained this pure offering at stake,
To cleanse man from sin if its stain was his fate ;
That all, by repentance, might come and be clean,
And be, through obedience, forever redeemed.

4 In process of time, as was ordained of God,
Cain brought fruit of ground, offering it to the Lord :
While Abel brought firstlings of flock in Chirst's name ;
God loved Abel's offering, but did not like Cain's.

5 Thus, Cain and his offerings, God did not respect ;
   Cain's countenance fell, he was wroth and sore vexed.
   The Lord said to Cain, " O, why art thou so wroth ?
   The Lord must judge offerings by goodness and worth.

6 If thou doest well, I reject thee no more,
   If thou doest not well, sin lies at thy door.
   If thou wilt do well, then will Abel desire
   To have thee rule o'er him, and ever aspire."

7 Then Cain talked with Abel, then came it to pass,
   When lone in the field that Cain slew him in wrath.
   Then God said to Cain, " where is thy brother dear?"
   Cain said, " I know not," as he trembled with fear.

8 Then God said to Cain, " O now what hast thou done ?
   The voice of thy brother's blood cries from the ground.
   Henceforth shalt thou from thy tilled ground get a curse,
   Which openeth her mouth for thy brother's blood first ;

9 A fugitive wretch shalt thou be in despair."
   Then Cain cried, " My punishment I cannot bear ;
   Because I am driven from all good in Earth :
   From God's love, while all men will slay me and curse."

10 Then God set on Cain this vile mark to remain.
   A vagabond guilty, and not to be slain.
   Cain fled with his wife, from the presence of God,
   And dwelt in the land east of Eden, called Nod.

11 Cain's wife bore him Enoch, which name gained great fame.
   Then Cain built a city, called by his son's name ; .
   Enoch begat Irad, Irad Mehujael,
   The grandsire of Lamech, sire of Methusael.

12 From Enoch to Lamech, these four sires connect
   Irad, and Mehujael, Methusael, Lamech.
   Then Lamech took wives, the one's name was Adah,
   The name of the other loved one was Zillah.

13 Then Adah bare Babal, in tents they did dwell.
   His children kept cattle, by which they lived well.
   His brother was Jubal, whose children at will,
   Could handle the harp and the organ with skill.

14 And Zillah bare Tubal-cain, skillful by birth,
   His sister was Naamah, a lady of worth.
   Then Lamech called Adah and Zillah, and said,
   "O ! wives hear my voice now, for I am afraid.

15   I've slain a young man, to my sorrow and hurt,
     If Cain merits vengeance, men will me desert."
     Then Eve bore to Adam a son they called Seth,
     Instead of good Abel, whom Cain put to death.

16   Eve said, "God appointed me true seed again,
     For seed of the righteous shall ever remain."
     To Seth was born Enos, of righteous reward,
     And men then began to call on the Lord.

CHAPTER V.

1   These are the generations from Adam to Noah,
    Since God made mankind in his image of yore,
    Both male and the female, in God's likeness best,
    And called their name Adam the same day, and blest.

2   At his hundred thirtieth year he did beget
    A son in his likeness, and called his name Seth,
    Then Adam lived eight hundred years from Seth's birth,
    And had sons and daughters to people the earth.

3   At nine hundred thirty years' age, Adam died ;
    His son Seth, had Enos, at age sixty-five.
    Thence eight hundred seven years from son Enos' birth
    Lived Seth, and had sons and fair daughters of worth.

4   Seth died in his nine hundred twelfth year, appears,
    Then Enos had Cainan, at age ninety years ;
    From thence Enos lived eight hundred fifteen years,
    And had sons and daughters, his long life to cheer.

5   Nine hundred five years, Enos on Earth did dwell.
    At age sev'nty, Cainan had Mahalabel.
    Thence eight hundred forty years from that son's birth,
    He had sons and daughters, and lived on the Earth.

6   Nine hundred ten years, were all Cainan's life had—
    Mahalabel's sixty-fifth year brought Jared.
    Years eight hundred thirty, from birth of Jared,
    Mahalabel lived and had children to wed.

7   Mahalabel lived eight hundred ninety-five years.
    At sixty-five, Jared's son Enoch appears.
    Jared lived eight hundred years from Enoch's birth,
    And had sons and daughters of goodness and worth.

8   In nine hundred sixty-two years Jared died.
Enoch had Methuselah at age sixty-five.
From birth of Methuselah, walked Enoch with God,
Full three hundred years in commands of the Lord.

9   When three hundred sixty-five years had passed by,
Good Enoch was not, for God took him on high.
Methuselah lived hundred eighty-seven years,
And had a son Lamech, from History appears.

10   Thence seven hundred eighty-two years from that birth,
Methuselah spread sons and daughters o'er Earth,
At nine hundred sixty-ninth year of his age
Methuselah died, oldest man on life's page.

11   When one hundred eighty-two years had passed o'er,
Then Lamech a son had, and called his name Noah.
This son shall us comfort in toil and in work
Of ground, which the Lord, for man's sin hath once cursed.

12   From Noah, five hundred and ninety-five years
Lived Lamach, and had sons and daughters to cheer;
When seven hundred seventy-seven years were all fled,
Then good Lamech died, and was laid with the dead.

13   And Noah was five hundred years old at that time,
And had three loved sons who were goodly inclined,
Named Shem, Ham and Japhet, who virtue's paths trod,
While Noah preached the faith of the gospel of God.

CHAPTER VI.

1   When mankind began to increase on the earth,
And daughters were born them of beauty and worth,
The sons of God saw their fair daughters of rose
And took to them wives of their love as they chose.

2   The Lord said, " My spirit shall not strive always
With man, for he also is flesh, yet his days
Shall be but an hundred and twenty years, when
I will call for him to account to me then."

3   'Twas then, there were giants in Earth in those days,
Also after that, when the sons of God clave
To daughters of men, then their children they found,
Became mighty men, goodly men of renown.

4   O'er one thousand years from this time, man grew **worse**,
His wickedness great, fast prevailed in the earth.
Then God felt repentant that he had made him,
And grieved at his heart on account of man's sin.

5   And said, " I'll destroy man, from off the earth
For working no goodness, but only a curse."
But Noah found grace in the eyes of the Lord;
He was a just man, having righteous reward.

6   His children so pious, vile men thought them odd,
While Noah preached them goodness and walked with his God.
Noah's three sons were Shem, Ham and Japhet of worth,
All flesh had corrupted its way on the earth.

7   For murder and violence stained earth with blood ;
God looked on this world and found none doing good.
He sorrowed and grieved, and He said, " 'tis a curse
To keep man to increase his sins on the earth."

8   Then God said to Noah, "Man's death is at hand,
They fill Earth with bloodshed and break all commands.
Their will, their accountable power, they control,
None else can control the will power of man's soul.

9   Man is man no more then, unless he hath power
To do good or ill in his life's every hour.
Accountable beings must have power of will
To take or reject either good or the ill.

10   I teach and admonish, to lead man to good,
I cleanse the obedient from sin by Christ's blood ;
I plead and entreat them to give me their heart,
'Tis all I can do them, their will is their part.

11   I long plead with Cain, his own brother to love,
I taught him well doings were all things above ;
I told him that Abel would have a desire
To have him rule o'er him in love, and aspire.

12   But all my entreaties, Cain treated with scorn,
And murdered his brother, and now, most forlorn,
And wretched, and marked, with a murderer's name,
No more among men, to be worthy of fame ! "

13   Then God said to Noah, " of the gopher wood take,
And build thee an ark, rooms in it shalt thou make,
And pitch it both outside and inside, with pitch—
Of fashions to make it, I'll now tell the which.

14 Just three hundred cubits in length will be right,
    And fifty in width and but thirty in height.
    A window above make thou in cubit size,
    A door of three stories thou shalt make likewise.

15 Behold, I bring waters on earth, even I,
    To drown the ungodly for sin, that they die.
    With thee is my covenant, and all righteous ones,
    Come thou in the ark, with thy wives and thy sons.

16 Of all living things, male and female, each kind,
    Bring thou in the ark, to keep live at this time;
    Of fowls, cattle, creeping things, after their kind,
    Two of every sort shall come to thee, inclined.

17 To keep all alive store thou food in the ark."
    Thus Noah did God's orders, ere they did embark,
    And Noah preached to man that they stay the great flood
    By yielding their hearts in obedience to God.

18 That God might repent the great flood he designed,
    And not destroy man as he now was inclined;
    But they heeded not Noah's entreaties, but cast
    Their vilest abuses on him, 'till the last.

19 Thus man can withstand the entreaties of God,
    Though arms of imploring extend for his good.
    The wrath of the sinner, oft leads him to death,
    The rage is infernal that burns in his breast!

20 " Were man to live on in his own wicked way,
    Then violence and bloodshed would stain every day;
    This race, now so wicked, must all come to naught,
    I'll save those eight souls, who my goodness hath sought.

CHAPTER VII.

1   The Lord said to Noah, " come, thou whom I approve,
    Come into the ark, all thy house whom I love.
    I have seen thee righteous before me this day,
    Thou hast taught my goodness, and learned men to pray.

2   Clean beasts male and female, by sevens shalt thou get,
    Unclean get by pairs, one pair each kind, except
    Of fowls get by sevens, male and female, to keep
    Alive on the earth, when all clothed with the deep.

3 For yet seven days, and I'll cause it to rain
On Earth forty days, forty nights, unrestrained:"
And Noah was six hundred years old, when the flood
Of waters, like ocean, all o'er the earth stood.

4 Then foul beasts, and clean birds, and all things that creep,
Went in male and female, their lives for to keep,
When seven days were past, as the Lord spoke at first,
The waters of flood then appeared on the earth.

5 When of Noah's life, in the six hundredth year,
And day seventeenth, second month, did appear,
The fountains of great deep broke up, and the rain,
From Heaven's open windows, poured floods unrestrained,

6 That day, Noah, and Shem, Ham and Japheth embarked
With all their wives to be saved in the ark.
Each creature first ordered, then went in the ark,
The male and female, as told in the start.

7 When all were safe entered, the floods did begin,
From rains dashing fiercely, the Lord shut him in.
The flood on the Earth, forty days did increase,
And bore up the ark, day and night, without cease.

8 The waters prevailed, and increased with great rage,
The ark, launching forth, did the billows engage.
The waters prevailed then exceedingly more,
'Till hills 'neath whole heaven, were all covered o'er.

9 Fifteen cubits upward, the floods more prevailed,
'Till mountains were covered, and all flesh did fail,
But Noah and his people, in God's ark were saved,
While floods covered earth one hundred fifty days.

10 A world of mankind, for their sin God hath slain,
Except eight of righteous he saved, to remain;
Which showeth that good, was the object of man,
To work out God's goodness in every land.

11 Then he who doth not unto good deeds incline,
Must feel that he fills not his Maker's design.
But like world of old, is God's subject of wrath,
If he is not found walking in wisdom's path.

CHAPTER VIII.

1 Then Noah was remembered of God in the ark,
   He made the wind blow, and the flood to depart,
   The fountains of deep, heaven's windows, and rain,
   By God's hand from Heaven, they were quickly restrained.

2 On Ararat Mountains the ark then did stay;
   'Twas in seventh month, on the seventeenth day.
   The waters dispersed far beneath what had been;—
   First day of tenth month, tops of mountains were seen.

3 At forty days' end, he a raven, let fly,
   Which went to and fro, till some land became dry;
   He sent forth a dove, for to find the bare ground,
   The dove, there no rest for her foot ever found.

4 In seven days more, he the dove did send forth
   Which brought back a green olive leaf in her mouth.
   Then, Noah knew that waters were dried from the earth,
   Stayed yet seven days, then the dove he sent forth,

5 Which came not again, then he was satisfied
   That waters from earth, were abated and dried,
   Then Noah removed the ark's covering by,
   And looked, and beheld that the ground was all dry.

6 Now in second month, on the twentieth day,
   God spoke unto Noah, and most kindly did say,
   "Go forth from the ark, sons and wives all with thee,
   And every creature, to multiply free."

7 Then Noah offer'd clean beasts, and fowls to the lord,
   Who blest Noah's offering, and pledged man his word,
   "Thine offerings of love, doth my heart so incline,
   I'll give man my Spirit of love most Divine.

8 I'll not drown the world any more for man's sake,
   Since thou dost such offerings of love to me make.
   But seed time and harvest, and summer and heat,
   And day, night, and winter, on earth shall not cease."

CHAPTER IX.

1 God blessed Noah and wife, their three sons and their wives,
Choice ones of His love, for obedient lives;
He bade them "be fruitful, and make fertile ground,
And birds, fish and beasts, all shall fear you around.

2 All living things may as the herb be your meat,
But flesh, with the blood thereof, shall ye not eat.
For surely. your offerings of blood I require,
Of clean beasts, and birds, shed for man, I desire.

3 To keep in your memory, the Lamb that was slain,
Ere earth had its foundings, man's life to regain;—
Who taketh man's life, surely he shall not live,
For God his own image, to man first did give.

4 God said I now cov'nant with man and with beast,
That by such a flood, they again shall not c ase.
The token I give, is my rainbow in clouds
Between Me and thee, brilliant sign of My Words.

5 And I will remember my covenant true,
That I with a flood will no more destroy you,
And when man hath lived out his life-time of days,
He then must account Me, his good or bad ways."

6 Then Shem, Ham, and Japheth forth from the ark came,
And Ham had a son, they called Canaan, by name,
Of these sons of Noah was earth overspread,
A husbandman he then became, it was said.

7 He planted a vineyard, and drank of the wine,
And did become drunken, and badly inclined;
When Ham, Canaan's father, saw Noah insane,
He told Shem and Japheth, who heard it with pain.

8 And went to relieve their good father's ill plight,
Caused by mocking wine, in which none should delight.
When Noah awoke from his wine, and did know
That Ham had thus told Shem and Japheth his woe,

9 He said, "Cursed be Canaan, to vile servile state,
A servant of servants shall hence be his fate;"—
He said, "God shall ever bless Japheth and Shem,
And Canaan shall ever be servant of them."

10 Hence, God was displeased with the drinking of wine,
Which so deranged Noah, in his great lovely mind,
Hence, God bade his people from wine to refrain,
If His Holy Spirit they wished to retain.

11 Hence, God ordered Hannah to drink not of wine,
That she might bring forth a true prophet divine.
Likewise did God's Angel, Manoah's wife tell.
" To drink either wine, or strong drink, is not well,

12 That thou bear son Sampson, true Nazarite to God,
Delivering his Israel from Philistie's rod."
God said to Elizabeth, " Thou shalt have a son,
He shall not drink wine, nor strong drink either one.

13 O, let my dear people from wine be refrained,
And seek for My Spirit, which shall them sustain.
Good Noah lived three hundred years, past the flood's rage,
And died, at his nine hundred fiftieth year's age.

CHAPTER X.

1 The generations born, since the flood on the earth,
Of Shem, Ham and Japheth, were, of Japheth first,
Gomer, Magog, Madai, Javan, Tubal, called,
And Meshech, and Tiras, these Japheth's sons all.

2 Of Gomer, Ashkenaz, Riphath, Togarmah
Of Javan, Dodanim, Tarshish, Elishah
And Kittim. From these have the Gentiles since sprung,
Their lands after families, and nations, and tongues.

3 Ham's sons were called Cush, Canaan, Phut, and Mizraim
Cush's sons, Seba, Havilah, Sabtah, and Sabtecha,
And Raamah, who had sons Sheba, and Dedan,
And Cush begat Nimrod, the first King o'er man.

4 He was a great hunter, of strength before God,
And often was called, Mighty hunter, Nimrod;
A Kingdom in Shinah, Nimrod did first get
And ruled Babel, Erech, Accad, and Calneeh.

5 From that land went Asshur, and built Nineveh,
The city Rehoboth, and Calah, those three,
And Resen, between Nineveh and Calah,
The same is a city, both prosperous and great.

6   Mizraim had six sons, Anamim, Lehabim,
Naphtuhim, Pathrusim, Casluhim, Ludim.
From whence came Philistim, likewise Caphtorim,
And Canaan had Sidon, and Heth, born to him,

7   Hivite, Jebusite, Amorite, Girgasite,
Arkite, Arvadite, Zemarite, Hamathite,
And Sinite ; these all did compose Canaanites,
Who soon were a nation of great wealth and might.

8   Their border touched Sidon, Gomorrah, Gaza,
And Sodom, Zeboim, Admah, and Lasha.
These are sons of Ham, after their families past,
Their tongues, and their nations and rich counties vast.

9   Good Shem, who was sire of the Jews, five sons had,
Elam, Asshur, Arphaxad, Aram, and Lud.
And Aram had four sons, Uz, Hul, Gether, Mash,
Arphaxad's first born son, he did call Salah.

10 Salah begat, Eber, of whom two sons came,
Named Peleg, and Joktan ; these Joktan's sons' names,
Almodad, Sheleph, Hazarmaveth, Jerah,
Hadoram, Uzal, Diklah, Obal, Sheba,

11 Abimael, Havilah, Ophir, Jobab,
These are thirteen sons, all of which Joktan had;
They dwelt between Mesha, and Mount Sephar, East.
Shem's sons after families and Nations the best.

12 Now these are the families of good sons of Noah,
From their generations in nations of yore,
By these were the nations divided in earth,
Long after the flood, through whom Christ had his birth.

CHAPTER XI.

1   The world now was of but one language and speech
It then came to pass, as they journeyd from East,
That they found a plain, within Shinar land fair,
So beautiful, that they all thought to dwell there.

2   They said, "let us make brick and burn hard as stone,
And have slime for mortar, cementing them one,
And build a great city and tower unto Heaven,
That we may not part or asunder be driven."

3 The Lord saw the work which his children began,
And said; "they will never more spread 'neath the sun,
For with but one language, this one thing is true,
They'll not spread o'er earth, as I would they should do.

4 So I will go down and their language confound,
And scatter them far o'er the earth, all around,
For man should not stay at the place of his birth,
But spread forth my glory a.l over the earth.

5 The name of that city, then, Babel was called,
Since God there confounded the language of all.
We now turn to Shem, who begat Arphaxad,
When hundred years old, two years after the flood.

6 Shem lived after that time, full five hundred years,
And had sons and daughters of worth it appears.
Arphaxad, at thirty-fifth year of his age
Had born a son Salah, of worth it is said,

7 Thence four hundred three years, from son Salah's birth
Arphaxad spread sons and fair daughters o'er earth.
Salah, had son Eber, at age thirty years,
Lived four hundred three years and had children dear.

8 Eber had son Peleg at thirty-fourth year,
Lived four hundred thirty years, had children dear.
At thirty years age Peleg had a son Reu,
Lived two hundred nine years, had sons, daughters too.

9 At age thirty-two Reu had son called Serug,
Lived two hundred seven years, had sons, daughters good.
Serug had son Nahor, at age thirty years,
Thence lived years two hundred, had children to cheer.

10 Nahor had son Terah, at twenty-ninth year,
Lived years hundred nineteen, had sons, daughters fair.
Terah lived years seventy, thence had these three sons,
Abram, Nahor, Haran, all righteous, each one.

11 And then Abram wooed Terah's daughter most fair,
Who was his half-sister, of virtues most rare,
His beauteous wife called they Sarai by name,
While Nahor's fair consort was Milcah of fame.

12 Haran had son Lot and had no more increase,
But died before Terah, in Ur of Chaldees.
Then Terah took Abram, and Lot, Haran's son,
And Sarai, the consort, whom Abram had won.

13   And went forth with them, out from **Ur** of Chaldees,
To go into Canaan, to dwell where they please.
They then dwelt in Haran, a land very fair;—
Terah lived two hundred five years, and died there.

14   With what nice precision this record was kept
Of noted men's birth, life and death most exact,
All bearing swift witness of record divine,
All touched by the Spirit of God and inclined.

CHAPTER XII.

1   To Abram God said, go from thy country free,
And kinsfolks, to that land which I shall show thee,
And I will make of thee a nation the best,
And make thy name great, and a world thou shalt bless.

2   I'll bless them that bless thee, and curse them that curse,
In thee shall all families be blest in the earth.
Abram went with Lot as the Lord did command,
At age seventy-five he did leave Haran's land.

3   Then Abram took Sarai, the wife he had won,
And wealth gained in Haran and Lot, brother's son,
And went for the land they called Canaan by name,
And into the land of that Canaan they came.

4   Abram came to Sichem unto Moreh's plain,
Where Canaanites then that fair land did retain.
The Lord then app ared unto Abram and blest,
And said, "To thy seed I give this land of rest."

5   There he built an altar, and worshipped the Lord,
Then moved to a mountain from Bethel Eastward.
He th re pitched his tent. Bethel was on the west,
Hai on the East, there he called God, and blest.

6   There Abram went onward, still journeying South;—
A famine was sore in the land by a drouth,
When near unto Egypt, he said to his wife,
"Thou being so fair may endanger my life;

7   Egyptians, may fancy and for thee may strive,
And hence, may kill me, but, will save thee alive,
Say thou art my sister, that it may with me
Be well, for thy sake, and I live cause of thee."

8 When Abram reached Egypt, they thought her so fair,
That Pharaoh took her to his own house with care,
And kept Abram well, for his fair sister's sake,
Pharaoh being rich, finest presents did make.

9 The Lord then plagued Pharaoh, perplexing his life,
On Sarai's account, Abram's beauteous wife,
Pharoah said to Abram, "did'st thou treat me right?
Why did'st thou not tell me Sarai was thy wife?

10 Lo! I might have taken thy wife for to wed,
Now take thy wife quickly, and go and be fled."
Then Pharoah commanded his men, to send him
And wife, and all things that he had, far from them.

11 Said Abram, "I feared that I here might be slain,
If strangers should wish my fair wife to attain,
Lo! she is my sister, on my Father's side,
But not on my mother's though she is my bride.

CHAPTER XIII.

1 Then Abram, with Lot, went from Egypt still South.
He had gold and silver, and cattle without;
Then went on his journey from South to Bethel,
The place of his tent, where he first used to dwell.

2 He found the old altar which he first built there,
And called on the name of the Lord God in prayer.
Now Lot, who went with him, had herds, flocks and tents,
The land could not bear them, while as one they went.

3 Their substance was great, so that they could not dwell
Together, since strife oft their herdsmen befell;
And Canaanite, Perizzite, dwelt in the land.
Said Abram to Lot, " Let no strife be at hand

4 Between me and thee, and my herdsmen and thine,
Because we are brethren, our love should incline.
Vast land lies before thee, divide me from thee,
And take thou the left hand, the right leave for me.

5 If thou wish the right hand, I will take the left.
That we dwell in peace, and of God may be blest."
Lot lifted his eyes and beheld Jordan's plain,
Well watered, where Sodom, Gomorrah doth reign.

6   Like as the Lord's garden, or Egypt of yore,
    As thou comest unto the regions of Zoar,
    Lot chose Jordan's plain, to go Eastward alone.
    In love they divided, and parted each one.

7   In Canaan dwelt Abram, Lot dwelt in the plain,
    Pitched tent toward Sodom, where he did remain.
    But men of that Sodom in sin did exceed.
    Before God were wicked, in word and in deed.

8   Then God said to Abram, "lift up thine eyes,
    Look North, Southward, Westward, and Eastward likewise,
    All land which thou sees't to thee will I give,
    To thy seed forever, as I the Lord live.

9   Thy seed is the righteous who in me do trust,
    Which no man can number more than number dust,
    Rise walk through the land, in the breadth in the length,
    For it will I give thee, as I, God, have strength.

10   Then Abram removed to the plain of Mamre,
    And built there an altar of worship we see.
    He bowed at that altar, and called on the Lord
    To strengthen the faithful, who trust in His word.

CHAPTER XIV.

1   Then Amraphel, Chedorlaomer came far
    With Tidal, Arioch against five kings to war.
    Bera, Birsha, Shinab, Shemeber, Bela,   [Salt sea.
    These five kings fought four kings down in Siddim's vale,

2   They served Chedorlaomer years numbering twelve,
    Then in thirteenth year these five kings did rebel
    In fourteenth year Chedorlaomer's kings came,
    And smote the Rephaims, in Ashteroth Karnaim.

3   Smote Emims in Kiriathaim, and Zuzims in Ham,
    And Horites in Mount Seir, unto El-paran,
    Returning to Kadesh, with Amalek did fight,
    In Hazezon-tamar, they smote Amorites.

4   Then went king of Sodom, king of Gomorrah,
    And king of Zeboiim, and king of Admah
    And king of Bela, and with war did assail
    These foreign invaders down in Siddim's vale.

5   'Gainst Chedorlaomer, the king of Elam,
    Tidal, king of nations and Amraphel, king
    Of Shinar, and Arioch, king of Ellasar,
    These four kings fought five, in the Siddim's-vale-war.

6   In slimepits, Gomorrah and Sodom's kings fell,
    And others not slain, fled to mountains, to dwell,
    Their foes took the goods of Gomorrah that day,
    And Sodom, and victuals and went on their way.

7   They also took Lot, Abram's own brother's son,
    Who then dwelt in Sodom, his goods, and were gone.
    Then one who escaped unto Abram did flee,
    Who dwelt in the Amorite's plain of Mamre.

8   The brother of Aner, likewise of Eshcol,
    These were all confederate with Abram, at call.
    Now when Abram heard Lot was kidnapped so mean,
    He armed his trained servants, three hundred eighteen.

9   And followed those kings unto Dan for to fight,
    He and his trained servants, and smote them by night;
    Pursued them to Hobah, Damascus the left,
    And brought back again Lot, and all things bereft.

10 'Twas then king of Sodom went out to meet him,
    To greet his return from the slaughter of kings.
    'Twas at Shaveh valley, which is the king's dale,
    Where Abram did fight in God's name and prevail.

11 Melchizedek, who then was high priest of God,
    Brought forth bread and wine, blessing them by his word,
    For he was a sworn priest, like Christ our blessed Lord,
    He said, " Blest be Abram. of the most high God."

12 He cried, "Ever blest be the true God, who hath
    Delivered his foes unto Abram at last."
    Then Abram gave tithes to Melchizedek there,
    While calling on God in devotion and prayer.

13 Then Sodom's king said unto Abram, " I would
    Thou give me the persons, and thou take the goods."
    Said Abram. " I lift up my hand to the Lord,
    That I will not take of thee one thread's reward.

14 Nay, I will not take anything, that for which
    Thou mayst after say, " I have made Abram rich."
    But for what the young men have eat, make thou right,
    And pay off the men which went with me to fight.

15 Mamre, Eschol, Aner, let them have their pay,
    But I will take nothing, but go on my way,
    The battle I fought, I have fought for the Lord,
    My trust is in Him, He shall be my reward."

16 A hero's example, good Abram hath shown,
    Not fighting for wealth, but for freedom alone,
    The rights of mankind, the true hero regards,
    The souls of such heroes the Lord doth reward.

CHAPTER XV.

1   Then God said to Abram, " Lo, I am the Lord,
    I will be thy shield, and thy greatest reward."
    Then Abram cried, " O Lord, what wilt thou give me ?
    How shall my seed, as thou saidst, as the dust be ? "

2   When Lo ! I am childless, and not blessed with seed.
    Shall my steward's offspring be mine heir indeed ? "
    " The child of thy steward," God said, " is not heir,
    Thine heir shall come forth from thy own body fair."

3   Then God brought forth Abram and said, " See the Heavens,
    Tell Me of the stars, can their number be given ?
    So numerous thy seed shall be," and he believed.
    Then God said, " True righteousness thou hast received.

4   'Twas I, the Lord God, who brought thee with strong hand
    From Ur of Chaldees, to inherit this land."
    Then Abram cried, " O Lord, whereby shall I know
    That I shall inherit this land, to and fro ? "

5   God said, " Take these three beasts, of each three years old,
    An heifer, a ram and a she goat, also
    One turtle dove, and a young pigeon to offer."
    He cut them in midst, laid each on the altar.

6   The doves he did not part, but whole did them lay,
    And when fowls came for them he drove them away.
    Then deep sleep seized Abram at sun going down,
    Great horror and darkness fell on him around.

7   " Now know of a surety," said God at my hand,
    " A stranger thy seed shall be, in a strange land,
    And serve them, while they shall thy children afflict,
    Full four hundred years, I the Lord now predict.

8 On those whom they serve, I in judgment will wait,
And after shall they come out with substance great,
And thou shalt go hence to thy Father's in peace,
Be buried, and in good old age, shalt decease.

9 But in fourth generation thy seed shall again
Come hither, this Canaanite land to retain."
At sundown and darkness, a burning lamp came
And passed by the offering and caught it to flame.

10 That day God made covenant with Abraham,
And said, "To thy seed have I given this land,
From river of Egypt to Euphrates river,   ·
Kenites, Kenizzites, Kadmonites, Hittites, ever.

11 The Perizzites, and the Rephaims, Amorites,
The Canaanites, Girgashites, and Jebusites.
Thy seed, which is Christ, shall be spread o'er all earth,
And shall Life inherit and heavenly worth."

12 Then God ordered Abram to make sacrifice
Of clean beasts, and birds, as an emblem of Christ,
Whom He had ordained once to die for man's sin,
That he through repentence might find grace in Him.

13 God's purpose, of man's earthly sojourn now know
Is that they conform to Christ's image below,
And thus become heirs of God through His dear Son
Inheriting all things of God's yet to come.

CHAPTER XVI.

1 Sarai, Abram's wife, him no children did bear,
But she an Egyptian hand maiden, had there,
Then Sarai said, "since I no children do have,
Take Hagar as wife, that thy seed may survive."

2 It was eighty-sixth year of good Abram's life,
When Sarai gave Hagar to him for his wife,
When Hagar conceived she her mistress despised.
"My wrong be on Abram," then Sarai replies.

3 "The Lord judge between me and thee," Sarai said
Then Abram said, "do what thou please with thy maid,"
When Sarai dealt hardly, she fled from her face;—
God's angel found her in the lone wilderness.

4   By fountain of water, in way on to Shur,
    He called Sarai's maid, saying thus unto her,
    "O, where wilt thou go?" and she said, "I do flee
    From Sarai my mistress, who dealt hard with me."

5   The angel said to her, "return to thy home,
    Submit to thy mistress, and no farther roam,
    Exceedingly, shall thy seed multiplied be,
    So great, that it cannot be numbered by thee.

6   Despising thy mistress hath brought thee much ill,
    Hadst thou been kind to her, she would have lov'd thee still,
    She gave thee her husband, such love scarce was known
    Had'st thou not despised her, she still would thee own."

7   The angel said to her, "thou shalt have a son,
    And call his name Ishmael, the Lord hears thy moan.
    Thy son shall be wild, and his hand against man,
    And every man's hand against him in the land.

8   He shall dwell in presence of his brethren all."
    The Lord that spoke to her she this name did call.
    "Thou God seest me, have I looked here for him,
    The well was called Beer-lahai-roi, God hath seen.

9   Between Kadesh and Bered, is there found that well,
    And Hagar bore Abram a son, Ishmael;—
    Impatient was Sarai to wait for God's time
    To bring her a true son of promise, Divine,

CHAPTER XVII.

1   When Abram was ninety-nine years old, the Lord
    Said, "Walk for Me perfect, for Me, the true God;
    And I will make covenant between Me and thee,
    And will multiply thee most exceedingly."

2   He fell on his face, and God said to him, "There
    Thou shalt be the sire of great nations afar!
    And thy name shall not any more be Abram,
    But thy name henceforth shall be called Abraham.

3   I will make thee fruitful, kings shall thy seed be,
    Establish My covenant between Me and thee;
    Each man child shall ye circumcise near and far;
    Call not thy wife Sarai, but call her Sarah.

4　She shall bear son Isaac, to theé thy true seed,
　　Be mother of nations as I have agreed ;"
　　Then Abraham said in his heart, "shall this be,
　　A son born when hundred years old, unto me ?"

5　Then God said, " I promise thee Isaac to cheer,
　　Which Sarah shall bear thee this set time next year,
　　From Sarah's distrust, thy son Ishmael did rise,
　　But was not thy true seed I pledged from the skies.

6　For thy sake son Ishmael shall hence be blest yet,
　　A great nation, twelve princes, shall he beget."
　　Then God ceased His speech and went from Abraham,
　　And Abraham did as the Lord did command.

CHAPTER XVIII.

1　The Lord appeared to Abraham
　　　In Mamre's plains, at heat of day,
　　He saw three men, to them he ran,
　　　Bowed himself down and bade them stay.

2　" Pray let me wash your feet," he said,
　　　" Come rest yourselves beneath this tree,
　　And I will fetch a piece of bread,
　　　Refresh yourselves. then pass on free."

3　They said, " so do as thou hast said."
　　　Then Abram hasted to his tent
　　And said to Sarah, " make some bread."
　　　Then quickly to his flock he went

4　And fetched a tender, fatted calf,
　　　And bade his servant dress it then:
　　And butter took, and milk, and last
　　　The roasted calf and gave to them.

5　There he stood by those men of Leife,
　　　As they did bless and eat his fare ;
　　They said, " where is Sarah thy wife ?"
　　　He said, " within her tent at prayer."

6　They said, " Sarah shall have a son."
　　　She heard their words through her tent door,
　　Her life had most a century run,
　　　Prospects of children were no more.

7 Then Sarah laughed and said, "shall I
    Or Abraham with seed be blest,
And have the pleasure e'er we die
    To have a son! it seems a jest.

8 Then God said, " why should Sarah laugh,
    Is anything hard for the Lord?"
She said, " when time of life is past
    How shall a son be my reward!"

9 Then Sarah said, " I did not laugh ;"
    She was afraid, but He said, " nay,
Thy time of life, though long 'tis past
    I'll give again without delay."

10 The men rose up, looked Sodom-ward ;
    Abraham thought to go their way.
" Shall I hide what I do," said God,
    From faithful Abram this day ?

11 Since Abraham shall surely be
    A nation great of might in Earth,
All shall be blest in him and free,
    Who seek by faith the heavenly birth.

12 For Abram will command his seed,
    So that they keep My ways," saith God,
"And justice do, and judgment deed,
    And give all men their just reward.

13 Since Sodom, and Gommorrah's cry
    Of murderous blood comes from the ground,
I must go down, that Sodom die,
    Lest murder in my skirts be found."

14 The men, their faces turned away,
    And straight for Sodom, they did go ;
But Abram, with the Lord did stay,
    And pray that he would mercy show.

15 Then Abram drew near, and said,
    " Wilt thou destroy the pure with vile ;
If Sodom furnish fifty good,
    Wilt thou for them not spare awhile ? "

16 " If Sodom furnish fifty good,
    Then I the Lord will Sodom spare,"
Abraham said, " if five lack, would
    The Lord destroy them without care ? "

17 God said, "if there are forty-five,
    I'll spare the city for their sake,"
  "Lord, if but forty they shall have,
    What mercy's offer wilt thou make?"

18 God said, "if forty there are found,
    I'll do it for the forty's sake."
  "If only thirty should abound,
    Lord, hast thou mercy at that rate?"

19 God said, "I'll spare for thirty's sake
    I am of tender mercy, kind,
  And pitiful, and wish to make,
    The souls of men to good incline."

20 "Lord, be not angry while I speak,
    Since I have taken it on me,
  To plead for mercy, for man's sake
    What if but twenty there should be?"

21 God said, for twenty I'll give o'er,
    And not burn Sodom for their sake."
  Then Abram cried, but this once more,
    Will I a pray'r for Sodom make.

22 If only ten shall be found there,
    Lord can thy mercy Sodom save?"
  God said, "I hear the righteous' pray'r,
    If ten are found then they shall live.

23 Six times I've yielded to thy prayer
    Which thou hast made for Sodom's sake,
  Wishing that yet they would have care
    For righteousness, that they be saved."

24 'Twas then the Lord went forth His way,
    And talked no man with Abraham;
  And Abraham returned that day
    Unto his home, in Mamre's plain.

CHAPTER XIX.

1 Two angels unto Sodom came,
    At eve. as Lot sat in the gate;
  He bowed down to those angels twain,
    And ran to meet and on them wait.

2 He said, " My lords, turn in, I pray,
      And tarry in my house this night,
    I'll wash your feet if you will stay,
      Then go your ways at morning light.

3 But they said, " Nay, we would abide,
      In Sodom's street, all though this night."
  He urged them till they did decide
      To stay with him 'till morning light.

4 Then Lot prepared a sumptuous feast,
      And break to them unleavened bread.
  Then Sodom's men, his house compassed,
      And called for Lot, and sternly said.

5 " Where are those men who came in here ?
      Come quickly, bring them out to us,
  That we may prove them, for we fear,
      That they came here to be a curse."

6 Then Lot went out and thus advised,
      " Brethren, do not wickedly,
  My children I would sacrifice,
      Ere you should harm these guests with me.

7 The Sodomites said in return,
      "Stand back," as thus they railed and cursed.
  " This fellow came here to sojourn,
      And wants to be a judge o'er us.

8 Now we will deal worse with thee than
      We would with these strange men, yea more ;"
  Then they prest sore on Lot the man,
      And rushed quite near to break his door !

9 The angels pulled Lot in the house
      To them, and quickly shut the door,
  And smote the Sodomites without,
      With blindness, small and great, most sore.

10 The smitten, wearied and annoyed,
      The men bade Lot, " warn out your friends,
  For God hath sent us to destroy
      The city for its grievious sins.

11 Then Lot forewarned his sons-in-law,
      And said, " up get you out this place,
  For God this city will destroy,
      But he seemed mocking as he spake.

12   And when the early morn arose,
  The angels hastened Lot away,
 Lest they should be consumed with foes,
  Within the burning of that day.

13   The angels seized Lot's hand in haste,
  And of his daughters and his wife,
 And pulled them from the city fast,
  And cried, " escape now for thy life.

14   Look ye not back, to mountains go,
  All who stay here must be consumed."
 Then Lot replied, " my lords, not so,
  I with your God have long communed ;

15   His mercy he hath magnified,
  Oft shewed it me, and heard my cry ;
 In Zoar City let me hide,
  Pray, lest ill take me and I die."

16   They said, " since God hath long loved thee,
  This city we will not o'erthrow ;
 Thy prayer of faith in God grant we,
  Then haste and quickly to it go.

17   For we cannot destroy this place,
  Till thou hast fled and gone before ;"
 This little city of God's grace
  Was then called by the name of Zoar.

18   At risen sun, Lot entered Zoar.
  Then brimstone rained and fire from heaven
 All Sodom and Gomorrah, o'er,
  For grievous sins and unforgiven.

19   Those cities, men, and things that grew,
  Were burned by fire from heaven rained,
 And when Lot's wife looked back to view,
  As a salt pillar she became.

20   At early morn, Abram went where
  He had conversed with God, most wise,
 Up from those cities of his care,
  He saw a dreadful smoke arise.

21   When God burnt cities of the plain
  He favored Abraham the brave,'
 And sent Lot out from midst of them.
  He fled from Zoar, dwelt in a cave.

22 Lot's daughters then dwelt with him there ;
    The first-born to the younger said,
  " Our sire is old, no swains here are,
    To seek us for their wives to wed.

23 We ought to save our father's seed,
    And not permit it to decay,
  Whom heaven hath blest in word and deed
    And saved from Sodom's burning day ;

24 Let us make him drink wine so long,
    That he know us not from his wife."
  Whence, each a son to him had born,
    Moab, and Amon, their delight.

25 The Moabites, and Amonites,
    Sprang forth from these two maidens' sons,
  Who made two nations great in might,
    Who first from Lot and daughters sprung.

CHAPTER XX.

1 In Gera dwelt Abram 'tween Kadesh and Shur,
  And called his wife sister, when speaking of her,
  Abimelech sent, and took home Abram's wife.
  God told him by dream, he endangered his life.

2 Abimelech said, " Will God slay me as one vile ?
  Since Abram and Sarah deceived me with guile.
  She was Abram's sister, I thought as they said,
  Hence justly I sought the fair Sarah to wed."

3 " Thou didst this sincerely," God said, " without sin,
  To give back to Abram his Sarah again."
  Abimelech reproved Abraham for this thing,
  And said, " Why bring on me so grievous a sin?"

4 Said Abram, " I thought none feared God in this place,
  And that men might slay me for my wife's sake.
  Sarah is my sister on my father's side,
  But not on my mother's, and she is my bride.

5 When God sent me far from my dear father's house,
  I said to her, pray show me this kindness now.
  Say of me to all, ' he is my brother true,'
  That it may be well with me, and with thee too."

6 Abimelech gave oxen, and servants and sheep,
   Restoring him Sarah his wife for to keep,
   And said unto him, "Now I give thee all these,
   My land is before thee, go dwell where thou please.

7 A thousand bright pieces of silver likewise
   I give to thy brother, thy covering of eyes,
   To all who are with thee, and others aloof."
   Thus did King Abimelech give Sarah reproof.

8 God blest King Abimelech and household with rest,
   Since he gave back Sarah as He did request.
   Thus men are oft frightened to vary from truth,
   To rescue from danger, in days of their youth.

9 Lie not one to another, our Maker enjoins,
   Buy truth, sell it not, truth is council divine,
   And do unto others this precept most true,
   Do that unto them ye would have done to you.

10 ,Mankind need long training to be truly good.
    God long counseled Abram, ere faith firmly stood,
    And Sarah long doubted her God's promised seed,
    Gave Hagar to Abram as though God had need.

11 And Abram and Sarah once laughed at God,s word   .
    Of promise, as though things were hard for the Lord! *
    But God is not slack every promise to fill,
    He never will fail those who trust in Him still.

12 God's purpose eternal, of man on the Earth
    Was that they be like Him in goodness and worth,
    Conformed to the meek, lowly mind of His son,
    That they might be joint heirs with Christ every one.

CHAPTER XXI.

1 Then Sarah bare Isaac, to Abram, true seed,
   At set time of promise, his true heir indeed.
   He circumcised Isaac, as God had him told,
   And Abraham then was an hundred years old.

2 Then Sarah said, " God hath so made me to laugh
   That all those who hear shall have joy in behalf,
   To think God made me to bare Abram a son
   In old age, when life had a century run.

*Read Gen. 17th chap., 16, 17 verses, and 18th chap. 12 15.

3 When Isaac was weaned, Abram made a great feast,
 Then Hagar's son mocked, as one illy possessed.
 Then Sarah said, "cast out the bond son from me,
 He shall not be heir with son Isaac, the free.

4 'Twas grievous to Abram, for Ishmael his son,
 But God bade him heed Sarah's voice, and 'twas done.
 "For in Isaac only thy seed shall be called,
 But for thy sake will I bless Ishmael's sons all."

5 Then Abram gave Hagar both water and bread,
 And sent her away with her child, and she fled,
 And wandered in wilds of Beersheba forlorn,
 And cast down her child for to die there alone.

6 Then over against him she good ways off went,
 To not see him die, then with loud voice she wept.
 An angel called Hagar, and thus to her spake,
 "God hears thee; rise, take thy child, he shall be great."

7 She found there a well, and gave drink to her child,
 Who grew up an archer in Beer-sheba's wilds,
 And dwelt in the lone wilderness of Paran.—
 His mother took wife for him from Egypt's land.

8. Abimelech, and Phichol, chief captain of host,
 Said thus unto Abram, "God aids all thou doest,
 Now swear by thy God, thou wilt be true to me,
 And my sons, and son's sons, and country, swear thee."

9 Then Abram said thus, "swear I, as thou didst tell."
 Then Abram reproved him concerning a well,
 Which servants in violence had taken away.
 The king said, "I knew not this thing till to-day."

10 Then Abram gave oxen and sheep to the king,
 And they both made covenant concerning this thing,
 And Abram set seven ewe lambs by themselves.
 The king said, "what doth these ewe lambs mean, pray tell?'

11 "These lambs shalt thou take of my hand, that they tell
 And witness of me that I did dig this well."
 He called that place Beersheba, since they there swore
 Thus covenanted they at Beer-sheba of yore.

12 Abimelech and Phichol, chief of his command,
 Then rose and returned to the Philistine's land.
 A grove Abram planted in Beer-sheba there,
 And called on the name of the Lord God in prayer.

CHAPTER XXII.

1 Then God tempted Abraham to " sacrifice
Thy younger son Isaac to bleed,"
Who was son of promise, the child of the skies,
And Abraham's only true seed.

2 God bade him unto Mount Moriah to go
And offer his son Isaac there.
Then Abram took servants with Isaac also,
And clave wood for burnt offering fire.

3 When he the third day saw the mount afar off,
He bade the young men stay nor fear,
And I and the lad will go yonder aloft,
And worship, then come to you here.

4 Then Abram took wood for the burnt offering fire,
And laid it in son Isaac's hands,
When Isaac of Abram did strangely inquire,
And say, " Father, where is the lamb ? "

5 Then Abram said, " Son, God a lamb will provide."
As thus he did all things prepare,
Laid wood on the altar as God had required,
Bound Isaac and laid him on there ;

6 Then Abraham reached forth his hand for the knife,
To do what the Lord ordered done.
An angel's loud voice from the sky saved his life,
And cried, " Abraham, spare thy son.

7 This proves to the world thou in God doth confide,
Since thou hast withheld not thy son."
Then Abram beheld in a thicket aside
A lamb for an offering had come.

8 Then Abram that place named Jehovah-jireh,
In mount of the Lord ever seen.
The angel who saved his son Isaac from death,
Spake thus from the heavens again :

9 " God tempted thee here for example to show
That all men should thus mind the Lord ;
And love Him so that they would give all below
If it is the known will of God.

10 I've sworn with the Lord since thou hast not withheld
   Thy younger son Isaac from death,
   That blessing, I'll multiply thee, and will swell
   Thy seed as the sands of earth.

11 Thy true seed are all those who keep God's commands,
   And put on the mind of His love,
   Which was God's eternal design and wise plan
   Ordained ere creation begun.

12 The gates of their foemen that seed shall detain,
   In it shall all nations be blest,"
   Then Abram returned back to his home again,
   And dwelt in Beer-sheba at rest.

13 Then his brother Nahor with eight sons was blest,
   Of wife Milcah, men did him tell,
   Named Huz, Buz, Kemuel, and Hazo and Chesed,
   Pildash, Jidlaph and Bethuel.

14 Bethuel was sire of Rebekah the fair,
   Whom Abram's son Isaac did wed;
   The mother of Esau and Jacob, twin pair,
   Of whom much in history is said.

15 New ages pushed, old ages rolling away
   Until promised time came to hand
   When on hill of Calvary as Abram did say
   His God there provided the land.

CHAPTER XXIII.

1 At age hundred twenty-seven years Sarah dying,
   Separated this life within Canaan's domain.
   Then Abram came mourning with weepings and sighings
   His tears for wife Sarah he could not contain.

2 Then he to the sons of Heth said, " I'm a stranger,
   And but a sojourner with you in this land ;
   Pray give me a burying place from all danger,
   To bury my dead out of sight from my hand."

3 Said Heth's sons, " 'mong us lord thou art a prince mighty.
   We give thee choice place here to bury thy dead."
   Then Abraham bowed down to Heth's sons politely
   And said, "let me do as your kindness hath said.

4 Entreat for me Ephron who is son of Zohar,
      That he give me cave Machpelah of his field,
    For just as much money as he shall it offer,
      That there undisturbed may my dead rest concealed "

5 Then Ephron the Hitite made him this expression,
      In presence of all of the city of Heth,
    " I give thee the field and its cave for possession,
      To bury thy dead in that undisturbed rest."

6 Then Abraham bowed down before all the people,
      And spake thus to Ephron, in presence of all ;
    " If thou give the field, then it can be no evil,
      If I give what money thou mayest it call."

7 Said Ephron, " the field is, and cave also on there,
      Worth four hundred shekels of silver to me ;
    But what is that sum between mine and thine honor ?
      Go bury thy dead, all is welcome to thee."

8 Abram heard to Ephron, and weighed him the silver
      Which he named, in audience of city of Heth,
    The four hundred shekels, as current forever,
      As any of money the merchants possess.

9 Before Mamre's plain lay this field of Machpelah,
      Which field with its cave and all trees therein left,
    In all of its borders about were they deeded
      Abram's possession, by children of Heth.

10 Abram buried Sarah his wife, with much weeping
      In field of Machpelah, of Canaan's domain,
    With bright hopes to meet her where angels are greeting,
      And enter God's rest, which for saints doth remain.

11 How wondrous was God manifest unto Sarah,
      In birth of son Isaac at age ninety years.
    Who would from the trust of that God ever vary,
      Must be false to knowledge, and reason, most dear.

CHAPTER XXIV.

1 Now Abram was old, and well stricken with age,
      Yet God blest his heart and his hand :
    His servant he swore not a wife to engage
      For son Isaac, from Canaan's land.

2 Go thou to my country and kindred, and find
     A wife there, for Isaac my son.
  The servant then said, " should the maid not incline
     To follow me, what will be done ?

3 Must I bring thy son to that land whence thou came ? "
     Then Abram said, " Nay, but beware,
  God's angel will go before thee and sustain
     And find a maid, lovely and fair.

4 The Lord God who sent me from my father's hand,
     From kindred and country swore me,
  That unto thy seed will I give all this land,
     And ever a God be to thee.

5 If she doth not follow thee, thou shalt be clear
     From oath, so depart ye this day."
  His servant with ten camels quickly did steer
     For city of Nahor away.

6 He paused at a well near the city, the time
     That damsels go water to draw ;
  He prayed, " O, Lord God of good Abram incline
     To speed what he sent me here for.

7 Now Lord, if a maid to draw water shall go,
     And I ask for drink when she comes,
  And she say, " drink, lord, and thy camels also,"
     Let her be for my master's son.

8 At length a young Syrian damsel came out,
     With pitcher, and was very fair,
  She ran to the well, filling it, turned about
     And met Abraham's servant there.

9 He said to the damsel, " wilt thou give me drink ?"
     " Yea, drink thou my lord," she replied,
  Which caused Abram's servant that moment to think
     God chose her for young Isaac's bride.

10 She said, I'll give drink to thy camels also,
     And drew water till all were done,
  While he held his peace as his heart did o'erflow,
     To think prayer was answered so soon.

11 He took two gold ear-rings of half shekel's weight,
     Two bracelets of ten shekels gold,
  Placed them on the damsel, and thus to her spake,
     " Thy name I have not yet been told."

12   She said, " I'm Bethnel's own daughter, and kin
     To Abram, that great man of prayer.
   My name is Rebekah, wilt thou please turn in,
     In welcome abide with us there."

13   The servant bowed down and in prayer did abide,
     And blessed Abram's God meekly then,
   For showing such mercy his servant to guide
     To people of Abraham's friends.

14   Rebekah then told to her parents these things,
     When Laban, her brother ran out,
   And saw on his sister the bracelets and rings,
     He wondered what had come about.

15   He ran to the servant who stood at the well,
     And cried, " hail thou, blest of the Lord,
   Why standest without, come abide where we drink,
     All things for thee there are prepared."

16   The servant turned in and they set for him meat.
     He said, " I'll not eat 'till I've told
   Mine errand;" they said tell, as thus he did speak,
     I'm Abraham's servant of old.

17   The Lord blest my master, and hath made him great
     In herds, flocks, and silver and gold;
   And Sarah, his wife, bear him son Isaac late,
     When he was full ninety years old.

18   My master then made me thus swear as I tell,
     " Thou shalt not take wife to my son ;
   Of Canaanite's daughters in whose land I dwell,
     From my kindred's house take thou one."

19   He said that " the Lord God before Whom I walk,
     For thee will send His angel on,
   Preparing thy way 'till a wife thou hast got,
     Of kindred for Isaac, my son."

20   He said, " if thy kindred shall not give thee one,
     Then thou from thine oath shall be clear,
   And I came this day meekly, trusting, alone,
     That his God will prosper me here.

21   I prayed thus, if maids to draw water shall go,
     And I ask for drink when one comes,
   And she say. drink, lord, and thy camels also,
     Let her be for my master's son.

22   When I had thus prayed for these things of my God,
      Rebekah for water did go,
      I asked her for drink; and she said, 'drink, my lord,
      I'll water thy camels also.'

23   I asked her whose daughter she was of such grace,
      'Bethuel's,' she said, 'Nahor's son.'
      Then placed I the golden ear-rings on her face,
      And bracelets of gold on her hands.

24   I bowed down my head and in prayer did abide,
      And blest Abram's God meekly there,
      Who sent forth His angel my way for to guide,
      To this maid of Abraham's friends.

25   If ye will deal kindly and truly tell me,
      If not, tell, for you must decide,
      That I turn to the right hand or left may turn free,
      Say, shall she be young Isaac's bride?"

26   Bethuel and Laban then answered and said,
      " For this doth the Lord God abide;
      We would not speak to it, for heaven hath thee led,
      Since God wills, make her Isaac's bride."

27   When these words were heard, Abram's servant of old
      Bowed down and did worship and pray ;
      Then brought forth rich jewels of silver and gold,
      And raiment and gave Rebekah.

28   Her mother and brother he gave precious things,
      They ate and drank merry as one,
      He tarried till morn, when he said, " let me bring
      A bride to my good master's son."

29   They said, " let her 'bide with us yet for ten days,
      Then after that time she shall go."
      He said, hinder not, since God prospereth my ways,
      Pray send me to my master now.

30   They said, we'll enquire of the damsel to know.
      Then called on Rebekah to say,
      " Go ye with this Man ?" and she said, " I will go."
      So they went their journey away.

31   Rebekah and damsels, with servants and men,
      With these blessings journeying did go.
      " Be mother of thousands of millions, let then
      Thy seed hold the gates of thy foe."

32 Rebekah with damsels rode in the convoy
    On camels and followed the man,
  Then Isaac came from way of well Lahai-roi,
    He dwelt in the south country then.

33 As Isaac did oft meditate in the field
    At eve, he far off did behold
  His camels approaching which soon did reveal
    A damsel in purple and gold.

34 Rebekah then saw afar off on the field,
    A sprightly young man coming on,
  She asked, " who is he ?" when the servant revealed
    " 'Tis young Isaac, Abraham's son."

35 She took purple veil and did cover her face,
    And off of her camel did light,
  The servant told young Isaac all that took place,
    And that he had brought him his wife.

36 Young Isaac approaching, her veil she removed,
    The servant said, " 'tis Abram's son ;"
  Then she on him smiled as they greeted in love,
    Saluting as lovers become.

37 Young Isaac conducted her to Sarah's tent,
    And loved her as dear as his life,
  She comforted him after his mother's death,
    Becoming his kind, loving wife.

CHAPTER XXV.

1 Abram took a wife called Keturah, again,
  Who bare Zimran, Jokshan, Medan, Nidian,'
  Then Ishbak and Shuah, six children in all,
  And Jokshan's two sons, Shiba, Dedan were called.

2 Dedan's sons Asshurim, Letushim, Lecummim.
  These were the three sons Dedan had born to him.
  Ephah, Epher, Hanoch, Abidah, Eldah,
  These are Midian's sons, children of Keturah.

3 Then Abram gave up all to Isaac, his son,
  His days being numbered, his work being done.
  His life was an hundred and seventy-five years,
  He died in old age, with God's blessing to cheer.

4   His sons Isaac, Ishmael, did bury him then,
    In cave of Machpelah, in field of Ephron,
    Which he had once bought of the rude sons of Heth.
    They buried him there with wife Sarah to rest.

5   Nebajoth, Adbeel, Mibsam, Kedar, Mishma,
    Dumah, Massa, Hadar, Jetur and Tema,
    Napish and Kedmah, all sons of Ishmael,
    Of towns, castles, nations, like wise princes twelve.

6   Ishmael lived an hundred and thirty-seven years,
    And dwelt before Egypt, 'tween Havilah and Shur,
    And Isaac was forty years old when he wed,
    Bethuel's fair daughter, the Syrian maid.

7   At length Isaac prayed to the Lord for increase,
    Which when the Lord granted, did Isaac well please,
    The Lord said, " two Nations shall come forth of thee,
    Two manner of people shall they also be.

8   One yet shall be stronger than the other one,
    And likewise the elder shall yet serve the young,"
    Their first-born was Esau a red hairy man,
    His other twin brother was Jacob by name.

9   Esau was a cunning huntsman of the field,
    A plain man was Jacob, in tents he did dwell
    And Isaac loved Esau for his venison meat,
    Rebekah loved Jacob, who made pottage sweet.

10 Esau said to Jacob, " come feed me I pray,
    With thy good red pottage, for I faint to-day."
    He said, " Sell thy birth-right then feed thee will I."
    Esau said, " It's worth naught, if hungering I die.

11 Then Jacob said, " Swear it to me," and he swear
    And sold him his birth-right, as oath did declare
    Then Jacob gave bread, drink, and pottage likewise,
    Esau ate, and went, and his birth right despised.

CHAPTER XXVI.

1   To Gerar went Isaac to King Abimelech
    The Lord bade him, " Not go to Egypt but yet
    Remain in this land, from it go not forth
    'Tis thine, and I'll bless thee, according to oath.

2   Which I sware to Abram, who heard to my voice,
And kept My commandments, My statutes and laws,"
Then Isaac did call his wife " sister " while there,
For fear of his life since she was very fair.

3   The King saw the wrong, and that she was his wife,
And told him, " This might bring reproach on my life,
My swains might have sought thy fair wife for to wed,"
Hence he told his men that through fear it was said.

4   Then Isaac did sow, reap, and get hundred fold,
God blest him, he waxed great, and grew strong and bold,
And gained great possessions of flocks, herds and stores,
The lords of Philistines, then envied him more.

5   They filled up the wells which his sire Abram made,
The king said, "Go from us of thee we're a'raid."
From thence Isaac went, pitched in vale of Gerar,
And opened the wells digged by Abram his sire ;

6   Which Philistines stopped up since Abraham's death,
And gave wells the same names his sire Abram left,
For wells Isaac digged, Gerar's herdsmen did strive
He then digged far off, and was prosperous and thrived.

7   He went to Beer-sheba, where God assured him
Of blessings for sake of his sire Abraham,
He there built an altar, God with him did dwell,
He there worshipped, as they did dig him a well.

8   Abimelech, from Gerar, with friends did come near,
Said Isaac, " Ye hate me, why come ye here ?"
They said, " God is with thee, we want love with thee,"
So each pledged to do good to each and agree.

9   He gave them a feast then they rose up betimes,
And swore to each other in peace to combine,
Isaac named the well which his men found that day,
Shebah, which was called " City of Beer-sheba."

10   At forty Esau took two Canaanite wives,
Adah, Elon's daughter, who was a Hittite,
And Aholibamah, Anah's daughter fair,
Whose grand sire was Zibeon, and a Hivite there.

11   Since daughters of Canaan, his parents pleased not,
Of Abraham's seed, for a third wife, he sought,
And went to the house of good Abram's Son there,
And took Ishmael's daughter, Bashemath the fair.

CHAPTER XXVII.

1   When Isaac was old so that he could not see,
    He said to son Esau, " I soon shall leave thee,
    Behold I am old and know not my death day,
    Go kill for me venison, without a delay,

2   And make me good savory meat such as I
    Do love, that I eat, and bless thee, ere I die.
    Esau then went hunting. for venison to bring,
    Rebekah heard Isaac tell Esau these things.

3   Then she told to Jacob what Isaac had said,
    And said, " Now obey me, and bring two good kids,
    And I for thy father will make savory meat,
    Which thou shalt bring him, that he bless thee and eat.

4   Then Jacob said, " Esau is hairy and I
    Am smooth, then my father will blessing deny,
    If he should feel me, a deceiver I'll be,
    And bring not his blessing, but curse upon me."

5   Rebekah said to him, " On me be thy curse,
    Obey me, and fetch them, thou shalt be blest first,
    He fetched them, and she made for him savory meat,
    And dressed Jacob in Esau's raiment complete.

6   And put skins of kids on his smooth neck and hands,
    And gave him the meat, with her word of command,
    He brought it, and said, " Father eat for I'm come."
    Then Isaac said, " Tell me who art thou my son?"

7   He said, "I am Esau, thy first born to thee,
    I've come with my venison, rise, eat, and bless me,
    " O ! how didst thou find it so quickly my Son?"
    " The Lord thy God brought it to me very soon."

8   Then Isaac said to him, " come near me I pray,
    That I may feel thee whether Esau or nay,
    When Jacob drew near, Isaac said, " Sure it seems
    To be Jacob's voice, but it is Esau's hands."

9   He did not discern him for his hairy hands,
    He said, " Art thou Esau?" said Jacob, "I am.
    He said, "My son Esau now bring it near me,
    That I eat thy venison, and also bless thee."

10   Then Jacob with meat, unto Isaac did come,
      He ate, and said, " Esau, come kiss me, my son."
      Then Jacob did kiss him, as Isaac did bless
      His then supposed Esau, with fondest caress.

11   And said. " my son Esau doth smell like a field
      Which God hath much blest with abundance of yield.
      Therefore, God give Esau the blest due of heaven,
      And corn, wine and fatness to him shall be given.

12   And let people serve thee and nations bow down,
      Be lord o'er thy brethren, and thy mother's sons,
      And cursed be every one that hateth thee,
      And those who shall bless thee shall ever blest be."

13   Then Esau soon came from his hunting, with meat,
      And said, " rise, my father, and bless me, and eat."
      Then Isaac cried, " who cometh now to be blest ?
      For I have blest Esau, my son, and curest."

14   Then Esau cried, " father, I am thy first-born."
      Then Isaac did tremble, exceeding forlorn,
      And cried, " where is he who brought venison and said,
      'I truly am Esau,' O where hath he fled ?

15   And Lo, I have eaten of all ere thou came,
      And blest one who said, Esau sure was his name."
      Then Esau exclaimed, with a most bitter cry,
      "O father, wilt thou not bless me, even I ?"

16   Then Isaac said, " Jacob hath subtilly came
      And taken a blessing in Esau's own name;
      I made that one lord o'er his brethren each one.
      I meant it for thee, then, O Esau, my son."

17   Said Esau, " hast thou but one blessing to give?"
      And wept, saying, " may I a blessing receive?
      Then Isaac did say, " Esau's dwelling shall prove
      The fatness of earth and the dew from above.

18   By sword thou shalt live, and thy brother shalt serve,
      But time cometh when thou dominion shalt have,
      And break his yoke off of thy neck, which he hath,
      He shall call thee lord, and bow to thee at last.

19   Because of this fraud Jacob shall have great fear,
      And dwell as exile for many a year.
      Then God shall recall him to greet thee again,
      And call thee lord Esau, and thy love attain."

20   Esau did hate Jacob for that blessing's sake,
    And threatened his life, which did much trouble make,
    Rebekah, in fright, bade him flee, and to stay,
    Until Esau's wrath should be turned far away.

21   Rebekah then said, " I am weary of life,
    Lest Jacob of daughters of Heth take a wife.
    Of such daughters as I do in this land see,
    What good shall my life ever be unto me."

CHAPTER XXVIII.

1 Then Isaac called Jacob, and blest him, and charged,
    And said, "thou shalt not take a wife
  Of Canaanite's daughters, whose sins are enlarged,
    Lest thou dwell in sin and in strife.

2 But go to thy kins-folks and take thee a wife,
    Of goodness, that God bless thy hand,
  And multiply thee, that thy sons may in life
    Inherit good Abraham's land."

3 Then Jacob did journey to Padan-aram,
    To Laban, the Syrian's son,
  To take there a wife of his father's own kin,
    Esau went to Ishmael for one.

4 And took fair Bashemath, his daughter, to wife,
    Since Ishmael was Abraham's son.
  And Jacob from Beer-sheba went forth, till night,
    Toward Haran till sunset had come.

5 He took stones for pillows of his head, at even,
    And lay down in that place to sleep,
  And dreamed of a ladder from Earth unto heaven,
    On which passing angels did keep.

6 Then God said, " To thee and thy seed will I give
    This land, from East, West, North and South,
  And bring thee again to it, and will not leave
    But do all the words of my mouth."

7 Then Jacob did wake from his sleep and did say,
    " The Lord's here, and I know it not."
  He feared as he cried, " O, how dreadful this place,
    It is heaven's gate, house of God."

8   The stone of his pillow he there did set up,
     And oil he poured forth on its top,
   And named that place Bethel, which first was called Luz,
     So that it should ne'er be forgot.

9   Then Jacob did vow, " if the Lord will sustain
     And give peace and raiment and food,
   So that I to my Father's house come again,
     The Lord shall be ever my God.

10 This stone which I set for a pillar, shall be
     God's house. So of all Thou shalt give
   To me I will then give a tenth unto thee,
     As sure as I by the Lord live."

CHAPTER XXIX.

1   As journeying eastward, Jacob came to a well,
   Where flocks came for watering, from where men did dwell,
   Said Jacob, "from whence are ye?" they said. "Haran's land.'
   He said, " know ye Laban?" they said, " we know that man."

2   He said, " How are Laban's folks?" they said, " ask Rachel,
   His daughter, now yonder, leads her flocks to the well."
   Said Jacob, " it is not time that cattle drink now,
   Let me water Rachel's sheep that they feeding go."

3   They said, " one cannot roll off the stone from the well."
   As Rachel arrived with flocks from where she did dwell,
   The stone Jacob rolled, and watered Rachel's flock there,
   Then kissed her and wept, for she was lovely and fair.

4   Then Rachel told Laban this was his sister's son,
   Then he ran and kissed him, and invited him home.
   Then Laban said, " now, since thou art bone of my bones,
   Please tarry in welcome here and make it thy home.

5   Because thou art brother shouldst thou serve for nought,
   Please tell me thy wages and I'll pay what I ought "
   His two daughters Leah and Rachel with him did dwell,
   The eldest was tender-eyed, but Rachel looked well.

6   Said Jacob, " for Rachel, I will serve seven years,
   For thy youngest daughter doth my heart ever cheer."
   Said Laban, " 'tis better that I give her to thee
   Than have some stranger swain abiding with me."

7 Seven years' toil for Rachel seemed to him but few days,
   For love which he had for her and her kindly ways,
   Then Jacob to Laban said, " make Rachel my wife,
   My day's works are ended, that she comfort my life."

8 Then Laban invited and a wedding feast made,
   At eve gave his Leah, and not Rachel to wed.
   Until morning light had come, he knew not his fate,
   How strong wine had blinded him until 'twas too late.

9 Then Laban gave daughter Leah, Zilpah his maid,
   And Jacob next morning did see 'twas Leah he had wed.
   Then Jacob to Laban said, " what means this of thee ?
   Did I not for Rachel serve, why thus cheat thou me ?"

10 Then Laban said, " 'tis not so in our country known,
   To wed younger daughter off before the first-born,
   Fulfill now her week, and we'll give Rachel also,
   For service which thou shalt serve with me seven years more."

11 So Jacob agreed, and wedded Rachel also,
   Bilhah, Laban's hand-maid, he then gave Rachel too.
   Then Jacob served Laban till seven years more were past,
   For Jacob loved Rachel more than Leah at last.

12 For Leah was hated since no beauty she hath,
   Yet she had sons Reuben, Simeon. Levi, Judah.
   How sinful to hate the looks of what God hath made,
   The good are the beautiful, whose beauty ne'er fades.

CHAPTER XXX.

1 Then Rachel did grieve because no children she had,
   So she gave her hand-maid to her husband to wed.
   Her hand-maid then had two sons, Dan and Naphtali.
   Then Rachel said, " God hath judged me, hearing my cry."

2 Then Leah, her hand-maid, gave to Jacob to wed,
   Who bear her two sons, whom they named Asher and Gad.
   Then Leah again did bear to Jacob two sons.
   The first they named Issachar, the next Zebulun.

3 Then Leah bear to Jacob daughter Dinah, most fair,
   And Rachel to Jacob bear son Joseph, true heir.
   Then Rachel said. " God will give me yet one more son."
   Said Jacob. " God calls me now to my father's home.

4 Give me wives and children dear, for whom I served thee.
   Then Laban said " tarry, for God with thee blest me,
   Tell me what thy wages are, to them I'll incline."
   Said Jacob, " I've blest thy house, now let me keep mine."

5 Said Jacob, " for speckled stock hence born from this date,
   And thou take all speckled ones out, I'll work at that rate."
   Said Laban, " agreed, I would that it were so done."
   That day Laban gave all speckled stock to his son.

6 He set three days journey then between their two flocks ;
   He peeled poplar, chestnut, hazel, in streaks and spots,
   Then set those peeled, streaked rods, at waterings of stock,
   To make them conceive a spotted, ringed, speckled flock.

7 Thus Jacob did Laban trap, by this curious trade,
   Which paid him for smuggling Leah in Rachel's stead.
   So Jacob exceeding gained, in riches untold,
   In men and maid-servants, cattle, camels and gold.

CHAPTER XXXI.

1 Then Jacob heard words of Laban's sons. saying thus,
   That Jacob took father's wealth and glory from us.
   When he saw that Laban's look toward him had changed,
   God said, " I'll be with thee, seek thy sire's land again."

2 Then Jacob said to his wives, " your sire doth incline
   To hate me, for he hath changed my wages ten times,
   Ye see how the Lord gave Laban's wealth in my hands,
   Since now that he hateth me, we'll seek Isaac's land.

3 God's angel spake to me in a dream and did say,
   ' I am God of Bethel, where on stone thou didst lay.
   Return to thy father's house, to Esau confess
   The wrong thou hast done him, and like brothers be blest.' "

4 His wives said, " there's naught left in our sire's house for us
   We are counted strangers, and our money is lost.
   The wealth God hath taken from our father is ours,
   So what God hath bid thee do, that do at this hour."

5 Then Jacob did journey forth, with all he possessed,
   To go to his father's house, which he had just left.
   Then Laban o'ertook him on his journey three days.
   God warned him while going not to stop Jacob's ways.

6   Said Laban to Jacob, " why hast thou stole away,
    And carried my daughters off as captives to-day ?
    If thou hadst but told me, I would blest thy depart
    With songs, mirth and kisses, and with tabret and harp.

7   Thou sufferedst me not to kiss my daughters I love,
    Kept me from saluting my loved sons I approve.
    Thou hast done unwisely not to bid us adieu,
    I have power to hurt you, but God bade me be true.

8   Said Jacob, " I feared that thou wouldst keep my two wives
    By force, and that such act might endanger our lives.
    I thought 'twas far better to depart still in peace
    Since I have long served thee, and long tried thee to please.

9   Then Rachel took Laban's golden gods when she left,
    In place of their wages, which their father had kept.
    Then Jacob did chide with Laban in much reproof,
    Till each made a covenant, and as friends went aloof.

10 Then Jacob made sacrifice, and feasted them all.
    They ate bread and tarried all the night, great and small.
    Then early next morning Laban kissed all his sons
    And daughters, and blest them all, and then journeyed home,

CHAPTER XXXII.

1   As Jacob did journey, God's angels met him,
    He called them God's host, named that place Mahanaim,
    And messengers sent to Esau ere he came,
    Who dwelt in Mount Seir, which is Edom by name.

2   He bade them tell Esau, "with presents I come
    To seek my Lord's favor, with flocks journeying home."
    His men came back, saying "thy brother we've seen.
    He cometh to meet thee with four hundred men."

3   Then Jacob feared greatly, and thus did divide
    His people and flocks, in two bands on each side,
    And said, " if he smite one, let other escape."
    Then called he on God, for his mercy and grace.

4   He said, " I'm not worthy thy mercies and truth,
    Which Lord thou hast showed me since days of my youth ;
    Deliver me, Lord, from my brother, I pray,
    From Esau, lest he come and smite me and slay.

5 The mother and children whom thou didst pledge me
   Should multiply like as the sand of the sea,
   O God of my fathers, Thou saidst unto me,
   Return to thy kindred, and all shall well be."

6 Then Jacob took two hundred twenty of goats,
   With same number sheep, thirty camels with coats,
   And fifty of kine, twenty asses with foals,
   And sent them to Esau to move insult old.

7 This flock Jacob placed in his servant's command,
   And said, " go tell Esau it's from Jacob's hand,
   A present he sends unto Esau his lord,
   And he is behind us who sent this reward."

8 For Jacob said, " I will my brother appease
   With presents before, that he may me receive,"
   Then Jacob that night took his women and sons,
   And crossed the brook Jabbok, with things every one.

9 And while Jacob stayed there that night in dismay,
   A man wrestled with him till breaking of day.
   And when the man saw that he did not prevail,
   He touched Jacob's thigh, and that moment it failed.

10 He said, " let me go, for the day breaks on thee."
   But Jacob said, " nay, not till thou hast blest me."
   The Man said to him, " tell Me, what is thy name."
   He said, " it is Jacob." He said, "thou hast fame.

11 As prince thou hast power with My God to prevail ;
   Thy name call not Jacob, but call it Israel."
   He then did bless Jacob, as God face to face,
   Preserving his life, and bestowing great grace.

12 He wrestled with Jacob, since he harbored fear,
   And crossed over Jabbok with wives and sons dear.
   The Man did him touch, for to show God hath power,
   That man should obey without fear, every hour.

CHAPTER XXXIII.

1 Then Jacob met Esau and four hundred men,
   And bowed himself down seven times to him then.
   Then Esau did run his twin brother to meet,
   Embraced him and kissed him, and they did both weep.

2   Then Esau said, "who are these whom ye here have?"
He said, "wives and children, God graciously gave."
Wives, children and hand-maids then all did draw near,
And bowed them to Esau, and did him revere.

3   Then Esau said, "what means this drove which I met?"
He said, "to find favor, my lord, in thy sight,
Since our mother once urged me thee to defraud
Of blessing which father meant for thee, my lord.

4   I now come with presents imploring thy grace,
In love I solicit the smiles of thy face."
Esau said, "my brother, I have enough wealth,
Keep that which thou hast, for thy children and self."

5   But Jacob said, "nay, lord, if I have found grace,
My present receive at my hand for love's sake,
For I've seen thy face as the dear face of God.
And thou wast pleased with me, so loving and good.

6   So take now I pray this my blessing brought thee,
Since God hath dealt graciously plenteous with me."
When he thus urged Esau, the drove he did take,
And said, "come, I'll lead thee, our journey we'll make."

7   Said Jacob, "my lord will please go before me,
And I will come slowly as our strength may be,
Until I shall come to my lord at Mount Seir."
So Esau turned home, leaving him in the rear.

8   When Jacob reached Succoth he built him a booth
For cattle, therefore was that place called Succoth.
Then Jacob to Shalem, Shechem's city came,
Pitched tent there, when he came from Padam-aram,

9   And bought there a parcel of Hamor's son's land
For an hundred pieces of money at hand,
And built him an altar near where he did dwell,
There prayed, calling it El-elohe-Israel.

CHAPTER XXXIV.

1   Then Dinah, the daughter of Jacob, did come
To visit the Canaanite daughters at home.
Then Shechem, a young Hivite prince, on her smiled,
And pledged her to wed, though he did her beguile.

2   Her brothers were wroth from disgrace, and sore grieved,
     And vowed to avenge sister Dinah, bereaved,
     But Shechem begged them to make Dinah his wife,
     And let all be peace, since he loved her as life.

3   To which they deceitfully pledged to comply ;
     If circumcision you will not deny.
     To which they agreed and were all circumcised.
     Then Simeon and Levi threw off their disguise.

4   And charged Shechem's city with drawn swords of death,
     Slew Hamar and Shechem, his son, with the rest.
     They then spoiled their city, took all for their own,
     And took sister Dinah from Shechem's house home.

5   " Ye are far more wicked then they," Jacob said,
     " To murder, and not keep the promise ye made,
     Such cruelty sure, will make me an offence,
     Among all the people of this land from hence.

6   Ye should have forgiven, since Shechem desired,
     Our Dinah for wife, they so meekly required,
     When they sought our friendship, 'twas vile to deceive
     My sons with such vengeance our God is displeased.

7   If they give such vengeance to us, we ere long
     May all be thus slain, we are few they are strong."
     They said, " Why should he then our sister defile?"
     He said, " They should not, nor should we them beguile."

CHAPTER XXXV.

1   To Bethel, God bade Jacob, " Go
     And build there an altar to Me,"
    Said Jacob, " Let all my house now
     Be clean, putting strange gods from thee."

2   They then gave him all their strange gods,
     And jewels which Jacob did hide
    Beneath an oak, by Shechem's wood,
     Then no more their foes did them chide.

3   And when he to Bethel forth came,
     He built altar El-bethel there,
    Since God there appeared to him, when
     From Esau he fled in despair.

4   Rebekah's nurse Deborah died there,
      Was buried neath altar Beth-el,
    The place called Allon-bachuth, where
      Again God with Jacob did dwell.

5   He said, " The land of Abraham,
      And Isaac, I to thee will give,
    And to thy seed from Mine own hand,
      What I gave them, thou shalt receive.

6   Then Jacob a stone pillar set,
      Where he held converse with the Lord,
    And called that place Bethel, God blest,
      To Ephrath he still went onward.

7   There Benjamin's birth, Rachel gave,
      And died, and he mourned her that hour,
    A stone pillar placed on her grave,
      Then journeyed beyond Edar's tower.

8   Now Jacob's sons did number twelve,
      Born to him in Padan-aram ;
    Then he came where his sire did dwell,
      In Hebron, land of Abraham.

9   At his hundred eightieth year,
      Died Isaac, to rest with the blest,
    Then Esau and Jacob in tears
      Did bury him in his last rest.

10   In Machpelah's cave, which Abram
      Once bought of the rude sons of Heth,
    Where Abram and Sarah were lain,
      Embalmed in their last quiet rest.

CHAPTER XXXVI.

1   Of daughters of Canaan, Esau took two wives,
    Adah, Elon's daughter, who was a Hittite,
    And one Anah's daughter, Aholibamah there.
    Likewise Ishmael's daughter, Bashemath the fair,

2   Bashemath bare Reuel, Adah bare Eliphaz,
    Aholibamah bare Jeush, Jaalam and Korah,
    These are sons of Esau, born unto him here,
    In Canaan.   Then he with all, moved to Mount Seir.

3 These are the generations of Esau the sire
  Of all of the Edomites, once in Mount Seir,
  Eliphaz and Reuel were both Esau's sons,
  Of Adah and Bashemath, in Canaan born.

4 These five sons were born then unto Eliphaz,
  Teman, Omar, Zepho, Gatam and Kenaz,
  Eliphaz had son Amalek of Timna.
  These are sons of Esau's first wife named Adah.

5 Reuel's sons were Nahath, Zerath, Shammah, Mizzah,
  All grandsons of Esau's wife named Bashemath.
  Aholibamah bare Jeush, Jaalam, Korah,
  These were dukes of Esau's sons of Eliphaz.

6 Duke Teman, duke Omar, Zepho, duke Kenaz,
  Duke Gatan, duke Amalek and duke Korah,
  These came from Eliphaz, in Edom's high land.
  These are sons of Adah, and dukes every man.

7 These are sons whom Reuel, Esau's son begat,
  Duke Nahath, duke Zerah, duke Shammah, Mizzah.
  These dukes came of Reul, Bashemath's first son,
  Who was Esau's wife in Mount Seir, called Edom.

8 Duke Jeush, duke Jaalam, duke Korah were sons
  Of Aholibamah, Esau's wife each one,
  These are sons of Esau, and called dukes each one,
  And these were the sons of Horites in Edom.

9 Duke Zibeon, Anah, Shobal and Lotan,
  And duke Dishon, duke Ezer and Duke Dishon.
  The children of Lotan were Hori, Heman,
  He had sister Timna also in that land.

10 The children of Shobal were these in that land,
  Manahath, Alvan, Ebal, Shepho, Onam.
  And Zibeon's sons were Ajak and Anah,
  This Anah found mules in the wildnerness there.

11 While feeding the stock of his sire, Zibeon,
  The children of Anah were Dishon, one son,
  And daughter, Aholibamah, and but one,
  And these are the children unto Dishon born.

12 Hemdan and Eshban, and Ithran and Cheran,
  Ezer's sons were Bilhan, Zaavah and Akan.
  The children of Dishan were Uz and Aran,
  And these are the kings that reigned in Edom's land.

13   Before any king over Israel did reign,
     Bela ruled Dinhabah of Edom's domain,
     Bela died, Jobab, Zerah's son, reigned 'tis said,
     Jobab died, Husham, Teman's son, reigned instead.

14   Husham died and Hadad, Bedad's son did reign,
     Who in field of Moab smote Midian of fame.
     Hadad died and Samlah of Masrekah reigned.
     Samlah died and Saul of Rehoboth then came.

15   Saul died and Baal-hanan, Achbor's son, did reign.
     Baal-hanan then died. Hadar took his refrain,
     His city was Pau, and this was his wife's name,
     Mehetabel, daughter of Matred of fame.

16   These are names of dukes, which from Esau once came,
     According to families and places and names,
     Duke Timnah, duke Alvah, duke Jetheth, Elah,
     Duke Pinon, duke Aholibamah, Kenaz.

17   Duke Teman, duke Mibzar, duke Magdiel, Iram,
     These are dukes of Edom, of their homes and lands.
     In all their possessions and kingdoms and rights,
     Esau is the father of all Edomites.

CHAPTER XXXVII.

1   As Jacob in Canaan did dwell,
     And Joseph his son was seventeen,
   He oft to his father did tell,
     His brethren's ill deed he had seen.

2   Now Jacob loved Joseph for sake
     Of Rachel's first love he attained,
   Since born in his age he did make
     His coat many colors contain.

3   They saw that their sire when grown old,
     Loved Joseph, and best of him spake,
   Then Joseph this dream to them told,
     Which when they heard, more did him hate.

4   " As we in the field did sheaves bind,
     Our sheaves rose and all stood upright,
   Your sheaves made obeisance to mine."
     They said, "shalt thou rule us with might ?"

5   They hated him then more by far.
      "I have one more dream," now said he.
     " I dreamed that sun, moon and twelve stars,
      All made their obeisance to me."

6   His father rebuked, and said, " son,
      Must I and thy mother bow down,
    And thy elder brethren to one
      That's younger ?" as they on him frowned.

7   His brethren to Shechem then went,
      Their good father's flocks to feed there.
    Then afterward, Joseph he sent,
      To bring word if all had good care.

8   From Hebron to Shechem he sped,
      A man found him wandering there,
    Who asked him " what seek ye ?" he said
      " My brethren, canst thou tell me where ?"

9   The man said, " to Dothan they're gone.
      They said feed was plenteous there."
    Then Joseph went traveling on,
      In Dothan found them in good fare.

10   And when they saw him far away,
      Before he came near, they conspired
    And said, " we will slay him this day,
      Then see if his dreams are inspired.

11   We'll then cast him into some pit,
      And tell that some beast hath him slain,
    But Reuben delivered him out
      Their hands, saying, " let us not stain

12   Ourselves, with our own brother's blood,
      But cast him here into some pit."
    This said he for young Joseph's good,
      To bring him to his father yet.

13   They stripped Joseph out of his coat
      Of colors, their sire made for him,
    And then cast him in a deep pit,
      All empty with no water in.

14   They then saw approaching afar,
      From Gilead an Ishmeelite band,
    With spicery balm, and with myrrh,
      On camel's bound for Egypt's land.

15 Then Judah said, " What shall we gain,
    If we should spill our brother's blood,
  To sell him will cause us less blame,
    And something may come of it good.

16 They then drew him up as a slave,
    And sold him to Ishmeelite men,
  For him twenty pieces they gave,
    And brought him down to Egypt then.

17 When Reuben returned to the pit,
    To save Joseph, he was not there,
  Then he in remorse his clothes rent,
    In demon like guilt and despair.

18 He went to his brethren and said,
    " The child is dead, what shall we do ? "
  They then dipped his coat in kid's blood,
    And sent to their father to show.

19 They said to him, " This have we found,
    Say is this thy son's coat or not ? "
  He said, " Sure this coat is my son's,
    Some wild beast devoured him no doubt."

20 Then Jacob for Joseph did mourn,
    His children to comfort him came,
  His spirit with anguish was torn,
    From weeping he could not refrain.

CHAPTER XXXVIII.

1 Then Judah went down from his brethren afar,
  To one Adullamite whose name was Hirah,
  He there to a Canaanite daughter did pledge,
  Whose name was called Shuah and took her to wed.

2 Then Judah of Shuah, had born these three sons,
  Er, Onan, and Shelah, who was the best one.
  Then Er, did wed Thamar, God slew him for sin.
  Then Onan did wed her, for sin God slew him.

3 Said Judah to Thamar, abide here with me,
  Till Shelah is grown, him I'll also give thee.
  When Shelah was grown Judah then would not wed
  Son Shelah to Thamar, as he had her pledged.

4 Then Thamar did Judah beguile for this wrong,
   She feigned a veiled harlot, as he passed along,
   Whence she, bare to Judah, twins, Zarah, and Pharez,
   More righteous than I, art thou, Judah declares.

5 This judgment on Judah did sink him with awe
   For breaking his pledge to his daughter-in-law.
   Inconstancy hath its rewards at the close,
   Had Judah been true he had not been exposed.

CHAPTER XXXIX.

1 Then Joseph to Egypt was brought,
      And sold into Potiphar's hands,
   Who him of those Ishmeelites bought,
      Which brought him into Egypt's land.

2 His master saw that he was bright,
      That God blest all things in his hands,
   So Joseph found grace in his sight,
      And over all things had command.

3 For Joseph's sake God blest their house,
      And fields and all things that they had,
   And Joseph ruled in doors and out,
      Was well favored, perfect and good.

4 His master's wife said, "Come love me,
      Which Joseph so kindly declined,
   "Since thy lord gave me all but thee,
      How can I so wicked incline?"

5 When Joseph her suit did deny,
      Her love turned to Hatred and wrath,
   She told to his master a lie,
      Which Joseph in prison did cast.

6 But God showed him mercy while there,
      The keeper of prison did trust
   Young Joseph with all of his care,
      His prisoners all by him were blest,

CHAPTER XL.

1 It came then to pass that the king
     Of Egypt, in prison did cast,
  His butler and baker for things,
     Offending their lord unto wrath.

2 He put them in prison near by
     To Joseph, and charged him with them,
  They both dreamed a dream in one night,
  And thus told to Joseph their friend.

3 The Butler said, "I saw a vine
     Of three branches, clustering in bloom
  Which shot clustered grapes, ripe with wine,
     I pressed them in Pharaoh's cup soon."

4 "These branches," he said, "are three days,
     When Pharaoh thy head shall lift up,
  Restore thee thy place and old ways,
     And thou fill to Pharaoh his cup.

5 When well with thee pray help thou me,
     To Pharaoh your influence use,
  And tell him when ye shall him see,
     The wife did me falsely accuse."

6 The chief baker said, "I thus dreamed
     Three white baskets stood on my head,
  One basket held Pharaoh's baked meats,
     The birds ate them out and then fled."

7 These baskets are days numbering three,
     When Pharaoh shall lift off thy head,
  And hang thee in wrath on a tree,
     Where birds on thy flesh shall be fed.

8 When birth-feast of Pharaoh came,
     The Butler and Baker he raised,
  Restoring the Butler again,
     The Baker he hanged in disgrace.

CHAPTER XLI.

1   Seven well-favored kine, Pharaoh dreamed did proceed
Up forth from the river, lean-fleshed, and did feed,
Then seven other ill-favored, lean-fleshed kine came,
And ate up the fat kine, his dream did first name.

2   Then dreamed of seven ears on one stalk rank and good,
Then seven thin ears blasted, on which was no food,
Then dreamed the seven thin ears devoured the full ears,
Then Pharaoh awoke from his dream filled with fears.

3   He then called magicians, and wise men and told
His dream, but its meaning they could not unfold.
Then spake the chief butler to Pharaoh and said,
" My faults I remember to-day with much dread."

4   When thou didst imprison the Baker and me,
We both dreamed a dream there one night about thee.
Those dreams were explained by thy Hebrew young man,
That thou wouldst me free, but the baker would hang.

5   He bade me remember him if I got free,
And speak truly for him when I should thee see.
He told me that he had been falsely accused,
And thrown into prison when faithful and true.

6   Then Pharaoh called Joseph and asked of his dream,
And said, " canst thou tell unto me what it means?"
Then Joseph him answered, " it is not in me,
But God shall give Pharaoh an answer of peace.

7   For God best directeth the way of a King,
His fear shall his Kingdom to honor forth bring,
Then Pharaoh told Joseph of his strange dreams two,
He said, "Pharaoh's dream shows him what God will do.

8   The seven fat kine, and the seven good ears,
Do in Pharaoh's dream represent seven years ;
The seven thin lean kine, and the seven blasted ears,
Shall be seven years famine, which God bringeth here.

9   First seven years of plenty shall bless every man,
Then seven years of famine shall curse all the land,
By thy double dream God this thing hath forecast,
And in His set time, He will bring it to pass."

10 Then Joseph bade Pharaoh to lay up in store,
One fifth of the seven years of plenty or more,
That we may have food while the famine doth rage,
Which Pharaoh much pleased, and his servants engaged.

11 Said Pharaoh, " Since God hath revealed thee these things,
No man is here like thee who would safety bring,
So thou shalt be ruler o'er all I have now,
Only in the throne I'll be greater than thou."

12 Then Pharaoh his ring fastened on Joseph's hand,
Arrayed him in vestures of fine linen grand,
And with golden chains 'bout his neck, he did ride
In Pharaoh's bright chariots, with his loving bride.

13 The amiable daughter of Poti-pherah there,
The beauteous Asenath, and lovely as fair.
Then Joseph went, gathered all food in the land,
Of seven years of plenty of grain, as the sand.

14 Then Joseph's Asenath did bare him two sons,
Before the dread years of the famine had come.
" God made me forget father's house grief and toil,
So I, my first born son, Manasseh will call."

15 He then called his second son, Ephraim by name,
Since God made him fruitful in lands of his pain.
The famine increased now all over the earth,
And all countries came to buy corn with their worth.

CHAPTER XLII.

1 Then Jacob did send his ten sons to buy corn,
Down in Egypts land whither Joseph had gone,
Who then was the ruler o'er all in that land,
When his brethren found him, they knew not the man.

2 But he knew his brethren, yet he did them shun,
And roughly said to them, prove whence have ye come.
They said we're from Canaan to buy food of thee,
He said, "Ye are spies come our famine to see."

3 They said, " Nay my lord, but for food are we come,
True men and not spies, we are all one man's sons.
Our sire had twelve sons, but his Joseph was slain
By wild beasts, but Benjamin with him remains."

4   Then Joseph said, " If ye have told me no lies,
Send, bring your young brother, and prove you no spies,
And I will bind one of you here till he comes.
Go carry ye corn for your household at home."

5   They said to each other, " We are guilty men,
Concerning our brother whose anguish we've seen.
When he so besought us and we would not hear,
Hence cometh this judgment on us so severe."

6   " Did I not," said Reuben, " entreat you in tears,
Sin not 'gainst young Joseph, but ye would not hear,
Therefore, of us now, is required Joseph's blood."
But they did not know that he them understood.

7   Then Joseph in weeping from them did refrain,
At length he bound Simeon before them in chains,
And put in their sacks each man's money with corn,
And victuals to eat on their journey when gone.

8   They showed to their father their money in sacks,
And told him they pledged to bring Benjamin back.
He said, " Of my children ye have me bereaved,
For Joseph is dead and for Simeon I grieve.

9   And Benjamin will ye now take all these three,
My sons, all these things are too hard against me."
Then Reuben cried, " Slay my two sons Father dear,
If I bring not Benjamin back to you here."

10   Said Jacob, " My son shall not with thee go down,
His brother is dead and my child is alone.
If mischief befall him afar on the way,
With sorrow ye shall bring me down to the grave,"

CHAPTER XLIII.

1   The famine pressed sorely, and Jacob did say,
" My sons go to Egypt, buy more food I pray."
They said, " We cannot for the man told us so,
That we should not see him lest Benjamin go.

2   Then Israel said, " Why told ye Benjamin's name."
They said, "He so asked us, we could not refrain.
Could we know that he would say bring him to me,
Pray send him and I will restore him to thee."

3 " If I let him go, now this plan I prefer,
  Send balm, spices, honey, and almonds and myrrh.
  Likewise send the money, brought home in your sacks,
  That he may send Simeon, and Benjamin back.

4 May Almighty God give you mercy before
  The man, that he bless, and my children restore."
  When Joseph saw Benjamin with them had come,
  He ordered them brought forth to dine at his home.

5 When they were brought in Joseph's house they did fear,
  And said, " it's for ill they have brought us in here,
  It is for that money we found in our sacks,
  They will make us bondmen and not send us back.

6 They spake to the steward thus, that he explain,
  " We all found our money in our sacks again.
  O, sir, who replaced it, know that thing we would,
  We have brought it back likewise more to buy food."

7 He said peace be with you, fear not, for your God,
  The God of your Father hath dealt you great good.
  Lo, I had your money ye found in your sacks."
  Then he brought out Simeon, whom Joseph kept back.

8 And then led them all into Joseph's house soon,
  Where they fixed the present to give him at noon.
  When Joseph came home, they the present gave forth,
  And bowed themselves down unto him to the earth.

9 He asked of there welfare thus, " is your sire well ?
  The old man of whom ye so often did tell."
  They answered, " thy servant, our sire's health is good."
  As they made obeisance and bowed down their head.

10 When Joseph his mother's last young son did see,
   He said, " is this Benjamin ?" and they said " yea."
   He cried, " God be gracious to thee, O my son,"
   All of you must dine here with me at this noon."

11 In haste Joseph sought place to weep, as he turned,
   For on his young brother his spirit did yearn.
   He entered his chamber, and there he did weep,
   At length he went out, washed, repaired and did eat.

12 They set meat for him and Egyptians alone,
   And then by themselves thus in order each one,
   According to birth-right from eldest to young,
   The men greatly marveled to see it so done.

13 Then Joseph sent messes to each as he pleased,
    But Benjamin's mess was five times one of these,
    They then ate and drank and were merry and glad,
    But knew not that Joseph among them they had.

CHAPTER XLIV.

1 Then Joseph said, " Fill ye up the men's sacks with corn,
    Likewise each man's money in his sack send along,
    Likewise put my silver cup in Benjamin's sack,"
    When done as was ordered, then they all journeyed back.

2 When they had gone from the city not far away,
    Then Joseph said, " Follow them. and unto them say,
    Why took ye the silver cup my lord drinketh in?
    Why do ye so ill for good, is this not great sin?"

3 His steward o'ertook and charged them all with this great sin;
    They said, " Wherefore saith my lord that we done this thing,
    Of money we found in our sack's mouth we have told.
    How then should we steal of thy lord's silver or gold?

4 With whom of thy servants lord thy cup shall bo found
    Let him die, and we will as thy bond-men be bound,"
    He said, "Let it now be done as you do agree,
    He with whom the cup is found my bond-man shall be."

5 He searched from the eldest to the youngest all round
    In Benjamin's sack the silver cup last was found;
    They then rent their clothes, and for the city were bound
    And at Joseph's house they fell to him on the ground.

6 Then Joseph said, " Why are ye against me inclined,
    To steal from me, know ye not that I can divine?"
    Then Judah said lord, " What shall we say to get free?
    For we are thy bond-men all this day unto thee.

7 He said, "God forbid that I should so do to thee,
    He with whom the cup was found my bond-man shall be,
    But as for you. get ye to your father in peace,"
    Then Judah cried, " O! My lord hear me once more speak.

8 Thou did'st ask us if a sire or brother we had,
    We told thee we had a sire quite old, with one lad,
    His last son, with brother dead, and mother, too, gone
    And he left alone, and father loves that young son.

9   Thou saidst ‘ bring him, that I might on him set mine eyes,’
    We said, ‘ If he leaves his sire the old man will die,
    Thou saidst if we bring not Benjamin to this place
    Along with us, that we should no more see thy face.’

10 Then came it to pass when we had reached Father’s house,
    We told him the words which thou my lord said to us,
    Then when father said to us, ‘ Go buy food again.’
    We said, we cannot unless thou send Benjamin.

11 Then father said, ‘ Rachel bare to me but two sons,
    And Joseph the eldest of some wild beast was torn,
    Now if ye take Benjamin from me far away,
    With sorrow ye shall bring my gray hairs to the grave.

12 Now since this is his last son of Rachel his wife,
    And my father’s life is bound up in this lad’s life,
    It shall come to pass then if the lad with thee stay,
    We shall bring our sire with sorrow down to the grave.

13 I pledged him my honor to bring Benjamin home,
    That if I did not let endless blame be my doom,
    I pray thee instead of him let me bond-man be,
    And let thou the lad go home his father to see.

14 O ! how can I journey home to my father dear,
    And Benjamin not with me, my heart faints with fear,
    How can I evil bear which killeth my sire ?
    My grief will be dreadful as unquenchable fire.”

CHAPTER XLV.

1   Then Joseph could not refrain himself before all,
    Then cried he, “ Let every man out from me withdraw
    Till none stood about him but his own brethren dear,
    Then he wept aloud and Pharaohs’s house all did hear.

2   He cried, “ I am Joseph doth my father yet live ?”
    They spake not, but troubled at his presence, they grieved,
    He cried, “ O ! my brethren come near to me I pray,
    I’m your brother Joseph whom ye sold far away.”

3   He said, “ Grieve not with yourselves that ye sold me here,
    God sent me before you, for to save life so dear,
    These two years hath famine raged, yet five more shall come,
    In which years a harvest shall no more hence be done..

4 So now 'twas not you that sent me hither but God,
   Who made me a sire to Pharaoh, ruling as lord;
   Haste ye to my father, tell him Joseph his son,
   Is lord o'er all Egypt tell him stay not but come.

5 Bid him come with children's children with all he hath
   And I will here nourish them while famine doth last,
   You and brother Benjamin, with open eyes see,
   'Tis your brother Joseph that now speaketh to thee."

6 Then Joseph caught Benjamin and kissed him and wept,
   And Benjamin too did weep, as Joseph him blest,
   He kissed all his brethren, as their joyous tears fell,
   The news reaching Pharaoh's house, it pleased them all well.

7 Then Pharaoh in kindness gave to Joseph command,
   To bring all his kindred down to Egypt's rich land,
   He gave each man change of clothes, but Benjamin five,
   And silver three hundred pieces gave him likewise.

8 Then Joseph sent presents to his sire, and did say,
   " Adieu, now see that ye fall not out by the way."
   They then journeyed to their sire by Joseph's command,
   And cried, " Joseph is alive, and rules Egypt's land."

9 Then Israel's heart fainted, them he could not believe
   But when Joseph's wagons came, his spirit revived.
   Said Israel, " It is enough my son is alive,
   I'll go and see Joseph if God will ere I die.

'CHAPTER XLVI.

1 Then Israel took all, and went son Joseph so see,
   And offered God sacrifice, when at Beer-sheba,
   Then God spake to Israel in the visions of night,
   And called Jacob and he answered, " Lord here am I."

2 God said, " Fear not going down into Egypt's land
   For I will go with thee and bring thee up again,
   I'll make thee a nation great, in goodness to rise,
   And Joseph thy son shall put his hand on thine eyes.

3 Then Israel's sons brought their sire and all that they had
   And settled in Egypt's land with all his seed, glad,
   These are Israel's children's names in Egypt they brought,
   Reuben with sons Phallu, Hezron, Carmi, Hanoch,

4   Jemuel, and Jamin, Ohad, Jachin, Zohar,
And Shaul, were the sons which Simeon brought down there.
Levi brought sons Gershan, Kohath, and Merari,
Judah brought sons Shelah, Pharez, Zarah, likewise.

5   Then Pharez brought sons Hezrom, Hamul, down to that land,
And Issachar, brought Tola, Phuvah, Job, Shimron,
And Zebulun brought sons Sered, Elon, Jahleel,
And all Jacob's sons and daughters were thirty-three.

6   All these are sons of Lea born in Padan-aram
With Dinah his daughter, Jacob brought to that land,
And God brought down Ziphion, Haggi, Shuni, Ezbon,
Eri, and Arodi, and Areli, his sons.

7   Asher brought sons Jimnath, Ishuah, Isui
Beriah with sister Serah, Egypt to try,
Beriah's sons Heber, Malchiel were of old,
Jacob's sons of Zilpah, making all sixteen souls.

8   Jacob's sons of Rachel were Joseph, Benjamin,
Joseph's of Asenath, Manasseth and Ephraim,
And these are the names of all young Benjamin's sons,
Belah, Becher, Ashbel, Gera, likewise Naaman.

9   Ehi, Muppin, Rosh, and Huppin, Ard are here seen,
All born unto Jacob of lov'd Rachel, fourteen,
Naphtali, brought Jahzeel, Guni, Jezer, Shillem,
His four sons to Egypt and Dan brought Hushim.

10 These are sons of Rachel's maid, which Bilhah did bare,
Whom Laban gave Rachel, all those souls seven are,
All souls out of Jacob's loins, in Egypt we fix
(Except wives of sons) their number three score and six.

11 In Egypt, of Joseph's sons there were but two men,
All souls there of Jacob's house are three score and ten.
He sent Judah on to guide them to Goshen's plains,
Where Joseph came on in haste and met Israel's men.

12 Then Israel embraced his son and kissed him and wept,
As Joseph wept in the arms of Israel caressed.
Then Israel cried, " O my son, I pray let me die,
Since God let me see thy face while thou art alive.

13 Then Joseph did bless them all in God's name and said,
" When Pharaoh shall call on you to know of your trade,
Then say ye, " our trade hath been much cattle to keep,
That ye dwell in Goshen, they hate keepers of sheep.

CHAPTER XLVII.

1   Then Joseph presented his five brethren and sire
    To Pharaoh, when they thus said, my lord, we desire
    To dwell here in Goshen, both ourselves and our flocks.
    Then Pharaoh said, "choose ye the best land for your stock."

2   Then Pharaoh asked Jacob's age, and did him revere,
    My days, said he, "are an hundred and twenty years.
    Both evil and few, and swift are days of my age,
    But have not attained yet to my sire's pilgrimage.

3   Maintenance and habitations he gave them there,
    The best land of Ramesses Pharaoh did them spare,
    All wealth of Egyptians and of countries that joined
    Was paid into Joseph and to Pharaoh for corn.

4   Then Joseph and Pharaoh bought all cattle and lands,
    Except land of priests, they had all else in command.
    Then Joseph the land let to them for one-fifth part
    Of increase and gave the rest for labor and art.

5   Then Israel did multiply exceedingly there,
    And lived in the land of Egypt full seventeen years.
    Then Israel's age was an hundred forty-seven years,
    When he said, "now I must die," and called Joseph near.

6   And said, "swear to bury me not in Egypt's plain,
    For I, in my father's sepulcher would be lain."
    So Joseph did swear, that he would bury him there.
    Then Israel bowed down and blest the Lord God in prayer.

CHAPTER XLVIII.

1   Then it did come to pass that the news spread at last,
      That good Israel was sick unto death,
    Then did Joseph prepare his two sons for the prayers,
      And the blessing of Israel's last breath.

2   And then Joseph took with him Manasseth and Ephraim,
      And unto his father he came,
    Who then said, "God Almighty in mercy hath taught me
      That he will the righteous sustain.

3   Now thy two sons I bless, Ephraim and Manasseth,
     Born in Egypt ere I heard of thee,
     As my Reuben and Simeon these blest sons are mine,
     All thy others I leave to thee free.

4   When I came to Padan, Rachel died in the land
     Of old Canaan, near to Ephrath's way,
     And I buried her there, with much weeping and prayer,
     And a stone pillar placed on her grave."

5   Joseph brought his sons near, Israel kissed them in tears
     And embraced them and to Joseph said,
     " I thought ne'er to see thee, but thy seed God shewed me,
     And hath raised thee as one from the dead."

6   Israel blest Ephraim first and Manasseth the last,
     And the young to the elder preferred.
     He blest Joseph and said, "trust in God who hath fed
     Me my life long, and all my prayers heard."

7   Then good Israel relying on God, said, " I'm dying,
     But he shall bring you up again,
     For the God of your Fathers, his people will gather
     Forever hence with Him to reign."

CHAPTER XLIX.

1   Then Israel did tell his twelve sons of their ways,
     And what should befall them in their after days,
     " O Reuben, my first born strength's excellence, now fell,
     Unstable as water, thou shalt not excel.

2   " O Simeon and Levi, as cruel as death,
     My soul be thou not into their secrets let.
     • For in cruel anger a man they have slain,
     I'll spread them in Jacob, and scatter them twain.

3   But Judah is he whom his brethren shall praise,
     The scepter from Judah shall not go away,
     Till Shiloh shall come, who is Christ, to make free,
     To Him shall the gathering of people then be.

4   And Zebulun shall dwell at the haven of seas,
     Near Zidon, an haven where ships ride at ease,
     And Issachar beareth great burdens by day,
     And boweth his shoulders to tribute, to pay.

5 And Dan, judging Israel, a servant reveals,
An adder that biteth a rider's horse's heels.
And Gad, though a great troop, shall him overcome.
He shall overcome at the last, every one.

6 From Asher his bread shall be fat which he gives,
And he shall yield dainties which princes shall crave,
And Naphtali is like a young hind let loose,
He gives goodly words which a good heart should prove.

7 And Joseph is fruitful as boughs by a well,
Whose branches with clusters of pome-granates swell.
The archers have him sorely grieved and have shot
At him, and him hated, but God left him not.

8 His bow did abide in the strength of his God,
His arms were made strong by the hands of the Lord,
For Joseph is Israel's shepherd and stone,
Which standeth by Almighty God, a true one.

9 But Benjamin shall ravin as wolves rage at morn,
Dividing the spoil and devouring the torn.
All these are the twelve tribes of Israel and sons,
And these things are what he spake to them each one,

10 And said, " bury me in the cave when I die,
Which Abram once bought of Ephron the Hittite.
Where Abram, and Sarah, and Isaac all lie,
And his loved Rebekah, and Leah my first wife."

11 When Jacob had ended commanding his sons,
He yielded his spirit, expired and was gone
Forth unto his people, to those who love Christ,
The true seed of Abram, in God's paradise.

CHAPTER L.

1 Then Joseph for Israel did mourn,
And wept o'er his father in grief,
His heart with keen anguish was torn,
  His spirit could find no relief.

2 Physicians did Israel embalm,
  And him in a coffin preserved,
Then three score and ten days they mourned,
  Ere they went forth him to inter.

3 Then Joseph when those days were o'er,
    Said, " let me now bury my sire,
In Canaan where he dwelt of yore,
    According as he made me swear.

4 Then Joseph, with all Pharaoh's house
    Of elders, and servants went forth,
With chariots and horsemen and horse,
    To Canaan's land of Israel's birth.

5 His brethren, with all kin they had,
    Rode forth with that company vast.
They paused at thresh floor of Atad,
    There mourning did seven days last.

6 When Canaan saw Egypt mourn there,
    They named that place Abel-mizraim,
Thus Joseph done as he did swear,
    And buried his sire in that land.

7 In cave, of the field of Ephron
    (The Hittite) which Abraham once bought,
For burying place, from Heth's sons,
    Where Sarah at death was first brought.

8 There Abram and Isaac now lie,
    And Jacob with wives in that rest,
Which four hundred shekels did buy,
    That Abram paid at Sarah's death.

9 His brethren, to Joseph thus spake,
    " Forgive us our trespass and sin
Which we done against thee in hate."
    He wept as they spake thus to him.

10 His brethren before him did fall,
    And said we are thy servants, lord,
Then Joseph said, " fear not at all,
    I am in the place of your God.

11 I know ye meant evil 'gainst me,
    But God meant it unto great good,
To bring it to pass as you see,
    To give unto His people food.

12 Fear not, I will now nourish you
    And your little ones with great care."
He done to them kindly and true,
    And lived to age hundred ten years.

13 He saw Ephraim's generations three,
     Manasseth's son's children also,
  Which were brought up at Joseph's knees,
     All Israel's seed prosperous did grow.

14 He said, " when I die then prepare,
     For God surely will bring out you
  From this land, for thus he did swear
     To Abram, Isaac, Jacob too."

15 Then Joseph had Israel's sons swear,
     To carry his bones up from hence,
  " At time when God calls you, prepare
     To go out with substance from thence.

16 At hundred tenth year Joseph died,
     Embalmed in a coffin, was he,
  And gathered to be glorified,
     Where saints of all ages shall be.

17 Here Genesis comes to a close,
     From creation till Joseph died.
  No record so perfect doth show
     A God of such goodness beside.

EXODUS.

CHAPTER XV—THE SONG OF MOSES.

1 " I'll sing to the Lord, He hath triumphed most glorious,
He cast down the war horse and rider, victorious.
The Lord is my strength, and my song and salvation,
My shield, and His house shall be my habitation.
    Praise our father's God, ever glorious.

2 The Lord is Almighty, in war and in slaughter,
He cast Pharaoh's chariots and hosts in deep water.
Lo in the Red sea his chief captains are drowned,
The depths have them covered as stones sank they downward,
    Praise our fathers' God, all victorions.

3 Thy right arm, O Lord, hath high power ever glorious,
   Thy hand dashed Thy foemen in pieces, victorious,
In greatness Thine excellency hath o'erthrown them,
Thou didst send thy scourge which as stubble consumed them.
    Praise our fathers' God, who hath conquered them.

4 With blast of thy nostrils the waters were gathered,
The floods stood upright, heaped within the sea centered.
Thy foeman then said, we'll pursue and annoy them,
Our lust shall have spoil, and our drawn swords destroy them.
    Praise our fathers' God, who hath constant been.

5 Thou didst blow thy wind and the sea did them cover,
As lead sank they in the deep waters all over.
Who is like the Lord, to the good glorious ever,
His holiness wondrous, His goodness forever,
    Praise our fathers' God, who deliverance brought.

6 Thy mercy hath led Thy redeemed to salvation,
Thy strength hath them guided to Thy habitation,
Thy foes shall have fear, Palestina have sorrow,
And Edom and Moab have trembling to-morrow.
    Praise our fathers' God, who salvation taught.

7 For Canaan shall melt and 'round foes fear shall hover,
Thy strength shall them still, till Thy people pass over,
Thy ransomed, whom Thou Lord shall plant in the mountain
Of Thy blest inheritance at Life's flowing fountain.
    Praise our fathers' God, who the righteous bought.

8 When in the sea-bed, Pharaoh's host charged to battle,
    While six hundred war chariots' thunders did rattle,
    Then God brought the floods of the Red sea upon them,
    While Israel's lov'd children on dry land went from them.
        Praise our fathers' God, all victorious.

9 Then Miriam and women, with timbrels sang glories,
    How God makes His people in goodness victorious;
    The war-horse and rider He cast in deep waters,
    Sing praise to the Lord, Zion's sons and her daughters,
        Praise our fathers' God, ever glorious.

CHAPTER XX.

1 God spoke to Moses in the mount,
    These words to call men to account,
    "I am the Lord your God, who brought
    You from Egyptian bondage out.

2 I am the Lord, the one true God,
    And heaven eternal my abode.
    To other gods shall none incline,
    Nor worship at an idol's shrine.

3 Speak not in vain the name of God,
    Keep his blest Sabbath holy, good,
    Give honor to thy parents dear;
  · Thou shalt not kill, but man revere.

4 Adultery thou shalt not commit;—
    Thou shalt not steal, 'tis most unfit;—
    Nor yet shalt thou false witness bear;—
    Nor covet neighbor's things, though fair.

5 What ye would have done unto you,
    Do ye to others kind and true;
    High way of life, that leads to God,
    Can, but by these commands, be trod."

ISAIAH.

CHAPTER LII.

1 Awake, put on Emanuel's strength,
   O Zion, beauteous garments wear,
Jerusalem shall no more hence
   Give the unclean an entrance there.

2 Arise thyself from dust and shake,
   With Shiloh's glory gird thee round,
And break the bonds from off thy neck,
   O Zion's captive daughter bound.

3 Saith God, "ye sold yourselves for naught,
   I without money will redeem.
My people were to Egypt brought,
   Their wrong oppressions I have seen.

4 My people, men have cursed, for naught,
   Caused them My Name oft to blaspheme,
But I'll make known I am the Lord,
   From all their foes I'll guard between.

5 How beauteous on the mount is he
   Who brings good tidings, and proclaims,
Who publisheth salvation free,
   And cries that Zion's God doth reign.

6 Thy watchmen with one voice shall raise,
   Their song as they see eye to eye,
When God shall Zion bring again,
   Let deserts' joy in songs reply.

7 Now God hath brought his people rest,
   And hath redeemed Jerusalem,
Made bare His holy arm most blest,
   And nations his salvation seen.

8 Press on my saints, touch naught of sin,
   Bear ye the burdens of the Lord.
I'll go before you, ye shall win,
   I, Israel's God, am your reward.

9   My servant Christ shall come most good.
    Astonished at Him men shall be,
He'll sprinkle nations with His blood,
    And cleanse them from iniquity.

10   He'll bring His bride safe home to rest,
    Where fruits ambrosial cluster fair,
Where saints with endless life are blessed,
    With all the righteous greeting there."

CHAPTER LIII.

1   O, who hath believed our report,
    To whom was the Lord's arm revealed?
For He before men shall grow up,
    As tenderest plant of the field.

2   Like unto a root from dry ground,
    Christ no form nor comeliness hath,
Men in Him no beauty have found,
    To make them incline to His path.

3   Despised and rejected of men,
    A man worn with sorrows and grieved,
Our faces we turned from Him then,
    Esteemed Him not, neither relieved.

4   Since surely our griefs he hath borne,
    And carried our sorrows to death,
We'll love him though stricken and torn,
    And praise Him with our latest breath.

5   Transgressions of ours did him wound,
    And our many sins did Him bruise,
Chastised for our peace, we have found,
    Great healing, by stripes on Him used.

6   Like sheep, we have all gone astray,
    And turned every one unto sin.
So God gave his son us to save,
    And laid all our sins upon Him.

7   Oppressed and distressed, He spake not.
    As lamb led to slaughter, was dumb,
From prison to judgment was brought.
    And died for our sins every one.

8 His grave with the wicked He made,
   Likewise with the rich at His death.
Because He no violence did;
   Nor yet was deceit in his breath.

9 God made Christ an offering for sin,
   That righteousness yet might prevail,
And penitent souls enter in
   Eternity's Rest without fail.

10 Come sinners and trust in His name,
    And keep his commands with delight,
That ye may be heirs with Him then,
   To righteousness and endless life,

THE SONG OF SOLOMON.

CHAPTER I.

1 Song of songs is Solomon's song,
   Better than all others,
Sung by saints with joyful tongues,
   Jesus is their lover.
Let Him greet me with love's kiss,
   That we ne'er may sever,
From whose lips flows righteousness,
   Yielding peace forever.

2 For His savors from above,
   Pour like precious ointment,
Wherefore do His people love,
   By divine annointment.
We'll run after thee, draw me
   In our King's blest chambers,
There we will rejoice in Thee
   And Thy love remember.

3 Better is Thy love than wine,
   How the upright love Thee,
  Lead our hearts to love divine.
   None hath love above Thee.
  I am meek but comely, fair
   Daughters of Jerusalem,
  As the tents of Kedar are
   Or the veils of Solomon.

4 Look thou not on me with shame,
   Since afflictions grieve me.
  Sinners held me in disdain,
   And they oft deceived me.
  They made me their vineyards keep,
   Mine I have neglected,
  Thy lost lambs did stray and bleat,
   I have them protected.

5 Tell me, Saviour, ever blest,
   Where thy flocks are feeding,
  That I lead these lambs to rest,
   And a joyful greeting,
  O, my bride, my fairest One,
   Seek my flock's steps onward,
  Feed thy lambs when thou reach home,
   By the tents of shepherds.

6 Thou resemblest, O. my spouse,
   Pharaoh's grand battalion,
  Jewels deck thy cheeks in rows,
   Thy neck-chains are golden.
  He will make thy borders gold,
   Set with studs of silver,
  Where the King His feast doth hold,
   Prayers of saints give savor.

7 My beloved is as myrrh,
   Near my heart most inward,
  As a cluster of camphire
   From En-gedi's vineyard.
  My love hath dove's eyes serene,
   Beaming with compassion,
  And our bed is vernal green,
   Clothed with flowrets blushing,

8 My beloved's house hath myrrh,
    Beams of lasting cedar ;
  And its rafters are of fir ;
    House of our Redeemer.
  All who seek His love shall rest,
    In His house forever,
  Crowned with endless life, and blest
    With unceasing pleasure.

CHAPTER II.

1 Christ is Sharon's rose of morn,
    Lily of the waters,
  As the lily 'mong the thorns,
    His love is 'mong daughters.
  As the apple tree 'mong trees,
    Of the wood, is better,
  So His shadow doth most please,
    And His fruit is sweeter.

2 He brought me to his blest feast,
    'Neath love's banner, joyful,
  Stay my soul with heavenly peace,
    Comfort me with apples.
  That I love for thy love's sake,
    Since Thy hand is 'neath me,
  And Thy right arm doth embrace,
    Jesus never leave me.

3 Stir not, nor disturb my love,
    Daughters of Jerusalem.
  He comes like the roe or dove,
    To all who pursue Him.
  My beloved, O behold,
    Leaping on the mountains,
  Skipping o'er the hills so bold,
    Like a young hart bounding.

4 My beloved said, " fair one,
    Rise, my love, come hither,
  Lo, the winter's past and gone,
    And the storms are over.

Singing birds and flowers are come,
  Vines and grapes smell sweetly,
Rise, my love, come way, fair one,
  I wilt lead thee meekly."

5 "O, my dove cleft in the rock,
    Speak thy voice so sweetly,
Let me see thy comely look,
  Of compassion meekly."
"My beloved hath we won,
  I am His forever.
Like a bounding hart, He comes,
  From the Mounts of Bether."

6 Sinners trust in Jesus' name,
    Seek your sins forgiven,
Win His everlasting gain,
  And a crown in heaven.
Then where e'er your death shall be,
  Jesus will run thither,
Like a bounding roe for thee,
  Down the heights of Ether.

CHAPTER III.

1 On my bed by night, I sought
    Him whom my soul loveth,
Sought Him, but I found Him not;
  Him, whom heaven approveth.
I will range the city through,
  In broad ways I'll seek Him,
Whom my soul doth love most true,
  Until I receive Him.

2 Thus I sought, but found Him not,
    When the watchmen found me,
Said I, "Have ye seen my love,
  Hath He been around thee?
Past the watchmen, I found Him,
  My love's not a stranger,
Him I held, and led Him in
  My dear mother's chamber.

3   Stir not, nor disturb my love,
        Daughters of Jerusalem,
    By the hinds and lovely roes,
        Till I interview Him.
    Who comes from the wilderness?
        Bearing smoke in pillars,
    'Fumed with myrrh, and frank incense,
        Types of heavenly savors.

4   Bound Him, as round Soloman,
        Shout His valiant Israels,
    All wield swords of spirit, one
        Guarding against all evils.
    Silver, cedar, paved with gold,
        Purple veils, did cover
    Chariots paved with love of old,
        For Jerusalem's daughters!

5   Then went Zion's daughters, where
        Solomon had his crowning,
    Which his mother gave him there,
        At his grand espousing.
    Daughters now seek Christ your King,
        Who died to restore thee.
    Crowned of God in heaven, He'll bring
        His lov'd bride to Glory.

CHAPTER IV.

1   "Thou art fairer love, than gold,
        Thou hast doves eyes charming,
    Thy hair like white goats of old,
        From Mount Gilead coming.
    Thy teeth like a flock of sheep,
        Even shorn from washing,
    All are white with mates complete,
        None 'mong them are wanting.

2   Thy lips like a scarlet thread,
        Thy speech sweet and lovely.
    Thy pomegranate temples, hid
        In thy locks most comely.

Thy neck like the tower so grand,
  Built for David's armory,
On which thousand bucklers hang,
  Worn by men of honor.

3 Thy form like the nimble roes,
  'Mong the lilies bounding,
Till day break and shadows go,
  Flee I to myrrh mountains.
To the hill of frank incense,
  Thou most pair and comely,
In thee there is no offence,
  Meek and mild and lovely.

4 Look love, from mount Lebanon,
  From mount Manna, round thee
Shemir, Herman, Lion's dens,
  And from Leopard's Mountains.
Feast me with thy look again,
  My lov'd spouse and sister,
With one of thine eyes, one chain
  Of thy neck with pleasure.

5 Most fair is thy love, my spouse,
  Sister, how much better
Is thy smile than wine to rouse,
  Calling sinners over.
Thy words drop as honey comb,
  Milk and honey bless thee.
Sinners if you pray and come,
  Heaven will caress thee.

6 In Christ's church are all the charms
  Of all flowers, and odors,
'Fountains, gardens, living streams,
  Compassing earth's borders.
Wake, O, north wind, south wind mourn
  All my garden over,
That its odors draw my love
  To His fruits with pleasures.

CHAPTER V.

1 I'm come in my garden, my sister, my spouse,
With myrrh, and with spices, beloved arouse ;
I have milk and honey, and fruits at this time,
Come eat ye, O saints, O beloveds of mine.

2 From sleep my heart wakes at the voice of my love,
Who knocks, saying, " Open to me, O, my dove.
I'm wet with the dew of the night all the while,
My coat is put off and my feet undefiled."

3 My love put His hand to the hole of the door,
Which caused me to ope, when my hands fumed with myrrh,
But my love had gone, and my spirit then failed,
When He spake, I sought Him, but could not prevail.

4 I called Him, but He did me answer no more,
The watchmen then found me, and wounded me sore,
The keepers of walls, then my veil did remove,
Tell Him Zion's daughters, I pine for His love.

5 " What is thy beloved, that thou charge us so ?"
The chief 'mong ten thousand, and lovliest, too.
His head as fine gold, with dove's eyes fitly set,
His cheeks beds of spices, His lips flowrets sweet.

6 His hands as gold rings, set with beryl stones bright,
His body as ivory, o'erlaid with saphires.
His legs, marble pillars, on feet of fine gold,
His visage excelling fine temples of old.

7 His mouth far more lovely than lilies that bloom,
His word giveth life, and restoreth from the tomb.
This is my Beloved, my Friend, Lord and King,
Jerusalem's daughters His love ever sing.

CHAPTER VI.

1 " Where is Christ, thy best beloved ?
    O, thou fairest of the fair,
. Tell me where he hath removed,
    That I seek for Him with care."

2 He has gone down in His garden,
    Feeding 'mong the spicy beds.
He who once hath bought our pardon,
    And hath sealed it with His blood.

3 I am my Beloved's ever,
    My beloved He is mine,
And our friendship ne'er shall sever,
    Since our love is most divine.

4 Hark, my Lord comes with His army,
    See their scarlet banners stream,
Bold and beautiful as Tirsah,
    Comely as Jerusalem.

5 "O my saints, thine eyes turn from me,
    They o'ercome and me confine,
And thy prayers are sweet as honey,
    Of a paradise divine.

6 How my bride looks fair as morning,
    As the moon, clear as the sun,
As an army in adornings,
    With their palms of victory won.

7 I went down in my love's garden,
    There to see the fruits and vines,
And if pomegranates had budded,
    There my Saviour I did find.

8 E'er I was aware, He gave me,
    Chariots of Ammi-nadib,
As we rode on high, He bade me
    Ever in His name be glad.

9 O thou Shulamite return ye,
    Thou our power, peace, and reward,
As two armies with us coming,
    Shiloh's people for to guard.

10 Sinners come and seek the Saviour,
    'Tis the Shulamite's return,
And repent all bad behaviour,
    Lest you should forever mourn.

11 That man might put on Christ's spirit,
    Is why God gives earthly stay.
All who seek Him, shall inherit
    Endless happiness and day.

CHAPTER VII.

1 Beauteous are thy feet, as flowers,
    Zion's prince's daughter.
  And thy neck like ivory towers,
    Eyes like Heshbon's waters,
  Thine head like mount Carmel high,
    Hair like Tyrian purple.
  Thou dost make the King draw nigh,
    Fairest most delightful.

2 Thy lov'd stature like a palm,
    Thy breast like grape clusters,
  And thy voice the spirits balm,
    Pleasant fruits and odors.
  Thy word doth the soul incline,
    Unto God's salvation,
  Leading sinners to the shrine,
    Of the new creation.

3 I am my Beloved's now,
    His desire is for me.
  Come dear Saviour with us go,
    We'll tell all men of thee.
  We will in thy vineyard toil,
    Trusting, never fearing,
  See if vines do flourish all,
    If young plants need cheering.

4 There will I give thee my loves,
    O my blessed Saviour,
  Odors from blest fruits shall move,
    Through thy vineyards ever.
  Fruits of doing good we'll lay
    Up for our beloved;
  Then we at the judgment day,
    Shall His word have proved.

5 Cause of man's sojourn in earth,
    Is the good he doeth,
  That he seek the heavenly birth,
    As the spirit wooeth;
  Of God's spirit, every man
    Hath a portion given,
  Whispering him through life's short span,
    Telling him "seek heaven."

CHAPTER VIII.

1   O that Christ, were as my brother,
      By my mother bred with me,
    I would love Him more than others,
      And would not despised be.
    Him I'd bring in mother's mansion,
      Where He should be blest most free,
    Feast, and drink, my choice pomegranate,
      And the world would not blame me,

2   But because Christ was a stranger,
      He was lov'd but by the good,
    Poor and cradled in a manger,
      Hence the world His words withstood.
    Let his left hand be my pillow,
      And His right arm, me embrace,
    And convey me o'er death's billow,
      There to see His Father's face.

3   Stir not, nor wake Him from sleeping,
      Who hath died, man to redeem,
    He from wilds His bride is leading,
      On her loving Lord she leans.
    Seal me on Thy heart and spirit,
      Let me lean, Lord, on Thine arm,
    Love is strong as death, and merits,
      Endless life and potent charms.

4   Many waters cannot quench love,
      Neither can the floods it drown;
    Nought but love, can e'er cement love,
      Nor can gold with love compound.
    If our sister, Gentile nations,
      Have no heart enlarged for God,
    How shall we cause their salvation,
      When the gospel call is heard?

5   God's eternal will and sentence.
      Is that Gentiles, may be heirs
    Of Salvation through repentence,
      And in Christ His kingdom share.
    When in God's great house shall center
      All the nations for their part,
    Equal part, shall have the Gentile,
      If she shall enlarge her heart.

6   If she be a wall, we'll build her
      A fine silver palace then,
    If a door, enclose, and gild her
      With the boards of Lebanon.
    Israel's wall hath breasts like towers;
      She with God will e'er prevail,
    And her heart is large with powers,
      And with love that never fails.

7   Thou, Who dwellest in high gardens,
      Let me hear Thy voice most sweet,
    Who once bled to gain our pardon,
      Make my heart Thy dwelling seat.
    O! make haste my best beloved,
      Like a bounding hart or roe,
    From high mounts of spices, coming,
      That my soul may with Thee go.

8   Jesus watches o'er His vineyard
      More than Soloman of old,
    Calling meekly unto sinners,
      "Come and reap My fruits of gold."
    Sing and shout your Lord and Saviour
      Daughters of Jerusalem,
    All who follow his behaviour,
      Shall eternal life attain.

THE FIRST BOOK

OF THE

NEW TESTAMENT,

OF OUR LORD AND SAVIOUR

JESUS CHRIST.

VERSIFIED,

ACCORDING TO MATTHEW'S GOSPEL.

MATTHEW.

CHAPTER I.

1 The book of generation of Christ, David's son,
In line down from Abram to Christ, every one.
From Abram to Jesus, the generations are
Abram, Isaac, Jacob and Judas, and Phares.

2 And Esrom, and Aram, and Aminadab,
And Naasson and Salmon and Booz of Rachab.
Then Obed of Ruth, Jesse, King David fair,
And David's son Solomon, Uria's wife bear.

3 Then Roboam, Abia, Asa, Josaphat,
Then Joram, Ozias, Joatham, and Achaz,
And then Ezekias, Manasses, Amon,
Josias, Jachoniae when to Babylon bound.

4 Salathiel, Zorobabel, Abiud,
Eliakim, Azor, Sadoc, Achim, Eliud,
Then Eleazar, Matthan, Jacob, Joseph last,
The husband of Mary the mother of Christ.

5 Generations from Abram to David, fourteen,
From David to Babylon fourteen intervene,
And fourteen from Babylonian bondage to Christ,
The blest birth of Jesus, it was on this wise.

6 When Mary was spoused unto Joseph then came,
On her heaven's favor which had been ordained,
Then as he thought privily to put her away,
An angel from heaven to Joseph did say.

7 "Fear not to take Mary to bless thine abode,
For she hath conceived by the Spirit of God;
She shall bare a son, Jesus shall be His name,
He shall save His people from sin, curse and shame.

8 For thus t'was long spoken by prophets of God,
A virgin shall bring forth a son to the Lord,
Emmanuel shall be His name which excels
All names, since it means that the God with us dwells.

9   Then Joseph arose in delight, and new life,
     And took his lov'd Mary, his God-favored wife,
     And waited most joyous for her first born son,
     And called His name Jesus, the blest, holy one.

10   Then Mary exclaimed, " I do glorifiy God,
     That I have brought forth the new man from the Lord.
     The first man is earthly, this man came from heaven
     To die for man's sins, that they might be forgiven.

11   All hail Holy Spirit, which made my reward,
     My Son and my Saviour; my High priest and Lord,
     And Rock of eternal salvation to all,
     Who keep His commandments on this earthly ball.

CHAPTER II.

1   When Christ was in Bethlehem of Judea born,
     In King Herod's days there came from eastward wise men,
     And said, " where's He Who is of Jews, born their King,
     His star we have seen, and come here to worship Him."

2   Jerusalem was troubled then, and Herod forlorn,
     He asked scribes and pharisees where Christ should be born,
     They said, " within Bethlehem, for prophets declare,
     That her new-born governor should rule Israel there."

3   Then Herod did privily call up the wise men,
     And asked when the star appeared that so led them on,
     He bade them, " go find the child and then bring me word,
     That I too may come and worship Him as my Lord."

4   The star led the wise men, till it stood o'er the child,
     Which made them rejoice with greatest joy all the while,
     With Mary they found the child, and worshipped Him there,
     And offered Him gifts and gold, frankincense and myrrh.

5   Then God warned them not to keep King Herod's command,
     He also warned Joseph to flee to Egypt's land,
     For Herod will seek for the young child, Him to slay,
     So he fled to Egypt, the young childs life to save.

6   He stayed there until the death of Herod had come,
     As prophets said, " I from Egypt called out my son."
     Then Herod was wroth since he the wise men ne'er found,
     And slew all young children then in Bethlehem round.

7 From two years of age and less, as wise men had told,
   And then was fulfilled what spake the prophets of old.
   In Rama a voice of lamentation was heard,
   Of Rachel's great mourning for her lov'd children dead,

8 And would not be comforted, because they are gone,
   While thousand fond mothers more fell weeping forlorn,
   God bade him at Herod's death go to Israel free,
   But he fearing Herod's son went to Galilee.

9 And dwelt within Nazareth, as long was foreseen,
   For prophets had given him the name " Nazarene."
   This Jesus brought life and immortality's light
   And God's glorious gospel He did preach day and night,

CHAPTER III,

1 When John the Baptist preaching came,
       In Judea's desert land,
   He cried repent, from sin refrain,
       God's Kingdom is at hand,

2 'Tis he of whom the prophets spake,
       The voice of one doth cry
   Within the wilderness make strait
       The paths of the most High.

3 John made his clothes of camels hair,
       With leathern girdle bound,
   Ate locusts and wild honey there,
       While multitudes came down.

4 From regions bounding Jordan's stream,
       And by him were baptized.
   And Pharisees, and Sadducees
       Sought him with weeping eyes.

5 Then John said who hath forewarned you,
       To flee the wrath to come?
   Bring forth fruits for repentence true,
       Say not, we're Abram's sons.

6 For God from your stone hearts can raise
       Up Abrahamic seed.
   If ye repent of sinful ways,
       And love the Lord indeed.

7　The axe, now laid at the tree's root
　　Proclaims that God requires,
　　That those which bring not forth good fruit,
　　Be cut and cast in fire.

8　With water, I baptize him,
　　Doth penitence desire ;
　　A mightier One shall baptize you
　　With Holy Ghost and fire.

9　Whose fan will purge His floor, and turn
　　His wheat in barns to fill,
　　But He the chaff will after burn
　　With fire unquenchable.

10　Then Jesus came from Galilee,
　　To be baptized likewise.
　　But John forbade, and said, " of thee
　　I need to be baptized."

11　Then Jesus said to John, " I would
　　That thou shouldst do so now,
　　For it becomes us, that we should
　　All righteousness allow."

12　When Jesus from baptism came,
　　The heavens did on him shine,
　　God's spirit as a dove-like flame,
　　Did light and Him entwine.

13　Then lo, a voice from heaven did say,
　　" This is my well loved Son
　　In whom I am well pleased this day,
　　Hear ye Him, every one."

14　Thus John the gospel did begin,
　　Christ after him did come,
　　To free obedient souls from sin,
　　And lead His ransomed home.

CHAPTER IV.

1　Then Christ was of the spirit led
　　Up in the wilderness,
　　Of Satan there to be tempted,
　　And fast in great distress.

2 When fortieth fast-day came to hand,
   The tempter to him said.
"If thou art Son of God command
   These stones to be made bread."

3 Christ said, " 'Tis written man lives not
   By earthly bread alone,
But by the word which comes from God,
   If it be truly done."

4 Then he set Christ on temple's top,
   And said, "Now cast Thee down,
For angel hands shall bear Thee up,
   Is written of the Son."

5 Christ said, " 'Tis written 'Tempt not God.' "
   Then satan took him up
Into a mountain's high abode,
   And spake exulting thus:

6 "Behold earth's glorious kingdoms fair,
   I'll give them all to Thee,
If thou wilt fall down and declare,
   That Thou wilt worship me."

7 Christ said to Satan, "Get thee hence,
   For it is written, thou
Shalt worship God alone, none else,
   To Whom all men must bow."

8 When He the tempter's hour had past,
   God's angels strengthened Him,
When John was into prison cast,
   Christ sought Capernium.

9 All men in darkness then saw light,
   In all earth's regions round,
And through sin's deathly shades of night
   Did roll the gospel sound.

10 Then Christ began to preach and, say,
   "Repent ye every man,
This is thy glorious gospel day
   God s kingdom is at hand."

11 So Peter, Andrew, called He, then
   From fishing in the sea,
And cried, "I'll make you fish for men,
   If you will follow Me.

12 Then He called James and John, who left
    Their nets, and ways of sin,
    Then Jesus traveled, preached, and blest,
    Vast multitudes sought Him.

CHAPTER V.

1 When Jesus saw the multitude
    He sought a mountain near,
    While His disciples round Him stood,
    He taught these words most dear.

2 Much blest the poor in spirit are,
    For theirs is peace and heaven;
    And blest are they that mourn, for there
    Shall comfort be them given.

3 Blest are the meek, for they shall heir
    All things, for 'tis God's will;
    Who thirst for righteousness, blest are
    For they shall all be filled.

4 Blest be the merciful, for he
    God's mercy shall obtain;
    The pure in heart God's face shall see,
    And blest with him to reign.

5 Peacemakers shall be called the blest,
    Dear children of our God,
    Those who are spurned for righteousness,
    Are blest with heaven's abode.

6 Most blest are ye, when men revile,
    And slander for My sake,
    Rejoice exceeding glad the while,
    Your prize in heaven is great.

7 For so spurned they the prophets old,
    Which long before you were,
    Ye are the salt of earth, the gold,
    The blest of heaven's care.

8 Ye are the light of earth's dark scene,
    A city on a hill,
    A candle is not lit by men,
    A bushel but to fill.

9 But to light all in the house,
     Then let your light forth shine,
    That all may see it far without,
     And unto good incline.

10 The law, I came not to deride.
     Or prophecies of old,
    But to fulfill, and lead my bride
     To crystal streets of gold.

11 Those who break one of these commands,
     And teach men so, wrong heaven,
    To those that do them, at her hand,
     Shall greatest praise be given.

12 Except your righteousness exceed
     The scribe and pharisee,
    Ye shall not enter heaven indeed,
     Nor have right to life's tree.

13 They who shall kill, said ancient laws,
     Endanger judgment sent,
    But he that's angry without cause,
     Shall die lest he repent.

14 Who calls his brother an ill name,
     Draws to the council nigher,
    And he that calls him fool, the same
     Hath danger of hell fire.

15 When thou dost gifts to altars bring,
     And know thy brother's grief,
    Be thou first reconciled to him,
     Then offer thou thy gift.

16 Let no wrong be 'tween him and thee,
     But ever live in peace,
    Lest thou in vile law-wranglings be,
     And oft in prison cast.

17 Adultery thou shalt not commit,
     Is a good law of old,
    But I say who so looks for it,
     Already stains their soul.

18 If hand or eye offend or ail,
     To cast them off is well,
    'Tis better that one member fail,
     Than all be cast to hell.

19   One may divorce his wife 'twas said,
       But I give no such laws,
     Let no man leave the wife he wed,
       Lest lewdness be the cause.

20   " Perform thine oaths to God of all,"
       'Twas said in times of old,
     But I say swear ye not at all,
       By heaven, or earth, or gold.

21   But let your words be yea and nay,
       For what is more than these,
     Forth cometh from an evil way,
       And doth your God displease.

22   Take tooth for tooth and eye for eye,
       Said they in old times odd,
     I say avenge not lest ye die,
       For that belongs to God.

23   If, at the law, one shall thee sue,
       And take away thy coat,
     The insult bear, for Me be true,
       And let him have thy cloak.

24   If one urge thee a mile to go,
       With him, then go thou twain,
     Give him that asketh thee also,
       The borrower's wish sustain.

25   Love enemies who false accuse,
       Do good to those who hate,
     Pray for them which despiteful use,
       And do you persecute.

26   That ye may be the children of
       Your heavenly Father God,
     Who makes His sun to rise upon
       The evil and the good.

27   If ye love but those that love you,
       Then what reward have ye ?
     Even the publicans so do,
       Love all since God lov'd thee.

28   For sinners must to judgment come,
       To God belongs reward ;
     Be truly kind to every one,
       As I who am your Lord.

29 Be perfect as your Father God,
 Who in high heaven doth reign,
 And walk the path which I have trod,
  And ye shall it obtain."

CHAPTER VI.

1 " Give not your alms for to be seen,
  Or glory have of men,
 But secretly give what ye mean,
  God shall reward thee then.

2 And when ye pray, mean what ye say,
  Speak not deceitful things,
 For what ye need, thus pray indeed,
  And God shall blessings bring.

3 Our Father God in heaven blest one,
  Hallowed be thy name,
 Thy kingdom come thy will be done,
  In earth and heaven the same.

4 Give us this day our daily bread,
  Forgive our sins we pray,
 As we forgive the trespass deed,
  Of each our fellow clay.

5 Lead us not to temptation's shrine,
  Keep us from evil then,
 The kingdom, power, and glory's thine,
  Forever more, Amen.

6 As ye forgive men's trespasses,
  So God will you forgive,
 If ye refuse men to forgive,
  No pardon shall ye have.

7 And when ye fast make no sad face,
  As hypocrites or fraud,
 To make men think that they have grace,
  But they have their reward.

8 But when ye fast, anoint thy head,
  And wash, that thou appear
 Not unto men to fast indeed,
  But unto God most dear.

9 Pray not as hypocrites, for they
     Oft make long prayers in streets,
  To make men think that they obey,
     In righteousness complete.

10 But when ye pray first shut thy door,
     Then pray to God alone,
  And he will bless thy secret hour,
     And make thy virtues known.

11 Lay treasures up for you in heaven,
     Where moth nor rust can go,
  For where ye have your treasure hidden,
     Your heart will be also.

12 The light of body is the eye,
     If thine eye single be,
  Thy body shall be full of light,
     A pleasure unto thee.

13 If thine eye evil be in thee,
     Great darkness shall thee fill,
  Therefore if thy light darkness be,
     That darkness is great ill.

14 If light, and knowledge which God gave,
     Be used, thy God to bless,
  Thou shalt be full of light and grace,
     And hopes of endless rest.

15 If light, and knowledge, God gave thee,
     Be used in sinful ways,
  In darkness thou shalt ever be,
     And far from heavenly grace.

16 If thy light, thou hast darkness made,
     Then take heed unto thee,
  If thou by sin make thy light shade,
     How dark that shade must be.

17 For God and mammon none can serve,
     One must be laid aside,
  Lest you from one of them should swerve,
     Or other be despised.

18 Trust God for food, and drink, and meat,
     Behold the fowls of air,
  They sow not neither do they reap,
     Yet God for them prepares.

19 If God clothe grass and lilies too,
        In glorious attire,
    Will He not much more then clothe you,
        As children doth require?

20 Grieve not about what ye shall eat,
        Or where withal be clothed,
    For all these things do Gentiles seek,
        Your need, your Father knows.

21 But seek ye first God's kingdom true,
        And His blest righteousness,
    And all these things I'll add to you,
        And take you to My rest."

CHAPTER VII.

1   "Judge not that ye should not be judged,
        Man cannot judge man good,
    Be kind to all, nor hold a grudge,"
        Leave judgment unto God.

2   For by the judgment, ye judge with,
        Ye shall be judged again,
    And just the measure that ye give,
        The same shall ye obtain.

3   The mote, seen in thy brother's eye,
        Through beams within thine own,
    Thou cans't not pull out if thou try,
        Till beams from thine are gone.

4   Give not things holy to the dogs,
        Nor cast your pearls to swine,
    Lest they defile pure things of God's,
        And you to rend incline.

5   Ask God, and He will give to you,
        Seek Him, and ye shall find,
    Knock, and it shall be opened too,
        For God is good and kind.

6   If son should ask his sire for cake
        Will he give him a stone?
    Or for fish give him a snake
        And think he blest his son?

7　If evil men will give good food,
　　　　When children ask of them,
　　　Will not your Father give things good,
　　　　When children ask of Him.

8　What ye would have men do to you,
　　　　That do ye unto them;
　　　This is the law and prophets true,
　　　　The duty of all men.

9　So enter in at the straight gate
　　　　That hath the narrow way,
　　　Which leads to life, ere 'tis too late,
　　　　Few find it in their day.

10　Wide is the gate and broad the way
　　　　Which leadeth unto death;
　　　Where many go therein astray,
　　　　In darkness and distress!

11　Beware false prophets in sheep's suits,
　　　　Who inwardly wolves are,
　　　But ye shall know them by their fruits,
　　　　For thistles no figs bear.

12　All good trees bear good fruit to suit,
　　　　Corrupt trees bear corrupt;
　　　Each tree that brings not forth good fruit,
　　　　Into the fire is thrust.

13　'Tis by their fruits ye shall them know;
　　　　Not all that saith, "Lord, Lord,"
　　　But they who do His will shall go
　　　　To heaven for their reward.

14　Some men will say to Me that day,
　　　　"We toiled, Lord, much for thee."
　　　I know you not, to them I'll say,
　　　　Ye work iniquity.

15　Who hears and does these words of mine,
　　　　Is like to a wise man,
　　　Who on a rock to build inclines,
　　　　And not upon the sand.

16　Who hears but does not my commands
　　　　Is likened to a fool,
　　　Who built his house upon the sand,
　　　　Regarding not my rule.

17 When on the house built on a rock,
 The winds and waters raged,
Then it fell not, nor felt the shock,
 Though tempests fierce engaged.

18 When on the house built on the sand,
 The tempest poured its weight,
It fell, alas! and could not stand,
 The fall thereof was great,

19 Christ to an end His sermon brought,
 When all astonished were,
For with authority He taught,
 And not as scribes declare.

20 'Twas thus the spotless Nazarene,
 On Juda's mount hath stood,
Whose words of love and looks serene,
 Did melt the heart with good.

[END OF SERMON ON THE MOUNT.]

CHAPTER VIII.

1 A leper said to Jesus then,
 " Lord if thou wilt, thou canst me cleanse,"
He said, " I will, so be thou clean,"
 Then nought of leprosy was seen.

2 When Christ into Capernium came,
 There a centurion said to Him,
" My servant, Lord, is sick at home,
 Of palsy, grievous and undone."

3 Then Jesus said, " I'll come and heal,"
 But he said, " nay 'tis just as well
To speak thy healing word of power,
 Which will him heal from this same hour.

4 I am not worthy, thou shouldst come
 Beneath my roof, speak, and 'tis done,
For I have soldiers under me,
 That go and come at my decree."

5 Then Jesus marvelleth, and saith,
 " In Israel I've not found such faith,
I say to you vast hosts shall come,
 From east and west and shall sit down.

6 With Abram, Isaac, Jacob there,
    In God's blest kingdom bright and fair.
    While children of the Jews, shall be
    Cast out in darkness, far from me.

7 Where weeping is, and gnashing teeth,
    Emblems of guilt, and pain, and grief,
    Then Christ said as thou hast believed,
    So be it unto thee received."

8 Then Jesus, Peter's mother healed,
    And cast out devils and fulfilled,
    As prophets spake, He healed and blest,
    And bore our sickness and distress.

9 When vast crowds round Him did abide,
    He said, " sail to the other side,"
    Then did a scribe say, " Master know
    I'll follow thee where thou dost go."

10 Christ said, " the foxes have their holes,
    And birds of air, nests many fold,
    But I've not where to lay my head,
    Nor yet a shelter for my bed."

11 One said, " to follow I desire,
    But let me bury first my sire.,
    " O follow me, now first," He said,
    " Lest thy Salvation should be fled."

12 Then they took ship, and tempests rose,
    And raging waves, their barque enclosed,
    While He did sleep, they were forlorn,
    And cried, " Lord save us from the storm."

13 He said to them, " why do ye fear ;
    Pray God for faith your hearts to cheer,"
    When He rebuked the winds and sea,
    There was a calm great as could be.

14 The men then marveled and did say,
    " What man doth winds, and sea obey ?"
    Then He sailed to the other side,
    In Gergesenes land to abide.

15 Two men possessed of devils, met
    Him from the tombs, for to beset,
    For they let no man pass that way,
    But they did cry and to Him say :

16   " What have we now to do with thee,
    Jesus thou son of God, we flee,
    Torment us not before the time,
    Let us go in you herd of swine."

17   He bade them go, when out they come,
    Went in the herd which violent run
    Down in the sea, till all were dead ;—
    Their herdsmen to the city fled.

18   The city then met Christ in haste,
    They feared and begged Him leave that place,
    This was to make men know and tell,
    How devels curse in whom they dwell.

19   For when they passed from men to swine,
    How soon the herd in death reclined.
    Thus all who do with devils dwell,
    Must feel the pangs of death and hell.

CHAPTER IX.

1   Then Jesus by ship to His own city passed,
    They brought Him a man sick of palsy, down cast,
    He seeing their faith, spake as one from high heaven,
    " Son be of good cheer for thy sins are forgiven."

2   Then scribes said, among them, this man doth blaspheme,
    He knowing their thoughts, said, " why doth it so seem,
    For which is the easier to say as I talk ?
    Thy sins are forgiven thee, or say rise and walk."

3   " But that ye may know that I can sins forgive,"
    He said, " Take thy bed, walk to where thou dost live."
    The sick man then rose, walking to his house, when
    They glorified God, who such power gave to men.

4   Then Jesus called Matthew from custom's receipt,
    Who followed to where Jesus did set at meat,
    With sinners, and publicans, dining with Him,
    Then Pharisees murmuring, did railings begin.

5   He said unto them, that, " the whole have no need
    To have a physician, but sick ones indeed,
    Now learn what this meaneth, I will mercy have,
    And not sacrifice, that I sinners may save.

6 For I came on earth, not the righteous to call,
But sinners' repentence is My mission all."
Then came John's disciples, and thus they besought,
" Why fast we while thy lov'd disciples fast not ?"

7 " Because I their bridegroom am with them to feed,
But when I am gone they shall hunger and bleed,
New cloth in old garments, will make the rent worse,
New wine in old bottles will cause them to burst.

8 New cloth in new garments the longest will serve,
New wine in new bottles will each one preserve."
A ruler then came who a daughter's death grieved,
And said, "pray, lay hands on her and she shall live."

9 Christ and His disciples then followed the man,
A woman diseased, then behind there came,
For lo, she had said, with belief in her soul,
" If I can but touch Him I shall be made whole."

10 She touched but the hem of His garment, when He
Turned round and said, " daughter thy faith hath saved thee."
The woman was healed then from that very hour,
And she glorified God as she felt healing power.

11 As noise in the rulers house rang, Jesus said,
" Come out, give me place, for the maid is not dead."
They laughed Him to scorn, as He took hold her hand,
When she did arise and before them did stand.

12 The fame thereof went far abroad of Him then,
But as He departed there cried two blind men,
" O, thou son of David, have mercy pray do."
He said, " now believe ye that I can heal you ?"

13 They answered Him, " yea Lord," then touched He their eyes,
And said as your faith is so God hears your cries.
Their eyes then were opened, He said, " tell no man,"
But they afterward spread His fame through the land.

14 A dumb man they found, of a devil possessed,
Which Christ did cast out when the dumb spake and blest,
All said, " this in Israel was never so done,"
But Pharisees said, " through the devil it come."

15 Then Christ preached the gospel, and kingdom of peace,
And healed every sickness and every disease,
Then Christ had compassion on fainting ones there,
All scattered as sheep having no shepherd's care.

10 Then saith He, " the harvest is plenteous 'tis true,
    But laborers in harvest, alas, they are few,
    So pray ye the Lord of the harvest, to send
    Forth laborers in harvest, to save the lost men."

CHAPTER X.

1 Christ gave His disciples power o'er unclean spirits,
    To cast out, and heal sickness, and all disease,
    The names of His twelve lov'd Apostles of merit,
    Were Peter, and Andrew, James of Zebedee.

2 John, Philip, Bartholomew, and Thomas, and Matthew,
    And James, son of Alpheus, Lebbeus, Thaddeus,
    And Simon the Canaanite, and Judas Iscariot,
    Who also betrayed Him and brought a great curse.

3 These twelve Christ sent forth saying, " go not to Gentiles,
    Nor yet shall ye enter Samaria's land,
    But go to the lost sheep of blest house of Israel,
    And preach that the kingdom of heaven is at hand.

4 Heal sick, raise the dead, and cast out demon curses,
    As ye have received freely, so freely give,
    Provide gold nor silver, nor brass, in your purses,
    Nor scrip for your journey, two coats, shoes, nor staves.

5 In what place ye enter inquire who is worthy,
    There shall ye abide with them till ye go thence ;
    At first coming in ye shall hail as a brother,
    If worthy your peace there let rest with content.

6 Who shall not receive you nor hear your blest mission,
    Depart ye from them who your words shall reject,
    Gomorrha and Sodom, hath better condition
    In judgment, than those who My gospel neglect.

7 I send you as sheep, where the wild wolves are crouching,
    As serpents be wise, and as doves harmless too,
    Beware ye of men who will bring you to councils,
    And oft before governors persecute you.

8 Think not what to answer, when they shall deliver,
    For it shall be given you, that hour what to speak,
    'Tis not ye that speak but the words of your Father,
    Which speaketh in you, for which pray ye and seek.

9   The brother to death, shall deliver his brother,
     The father, the son, son his sire to the grave,
     All men shall you hate, for My sake not another,
     But he that endures to the end shall be saved.

10 If one city hate you flee ye to another,
     For cities of Israel shall last till I come,
     Disciple can never be over his master,
     Nor servant o'er Lord 'tis enough they are one.

11 If men give the name " Beelzebub " to the master,
     They also will give to his household that name,
     Fear not for things secret shall all be hereafter,
     Divulged from the darkness and made very plain.

12 What I tell you here, preach on house-tops forever,
     Fear not them which only this body can kill,
     But I will fore-warn you whom ye should fear rather,
     Him who can destroy soul and body in hell.

13 The least things are noticed of your heavenly Father,
     The hairs of your head are all numbered and given,
     Two sparrows which only are sold for one farthing,
     One shall not fall down but God sees it from heaven,

14 I'm come to set men 'gainst the sins of their fathers,
     Who oft will contend 'gainst the sons whom I draw,
     I come to set mothers 'gainst sins of the daughters,
     And daughter-in-law 'gainst the mother-in-law.

15 A man's foes shall be of his household and clamor,
     Round those who love Me and My gospel the best,
     Who loveth Me not more than mother or daughter,
     That one is not worthy to enter My rest.

16 He who loves his life more than Me, he shall loose it,
     Who loseth his life for My sake shall it find ;
     He that receives you, it is Me that he choseth,
     And him who hath sent Me, the Father divine.

17 Who feedeth a prophet, in name of a prophet,
     Such one shall receive a true prophet's reward,
     Who feedeth My servants, though men think light of it
     Who doth it, his goodness the Lord doth regard.

18 He who shall give drink to one of My disciples,
     A cup of cold water in name of his Lord,
     It is a blest deed far above earthly trifles,
     And such one shall reap My disciple's reward."

CHAPTER XI.

1 When Christ ceas'd commanding His twelve, He went preaching
   When John heard in prison, Christ's works, he did send
   His two lov'd disciples, who came thus beseeching,
   Art thou the true Christ on whom we should depend?"

2 Christ said, " go shew John what ye hear and see sacred,
   How blind see, the lame walk, and lepers are cleansed,
   And how that the deaf hear, the dead they are raised,
   The poor have the gospel now preached unto them.

3 Most blest is he who in Me is not offended,
   More great than a prophet is My servant John,
   And at his blest preaching ye should have repented,
   None greater than John ere among men was born.

4 From John until now doth the kingdom of heaven,
   Oft suffer the violent to take it by force,
   The law and the prophets until John were given,
   John is the Elias which was to come forth.

5 With what is this pert generation contented,
   We piped unto you and lo ye have not danced,
   We wept over you and ye have not repented,
   Believe and repent and My kingdom advance.

6 Ye murmured when John preached not eating or drinking,
   My eating and drinking ye now both deride,
   Ye taunt Me with wine and of eating with sinners,
   Ye said, " that a devil with John did abide."

7 Now woe to thee Chorazin, woe to Bethsaida,
   My works here would made Tyre and Sidon repent,
   It shall be far better for Tyre and for Sidon,
   In great day of judgment unless ye relent.

8 Capernaum which now art exalted to heaven,
   Shall come down to hell for if mighty work's sake,
   Which were done in thee had to Sodom been given,
   To-day, she would stand in her glory and state.

9 Then Christ answering said now I thank thee, O Father
   Lord of heaven and earth that thy pleasure hath hid,
   These things from the self-wise and prudent forever,
   And that it pleased thee to reveal them to babes.

10 No man knoweth God but the Son who is Saviour,
    And He to whom Son shall the Father reveal,
    Come ye heavy laden find rest from your labor,
    The meek and the lowly shall Jesus' love feel.

CHAPTER XII.

1 As Jesus' disciples passed on Sabbath day,
    By corn-fields, while hungered they eat on their way,
    Then Pharisees said, "'tis an unlawful deed,
    But Jesus said know ye not what David did.

2 When he was an hungered and those men with Him,
    They eat the shew bread in God's house without sin,
    As priests in the temple, the Sabbath profane,
    When they are an hungered and yet without blame.

3 One greater than temples behold now is here,
    With mercy the guiltless to feed and to cheer,
    For I am the Lord even of Sabbath days,
    Then He in their synagogues preached of God's ways.

4 Where one with a hand withered there was revealed,
    They asked is it lawful on Sabbath to heal,
    He said if on Sabbath it should come about,
    A sheep fall in pit wilt thou not lift it out.

5 Much better by far is a man than a sheep,
    Well doings will lawful the Sabbath day keep,
    Then bade He the sick man to stretch his hand forth,
    When lo, it was whole like the other restored.

6 When Pharisees counciled 'gainst Him to destroy.
    With multitudes great He from them did withdraw,
    For thus was fulfilled what the prophets foretold,
    Behold My choice servant, beloved of My soul.

7 I will put My spirit on Him for He must
    Show judgment to Gentiles and they in Him trust,
    A bruised reed He'll break not, nor smoking flax quench
    'Till judgment to victory be forth by Him sent.

8 One came blind and dumb of a devil possessed,
    Christ healed him, then spake he and saw and was blest,
    The people amazed asked is this David's son?
    The Pharisees answered, " by Satan 'twas done."

9 Christ said, "any kingdom that fights its own self,
   Works its own destruction and dies by none else,
   If Satan fight Satan destruction is his,
   A self fighting kingdom must ruin receive.

10 If by Beelzebub I bring good things about,
   Then judge ye by whom your son cast devils out,
   If I cast them out by the Spirit of God,
   The kingdom of God is to you come abroad.

11 Else how can one rob a strong man of his goods,
   Except he first bind him, he will spill his blood,
   He that is not with Me against Me is then,
   All blasphemies shall be forgiven of men.

12 Except the reviling of the Holy Ghost,
   Which God ne'er forgives, 'tis of all sins the worst,
   He who speaks against Me it may be forgiven,
   But sin against the Holy Ghost shuts one from heaven.

13 Make ye the tree good and its fruit good also,
   If it be corrupt, then its fruit will be too,
   A tree is well known by the fruit which it brings,
   Nor can evil hearts ever bring forth good things.

14 By words from good hearts men shall be justified,
   Bad words from bad hearts causeth guilt to abide,
   For all idle words men shall speak, they shall give
   Account in the judgment day, sure as I live.

15 By words man shall be justified or condemned,
   Who sins not in word is a perfect man then."
   Then Phar'sees and scribes said, "Lord show us a sign,"
   He said, "the adulterers to signs do incline.

16 All signs but of Jonas the righteous do scorn,
   Three days from My death is the resurrection morn
   As Jonas lay swallowed up three days of death,
   I shall be three days in the heart of the earth.

17 Old Nineveh's men in the judgment shall rise,
   To this unbelieving generations surprise,
   For Jonas's preaching drew penitent tears,
   But ye have a greater than Jonas now here.

18 The queen of the south, in the judgment shall rise,
   Against this generation to their sad surprise,
   For she did the wisdom of Solomon revere,
   But lo, a far greater than Solomon is here.

19 When an unclean spirit is gone from a man,
    It walketh dry places for rest finding none,
    It saith, " I will enter my house I once kept,
    He findeth it empty and garnished and swept.

20 He took seven spirits with him that were worse,
    They entered and that man was worse than at first.
    So shall it be with this generation now here,
    Because that My gospel ye do not revere.

21 Then one said, Thy mother and brethren seek Thee,
    He said, " none are brethren lest they follow Me,
    For who so shall hence do God's will to His praise,
    The same is My brother and sister always.

CHAPTER XIII.

1 When Jesus sat upon the sea,
       And multitudes did throng that shore,
   He spake in parables like these,
       Of harvest fields, and seeds and sowers.

2 What seed fell wayside fowls devoured,
       What fell on stones did spring up soon,
   Some fell 'mong thorns, which them o'erpowered,
       Those plants on stones were scorched at noon.

3 Some fell on good ground and brought fruit,
       Some thirty, sixty hundred fold.
   Who hath an ears hear ye the truth,
       In easy parables of old.

4 They said, " in parables why speak ?"
       He said, " to make all mysteries known,
   Of God's blest kingdom, men should seek,
       Through parables great light is shown.

5 Those who have light can comprehend
       And know the truth of all I say,
   To those in darkness I extend
       By parables, the heavenly way.

6 They fill the prophecy which saith,
       Ye hear but understand not full.
   They see and yet do not perceive,
       Their heart is gross, their ears are dull.

7 Their eyes they close lest I reveal
     The truth, so that they understand,
   And be converted, and I heal
     And bring them to the heavenly land.

8 How blest are ye who see and hear,
     For many righteous have desired
   To see the things which we revere,
     And have not seen them, neither heard.

9 When one to keep God's word doth start,
     And understands it not, then comes
   His foe, who steals it from his heart,
     This is that seed by wayside sown.

10 He that receives with joy and haste,
      And doth not firmly then endure,
    He is that seed on stones forth cast,
      Whose harvest never will be sure.

11 He that receives the seed 'mong thorns,
      Is he that hears God's word with joy,
    Whose heart is to earth's pleasures drawn,
      So that they do that seed destroy.

12 The seed in good ground is that soul
      Who hears and keeps God's word with care,
    Where thirty, sixty, hundred fold
      Of heavenly fruits clustering there.

13 One sowed good seed within his field,
      But while he slept his foe sowed tares,
    So when the blade sprung forth to yield,
      The servants grieved to see them there.

14 They said. "didst thou not sow good seed,
      From whence doth tares so cloth the ground ?"
    He said, " my foe hath done this deed,"
      They said, " lord, shall we cut them down ?"

15 He said, " nay, lest ye spoil the wheat,
      Let both be till the harvest time,
    Then I will bid my servants reap
      My wheat, but bind the tares to burn."

16 Like as a grain of mustard seed,
      Again God's kingdom I compare,
    Which is the least 'mong all seeds indeed,
      But greatest of all herbs there are.

17   Like leaven, which a woman hid
  In meal, till leavened all became
Just as the spreading leaven did,
  My kingdom shall this world inflame.

18   Plain parables to you I set,
  As spake the prophets oft of old,
I'll utter things which have been kept
  From the foundation of the world."

19   As Christ to them these things did say,
  Then His disciples said, " declare
To us the parable this day,
  Both of the sowers, wheat and tares."

20   The sower of good seed is Christ,
  The field it is this world below,
The good seed keeps God's word of life,
  The tares, are wicked men of woe.

21   'Twas Satan sowed them in the field,
  The harvest is end of the world, ;
The reapers, angels are revealed,
  Who gather tares in fire to hurl.   ·

22   Christ shall send forth his angels then
  And gather them who do not keep
His blest commands. and will them send
  Where weeping is and gnashing teeth.

23   Then shall the righteous ever shine,
  Fair as the sun in heaven above,
Who hath an ear, let him incline
  To seek God's kingdom, peace and love.

24   So heaven is like a treasure hid,
  Found in a field, which one had left,
When he for joy, sold all he had,
  To buy that field, that prize to get.

25   And like a merchant's goodly pearl,
  When he had found one of great price,
Gave all he had here in this world
  For that choice pearl.   So choose ye Christ.

26   Like as a net cast in the sea,
  God's kingdom draws all to that day
When at the judgment shore shall He
Select the good, cast bad away.

27 So shall it be when this world ends
        God's angels shall part vile from just,
    And cast in outer darkness them
        Who do not in their saviour trust.

28 He said, " now know ye all these things ?"
        Then they said unto Him, " Yea, Lord."
    He said, " let each man good things bring
        Forth from his treasures of reward."

29 In synagogues he preached and talked,
        So that they all astonished were,
    They said, " who hath Him wisdom taught ?
        Who did such good for Him prepare ?

30 Is this not Joseph's son we know,
        Whose mother Mary here remains ?
    And sisters likewise, brethren, too,
        Joseph and Simon, Judas, James."

31 And they offended were in Him,
        But Jesus spake and said to them,
    " A prophet hath no honor in
        His country and among his friends."

CHAPTER XIV.

1 King Herod thought Christ to be John
       The Baptist, whom he put to death,
   Since mighty works by Christ were done,
       He thought 'twas John rose from the dead.

2 For Herod thought to take John's life,
       For saying 'twas unlawful deed
   For him to wed his brother's wife,
       But he did fear the multitude,

3 On Herod's birthday He made oath,
       Herodias' daughter's wish to give,
   When she had danced and pleased them both,
       "John Baptist's head," she said, " I'll have."

4 John's head, to her, he gave that day,
       And his disciples buried him.
   Then Jesus did depart away,
       And heal the sick that to Him came.

5   Then His disciples to Him said,
     " Lord send the multitude away,
    That they may buy themselves some bread,"
    But Jesus said, " O, let them stay."

6   He said, " ye ought to give them meat,"
     They said, "five loaves will never last,"
    He said, " bring ye the food to me,
    And make the men sit on the grass,

7   Then Jesus blest the bread, and brake
     To each disciple of the food,
    While they did carry round, and make
    Provision for the multitude.

8   They all with pleasure ate their fill,
     Then took up fragments that remained.
    There being left twelve baskets full,
    When they had fed five thousand men !

9   He said to His disciples then,
     " Take ship unto the other side,
    While I the multitude do send
    Away, and for their wants provide."

10   Their ship now rolled afar at sea,
     High tossed on waves, mid wind and rage,
    Then Jesus went forth them to free,
    And still the tempest that engaged.

11   For He went walking on the sea,
     'Til He came to their floundering barque,
    Each cried, " have mercy Lord on me,"
    For mighty dread had seized their hearts.

12   He said, " my children have no fear,
     For it is I, be not afraid."
    Then Peter cried, " let me come near,
    Lord to thee, on the water's edge."

13   He bade him come, and he went down
     Out of the ship upon the wave,
    But when he feared the billows frown,
    He then did sink, and cry, " Lord save."

14   Christ caught, and said, " O little faith,
     Wherefore thy fear ? why dost thou doubt ?"
    When in the ship the storms were laid,
    And all adored Him most devout.

15 When to Gennesaret they came,
    They brought Him those that were diseased,
    And those who touched His garment's hem,
    Were healed as many as were pleased.

CHAPTER XV.

1 Then from Jerusalem came foes,
    Both scribes, and priests, did thus contest,
    Why transgress thy disciples those
    Traditions, which the elders kept.

2 For they wash not, when they eat bread,
    Christ said, " why do ye disobey,
    Transgressing the commands of God,
    By your traditions here to day.

3 For God commanded, telling you,
    To honor father, mother dear,
    They who curse them shall die, 'tis true,
    The child his parents shall revere.

4 But ye say, " who saith 'tis a gift,
    If parents shall be blest of child,
    He who to parents nought doth give,
    Him ye set free, and on him smile.

5 These, God's commandments ye reject,
    By your traditions which ye have,
    Ye hypocrites whom God neglects,
    How from hell fire can ye be saved?

6 Well spake the prophets old, how ye
    Draw nigh unto me with your mouth,
    And with your lips ye honor me,
    While yet your heart is far, far out.

7 In vain ye worship me, and teach
    For doctrines the commands of men."
    He did the multitude beseech
    And bade them, " hear and understand,

8 Not that which entereth man defiles,
    But that which cometh from his heart."
    The Pharisees were angry while
    Our Lord these sayings did impart.

9 " All plants not planted to God's mind,
       Shall be torn up both one and all,
   Let 'lone blind leaders of the blind,
       For they both in the ditch will fall."

10 Then Peter answering thus demands,
        " Declare this parable the while."
    Christ said, " Do ye not understand
        That what man eats doth not defile ;

11 But things proceeding from the mouth
        Must come forth from the heart, while
    If thefts or blasphemies come out
        Of hearts, they do the men defile."

12 When on the coast of Tyre there pray'd
        A Canaan daughter, crying thus,
    " Have mercy on us Lord," she said,
        "My daughter's vexed of devils cursed."

13 His followers said, " Send her away,"
        He said, " To lost sheep I am sent
    Of house of Israel, this day,"
        She cried, " Lord help me, I repent,"

14 He said, " It is not meet to take
        The children's bread and cast to dogs,"
    She said, " Truth Lord, yet dogs have ate
        Crumbs from the tables of their lords."

15 He said to her, " Great is thy faith,
        Be it unto thee as thou wilt."
    Her daughter, from that hour found grace,
        And healing for all pain and guilt ;

16 Then Christ, to Galilee forth came,
        Great multitudes pursued Him, where
    Were lame, and blind, and dumb, and maimed,
        At Jesus' feet, who healed them there.

17 Then, when the people saw that He
        Made lame to walk, and maimed made whole,
    The dumb to speak the blind to see,
        They glorified the God of all.

18 Christ said, " I feel compassion here
        For multitudes, who for three days
    Have followed me, but for to hear,
        How can I send them faint away ? "

19 Then His disciples said, " Whence should
    We have bread in this wilderness,
    To feed so vast a multitude ? "
    He said, " How much have ye at best ? "

20 They said, " Seven loaves with few of fish."
    He bade them all sit on the ground,
    He took the food, gave thanks and give,
    To all the multitude around.

21 They ate in love, and were all filled,
    They took what broken meat was left,
    Which did make seven basketsfull
    When, o'er four thousand ate at best.

22 Women and children ate also,
    He sent the multitude away,
    And took a ship forthwith to go
    To the fair coasts of Magdola.

CHAPTER XVI.

1 Then Pharisees and Saddusees
    Urged Him from heaven to shew a sign,
    He said, " when red sky comes at eve,
    Ye say, " fair weather it divines.

2 At morn ye say foul day is nigh,
    Because the sky is low'ring red,
    For hypocrites can see the sky,
    But not the signs of times ahead.

3 A wicked people seek a sign,
    Yet no sign shall be given, but
    The sign of Jonas, of old time."
    Then He left them and journey'd out.

4 As on their voyage they did proceed,
    They had forgotten to take bread,
    " Of Pharisees and Sadducees
    Beware their doctrine," Jesus said.

5 He said, " Whom do men say I am ?"
    They said, " Elias, some say John,"
    " Tell ye who I am if ye can."
    They said, " the Christ of God, His son."

6   " Blessed are ye, for flesh and blood
    Hath not revealed this unto thee,
But He who is in heaven, your God
    Hath taught you thus concerning me.

7   A rock is Peter which ne'er fails,
    I'll build my church on it to stand,
And gates of hell shall not prevail,
    I'd give thee keys of heaven's land.

    What thou shalt bind on earth, is bound
      In heaven, and what thou loose, be loosed."
He charged them not to make Him known,
    His sufferings thus to them He shows.

9   " I to Jerusalem must go,
    There suffer for all sins, they say,
Of elders, priests, and scribes also,
    Be killed and rise on the third day."

10   Then Peter Him rebuked we find,
    And said, " Lord be this far from Thee."
He said to Peter, " get behind
    Me Satan, thou offendest me.

11   Thou loveth not the things of God,
    But things of man thou dost approve,
Who hath My love, My paths have trod,
    The way of goodness, peace and love.

12   Who loves life more than Me, shall loose,
    Who loves Me more than life, shall find,
What gain if thou, O man, should choose
    The world, and loose this soul of thine ?

13   For soon the son of man shall come
    In glory of His Father God,
With angels then to give each one,
    According to his works reward.

14   I verily say now, there be
    Some standing here, who shall not die,
'Till they the Son of man shall see,
    Come in His kingdom, very nigh."

CHAPTER XVII.

1 Then Christ took Peter, James and John,
   Up in a mount within six days,
 And was transfigured unto them ;
   His face did shine as sun-light blaze.

2 White was His raiment as the light,
   Elias, Moses, talked with Him.
 Then Peter said to Jesus Christ,
   " Lord, it is good to be here in.

3 Let us three tabernacles make."
   While He was talking, lo a cloud,
 From which a voice thus to them spake,
   " Hear My loved Son, the Son of God."

4 His brethren fell most sore with fright,
   Then Jesus touched and bade them rise,
 Then as they looked, none were in sight,
   Save Jesus, to their great surprise !

5 When they came from the mount He said,
   " Tell ye the vision to no man,
 'Till I am risen from the dead,
   And proved the resurrection plan.

6 Elias is already come,
   And persecutors have him slain ;
 Likewise shall they do to God's son,
   But see that faithful ye remain."

7 Then one came kneeling down to Him,
   And cried, " have mercy on my son,
 All vexed with dread disease and sin,
   From thy disciples I have come."

8 Then Jesus said, " O faithless men,
   Bring ye him hither unto Me."
 So He rebuked the devil then,
   And he did from the sick man flee.

9 Then Christ's disciples came to Him,
   And said, "why could we not him heal ?"
 " The cause is unbelief and sin ;
   Fasting and prayer, true faith reveals."

10 He said, the son shall be betrayed
    Into the hands of wicked men,
Be killed and rise on the third day ;
    They wept, exceeding sorry then.

11 Then tribute men did Peter ask,
    " Doth Jesus any tribute pay ?"
Then Jesus said to Peter, " cast
    A hook for me into the sea.

12 The fish first on the hook then take,
    And in his mouth shall money be,
Which take and go and payment make
    To tribute men for Me and thee,"

CHAPTER XVIII.

1 Then Christ's disciples asked Him " who
    Is greatest in Thy kingdom, Lord ?"
He called a little child to prove
    That heaven's greatest is the small.

2 " Except ye be converted and
    Become as little children are,
Ye cannot see the heavenly land,
    For greatest is the humblest there.

3 Who shall receive such little child
    In My own name, receiveth Me ;
Or who shall such an one beguile.
    'Twere better that he drowned be.

4 Woe to this world for its offence,
    Though its offences oft may come,
But those who do the good offend,
    Had better not live 'neath the sun.

5 If hand or foot shall thee offend,
    Cut off, though they are thy desire,
More dear is life, though halt or maimed,
    Than limbs in everlasting fire.

6 Cast off offences without strife,
    Even if thine eye God's will requires,
'Tis better with one eye to have life
    Than with two eyes cast in hell-fire.

7   Hate not one of My little ones,
      In heaven their angels do behold
   The face of God, who gave His Son
      Where angels walk the streets of gold.

8   To save the lost, God's Son inclines,
      As one that hath an hundred sheep,
   He leaves the ninety and the nine,
      And 'mong the mountains doth it seek.

9   When finding it, He doth rejoice
      More of that sheep, than ninety-nine,
   Which did not stray far from His voice,
      So God to save lost men inclines.

10   If 'gainst thy brother thou complain,
      Tell thou his fault to him alone ;
   If he hear thee, then thou hath gained
      Thy brother's love, and he thine own.

11   If He will not hear thee, take two,
      That three may all his words sustain.
   If He hear not those three, then you
      May to the church of Him complain.

12   If he neglect to hear the church,
      Let him be as the heathen 'round,
   For what ye shall bind here on earth,
      Or loose in heaven, is loosed or bound.

13   If two of you agree on earth
      As touching thing, ye ask in faith,
   It shall be done for them in worth,
      For God in heaven hears prayers of saints.

14   Where two or more met in My name,
      There am I in the midst of them."
   Then Peter asked as he forth came,
      " How oft shall I forgive a sin ?"

15   Christ saith, " not until seven times,
      Seventy times seven shalt thou forgive.
   Therefore God's kingdom doth incline,
      To what a king's men had received.

16   Ten thousand talents one man owed,
      With nothing left his Lord to pay.
   He ordered wife and children sold
      With him, and payment made that day.

17 That man fell down, and prayed his Lord,
    " Have patience and I'll pay in full."
His Lord was moved with great regard,
    And loosed him, and forgave him all.

18 That servant found me, who him owed
    An hundred pence, with nought to pay,
He quickly seized him by the throat,
    And cried, " now pay me all this day."

19 His fellow servant then fell down,
    And said, " wait, and I'll pay thee yet."
But he cast him in prison, bound
    'Till he should pay him all the debt.

20 His fellows then were sorry all,
    And told their Lord what he had done,
And then their Lord for him did call,
    And said to him, " thou wicked one.

21 Lo, I forgave all thou asked me,
    Should not thou then compassion had
On others, as I had on thee,
    When I forgave and made thee glad?"

22 His Lord then made him pay his due,
    And gave him to tormentors then,
So shall my Heavenly Father use
    Those who forgive not brethren's sins.

CHAPTER XIX.

1 Then Jesus to Judea came,
    And many sick folks healed He there.
The Pharisees came tempting Him,
    And questioned Him thus to ensnare.

2 " May men divorce their wives?" they asked.
    He said, " God bade them cleave to her,
That they be not twain, but one flesh,
    Whom none shall part, but her prefer."

3 They said, "did Moses not impart
    Commands, that they might her divorce?"
He said, " for hardness of your hearts
    Did Moses let you take this course.

4 From the beginning 'twas not so,
    Hence he who shall his wife divorce,
  And marry, shall to all men show
    Sins of adultery the worst."

5 Then they brought children that He bless
    And lay His hands on them and pray.
  As His disciples did protest,
    He said, " keep ye not them away.

6 Forbid them not to come to Me,
    The heavenly kingdom is the same."
  One said, " Good Master, I ask Thee
    How I eternal life shall gain ?"

7 He said, " why callest thou Me good ?
    There is but One good, that is God.
  If enter endless life ye would,
    Walk ye the path that I have trod,

8 Steal not, nor lie, nor murderous prove,
    Adultery thou shalt not commit,
  Honor thy parents, neighbors love."
    He said, " I've kept these, what lacks yet ?"

9 Christ said, " if thou wouldst perfect be,
    Sell that thou hast and give the poor,
  And take thy cross and follow Me,"
    But he his riches sorrowed o'er.

10 He said, " How hardly shall the man
    Who loves wealth more than Me, find heaven,
  Such cannot gain the heavenly land,
    Nor ever have their sins forgiven."

11 He said, " ye who have followed Me
    In the new path, shall sit on thrones
  And judge the tribes of Israel free,
    Within the kingdom of God's son.

12 He who leaves all earth's things of strife,
    For Me, shall have an hundred fold,
  Inherit everlasting life,
    And walk the heavenly streets of gold.

CHAPTER XX.

1   God's kingdom is like one at morn, hiring all
    For penny a day, in his vineyard to toil,
    Also at third hour, did all others engage,
    And say, "go and work, what is right shall be paid."

2   At sixth, and ninth hour, he also did thus hire,
    And at the eleventh did entreat and desire,
    And say, "what is right, ye also shall receive."
    Then he called up his servants and paid them at eve.

3   Beginning from last to the first, he did pay
    To each man a penny for work done that day,
    But when the first came, who the day's burdens bore,
    They thought that they should of their Lord been paid more.

4   They murmured against the good man, and did say,
    "These wrought but one hour, and have had equal pay,
    To us who have all the day's burden well bore,
    Should thou not in justice have paid to us more."

5   He said, "didst thou not for a penny agree?
    I give to this last as I gave unto thee.
    With mine, is it not right to do as I will?
    Because I am good, doth it make thee think ill?"

6   Then Christ took disciples apart from the way,
    And said, "at Jerusalem, priests shall Me betray,
    And scribes shall condemn Me to death on the cross,
    And give Me to Gentiles to scourge and to mock.

7   But I on the third day in triumph shall rise,
    And sit on the right hand of God in the skies,
    From whence I shall come here to judge quick and dead,
    According to works, and all words they have said."

8   The mother of Zebedee's children did bring
    Her two sons, and worshiped Him, asking one thing,
    "That these sons may sit on thy right hand and left,
    In Thy blessed kingdom of heavenly rest."

9   He said unto her, "ye know not what ye ask,
    Can ye take My cup, My baptism, and fast?"
    When they said, "we're able," He to them declared,
    "It is for them only, God hath it prepared."

10 And when the ten heard it, indignant they were,
But Jesus called to them and said, " do not care
To reign in dominion, like Gentiles o'er men,
Or have great authority by ruling o'er them.

11 Him greatest among you, shall minister be,
He who will be chief shall be your servant free.
God's Son came not here to be ministered to, then,
But He came to minister His life unto men.

12 Then as they from Jericho went on their way,
A multitude great followed Him on that day,
Then two blind men sitting by way-side did cry,
" O Lord, Son of David, help us or we die."

13 The multitude bade them be still, hold their peace,
But they cried the more, " Lord have mercy on us."
He stood still and said, " tell Me why do ye cry ?"
They cried to Him, "Lord that thou open our eyes."

14 Then He had compassion and touched both their eyes,
Immediately they received sight in surprise,
And straightway they followed Him, praising the Lord,
That He had bestowed on them such great reward.

CHAPTER XXI.

1 When nearing Jerusalem to Bethphage we came,
Unto mount of Olives, Christ sent two men on.
Go to the city on the other side,
To find there an ass with her colt also tied.

2 And bring them, and if one say ought unto thee,
Say ye, "the Lord needs," and he'll send them to me.
Tell ye Zion's daughter, thy king comes to thee,
As prophets hath said, " meek and lowly is he."

3 Then branches and garments they cast in His way,
While hosts, fore and after, exclaimed Hosanna.
Blest is He that cometh now in the Lord's name,
" Hosanna in highest," the hosts did proclaim.

4 Jerusalem was moved, saying, "O who is this ?"
The multitude cried, " Jesus, our king and priest."
He entered God's temple, cast out merchandise,
And those who sold doves, money-changers likewise.

5 'Tis written, "my house is where pray'r is received,
   But lo! ye have made it a vile den of thieves."
   The blind and the lame, then were both healed of Him,
   The chief priests and scribes saw these wonderful things.

6 And heard in the temple, Hossanna and praise,
   And David's Son worshipped, which did them displease.
   They said, " hearest Thou what these say?" He said, " yea,
   Have ye not read how children give perfect praise?"

7 Then He went to Bethany, and did lodge there,
   Next morn saw when hungered, a fig tree most fair,
   And finding no fruit there, He said to that tree,
   " Let no fruit henceforth evermore grow on thee."

8 As that fig tree withered, they did marvel all.
   He said, "if ye have faith, not doubting at all,
   What ye shall ask God for, it shall to you come,
   For in faith believing all things shall be done.

9 The chief priests and elders then said unto Him,
   " Tell by what authority Thou dost those things."
   He said, " I will ask one thing, if you tell me,
   I also will tell you my authority.

10 John's baptism, was it from heaven or men?"
   They reasoned among themselves wittingly then.
   " If we say from heaven, unbelief will us stain,
   For He will say, why did ye of John complain !

11 If we say of men, then the people, we fear,
   For they all do John as a prophet revere."
   So they said to Christ, "we cannot tell you true."
   Then He said to them, " neither do I tell you."

12 Said Christ, " once a man to his two sons did say,
   ' Come eldest, go work in my vineyard to-day.'
   He said, ' I will not, though my father hath sent.'
   But afterward that son repented and went.

13 He came to the second, and likewise besought.
   He said, ' I will go sir,' and yet he went not."
   He asked of the twain, which did his father's will ?
   They said unto Him, " the first son he did tell."

14 Then Jesus said, "say I unto you most true,
   That publicans enter God's kingdom 'fore you.
   In righteousness John came, and ye believed not,
   But harlots and publicans John's goodness sought.

15   And after ye saw it ye did not regard,
Believe, nor repent, neither glorify God.
One planted a vineyard and hedged it about,
And digged a wine press and in in built a tower.

16   And let it to husbandmen ere he did leave,
And then sent his servants the fruit to receive.
The husbandmen killed, beat and stoned those he sent;
He sent more whom they slew, and did not relent.

17   At last he did send to them his darling one,
And said, 'it must be they will reverence my son.'
When they saw the son they said, 'this is the heir,
Come let us kill him, then all will be ours there.'

18   Then they cast his son from the vineyard and slew.
Now what will that lord to those husbandmen do?"
They said, " he will miserably kill those vile men,
And let out his vineyard to better ones then."

19   " In scripture," he said, " have ye read how the stone
Rejected, the head of the corner become ?
This is the Lord's doing, so strange in our eyes,
God's kingdom from you shall be taken likewise.

20   Who falls on this stone he shall broken be found,
Him on whom it falls will to powder be ground.
When Pharisees and priests heard His parables then,
They plainly perceived they had spoken of them.

21   But when they would slay Him, the people they feared,
For He was a prophet by them much revered.
" My vineyard," He said, " shall be taken from you
And given to husbandmen rendering my due."

CHAPTER XXII.

1   Again, certain king, marriage made for his son,
And sent servants, calling the bidden to come,
And when they would not, He sent others to tell
The bidden to come, I have made all things well."

2   But one went to merchandise, one to his farm,
Some treated his servants with ill and great harm.
That king sent his armies in wrath and destroyed
Those murderers who had thus his servants annoyed.

3 Those bid to the wedding were evil inclined,
  " Go ye to the highways, bid all that you find."
  His servants made guests then, of all that they found,
  The king found one there with no wedding clothes on.

4 The king said, " why no wedding garment hast thou?"
  And lo, he was speechless; the king cast him out
  Into outer darkness, mid gnashing of teeth,
  And weeping, the emblems of guilt and great grief.

5 For many are called, but the good God doth choose.
  Then Pharisees planned how they might Him abuse,
  They sent with disciples Herodians likewise,
  And said, " thou art true, and dost teach no disguise."

6 But God's way in truth ; neither carest thou now,
  For persons of men ; therefore what thinkest thou ?
  Shall we pay to Cesar the tribute or not.
  He said, " hypocrites why so tempt Me for naught.

7 Shew ye Me, the tribute," a penny they laid.
  He said, " whose inscription is this, and whose head?"
  They said to Him, " Cesar ;" He said then, " 'tis good
  To give Cesar his things, and God's things to God."

8 They marveled and left Him, and all went their way,
  The same day the Sadducees came, and did say,
  " If one shall die childless, his brother shall have
  His wife, to raise seed to him gone to the grave.

9 Sev'n brethren to one wife, were thus once all wed,
  In turn each died childless, the wife also died,
  Now in the res'rection whose wife shall she be ?
  Of those seven brethren, all had her we see."

10 " Not knowing God's power nor the scriptures ye err,
  In res'rection, marriages never occur,
  For all counted worthy of life shall be given,
  To be in res'rection, as angels in heaven."

11 When Sadducees hushed them the Pharisees came,
  And one of their lawyers did thus question him,
  " Which is the commandment great in the law,"
  " Thou shalt love the Lord, the true God over all.

12 This is first, and greatest command o'er all else,
  The next is, thou shalt love thy neighbor as self.
  On these two, the law and the prophets all hang,"
  Then when Pharisees came, he asked them this thing :

13 " Tell me who is Christ ?" and they said, " David's Son."
He saith, " how can he call him Lord, and Blest One ?
How can Christ be both David's Lord, and his son ?"
And no man was able to answer that one.

CHAPTER XXIII.

1 Christ said, " scribes and Pharisees sit in Moses' seat,
What they bid you do, do it but not their deeds,
For they say and do not, but bind burdens great
On men, which they move not with one finger's weight.

2 They do all their works of mankind to be seen,
Make broad their phylacteries, enlarge garment hems,
Love high rooms at feasts, and chief synagogue seats,
And greetings, where men to them Rabbi repeat.

3 Let not the name ' Rabbi ' to you ever be given,
Call no man your father but the God of heaven ;
Be ye not called masters, Christ is one to thee,
But he that is greatest shall your servant be.

4 For he that exalteth himself is abased,
But he that doth humble himself findeth grace.
But woe, scribes and Pharisees, hypocrites, who
Shut up heaven's kingdom 'gainst men who would go.

5 Woe to you, for ye widow's houses devour,
And all for pretence do ye make your long prayers,
So greater damnation ye hence shall receive,
Ye compass both sea and all land to deceive.

6 To make ye one convert, your sins to excell,
And be two fold more child of hell, than yourselves,
Woe to you, ye blind guides, who teach men to swear,
By Gods, gold and temples, and all things there are.

7 I say, who swears by these things, swears by his God,
Who holdeth him guilty, and will him reward.
Woe scribes, Pharisees, who heed but earthly tithes,
And break laws of faith, judgment, mercy likewise.

8 Ye strain at a small thing but swallow a great,
Ye make clean the outside of cups and the plait,
While inside is full of extorsion, excess,
Cleanse inside, then thy outside God will respect.

9   Now woe to you scribes, Pharisees, hypocrites,
As sepulchres seem ye, both beauteous and white,
While inside is filled with uncleanness and bones,
So ye scorn most righteous outside to each one.

10   Woe unto you scribes, whose hypocricies curse,
Ye build prophet's tombs, and deck graves of the just,
And say had we but in our sire's days have stood,
We would not partook with them of prophet's blood.

11   Now ye are dread witnesses unto yourselves,
That ye are the sons by whose sires prophets fell,
If ye fill the measure your sires filled, pray tell
How ye can escape the damnation of hell.

12   Lo, I send you prophets, and wise men, and scribes,
Ye kill them, and crucify, scourge, and deride,
That all righteous blood shed on earth fall on you,
From Abel unto Zacharias ye slew.

13   On this generation shall all this curse wait,
Jerusalem, Jerusalem, who prophets did hate,
And kill them which God hath oft sent unto thee,
How oft would I gathered thy children to Me?

14   Even as a hen gathereth her brood 'neath her wings;
But since ye would not, all these curses God brings.
Your house now is long to your desolate left,
Hence ye shall not see Me, but long be bereft.

15   'Till ye be converted and say, blest is He
Who comes in the name of the Lord unto Me,
For soon shall dread armies deal death to you 'round,
And smite your impregnable walls to the ground.

16   Who fights Me doth kick his bare foot 'gainst the thorns,
Who serveth Me God will with white robes adorn.
For I am that stone set at nought, which was found
That whom it falls on, will to powder be ground."

CHAPTER XXIV.

1   Then Jesus' disciples as He left the temple,
Said, "Come, Master, see these good buildings around."
He said "let not these fine things take your attention,
For soon they shall all be thrust down to the ground."

2   And then His disciples when at Mount of Olives,
      Said privately, " tell us when these things shall be ?
   And what, also, shall be the sign of Thy coming,
      And end of the world ?" Jesus said then, " take heed,

3   For many shall come in My name, most deceiving,
      And say, ' I am Christ,' but believe ye them not,
   First shall war's dread rumors fill men's hearts with grieving
      And proud, clashing kingdoms to famine be brought,

4   Then they shall you kill and to prison deliver,
      And ye shall be hated of all for My sake,
   Then men shall deceive and destroy one another,
      But he that endures to the end shall be saved.

5   My gospel and kingdom shall go to all nations,
      For witness to all, when the end it shall come,
   When ye shall see Daniel's foretold desolation,
      Let all within Judea to mountains be gone.

6   Let him on the housetop escape and not enter,
      Nor him in the field turn to take clothes away ;
   Pray ye that these troubles come not in the winter,
      Nor yet that your flight should be on Sabbath day.

7   No flesh should be saved, lest those days now are shortened,
      It is for My children God shortened those days,
   False Christs shall come teaching, and likewise false prophets,
      And show signs and wonders to lead you astray,

8   If they shall say Christ is in chamber or desert,
      Then go ye not after them, neither believe ;
   As lightning comes out of the east and shines westward,
      So also shall coming of Son of Man be.

9   Immediately after this great tribulation,
      The sun shall be darkened and the moon not give light,
   When stars fall and powers of heaven are shaken,
      Then Christ's sign in heaven shall appear ever bright.

10   Then all tribes of earth shall be clad in great mourning,
      To see Jesus' coming in glory and power,
   He shall send His angels with great sound of trumpets,
      To gather His children around Him that hour.

11   When trees put forth leaves, then ye know 'tis near summer,
      So when these things come, know 'tis not far away,
   This generation, it shall not pass for another,
      'Till all be fullfilled I have told you this day.

12 Of that day and hour knoweth none but My father;
    'Tis as Noah's day, when God set him apart;
    They ate, and they drank, and they married each other,
    Until that day Noah did enter the ark;

13 And knew not till floods came on them so amazing.
    So shall it then be, when the Son of Man comes,
    Two men shall be in the field, one shall be taken,
    Of two women grinding, there shall be left one.

14 Watch then, for ye know not what hour your Lord cometh,
    Therefore, be ye ready at every hour;
    The servant found watching, his lord him approveth,
    To faithful, wise servants, their lord giveth power.

15 If one say, my Lord now delayeth His coming,
    And eat, and be drunken, and fellow-men beat,
    His Lord shall come then, when he looketh not for Him,
    And cut him asunder, and mind not his grief.

16 And point him his portion, with all unbelievers,
    With false prophets, hypocrites, liars and deceivers,
    Whose guilt, pain and anguish give them no relief,
    When there shall be weeping and gnashing of teeth.

CHAPTER XXV.

1 Then the kingdom of heaven shall be like ten virgins,
   With lamps, looking for the bridegroom,
   When of them five were wise, also foolish were five,
   And the foolish took no oil with them.

2 Then the wise kept their oil in their lamps all the while,
   When the bridegroom was gone they all slept,
   'Till the midnight cry came, "go to meet the bridegroom,"
   To trimming their lamps they all went.

3 Then the foolish did call, saying, "give of your oil,
   For our lamps are gone out," they did cry.
   But the wise said, "not so, 'lest it last us not both.
   Go to them who do sell, and it buy."

4 Then, when they went to buy, the bridegroom did draw nigh,
   Wise ones came, and the door it was shut.
   Then the foolish ones came, afterward making claim,
   Saying, ' Lord, Lord, now open to us."

5   He said, 'I know you not, since for me ye ne'er watched,
     Watch, for ye knew not what hour I come,
  For the watchful I love, and the good I approve,
     So depart from me, ye wicked ones.'

6   For the kingdom of heaven is as a man traveling,
     And giving his servants his goods,
  Some he gave talents five, others two, one likewise,
     Just as each man's ability stood.

7   Then he that had the five, gained five on them likewise,
     And he that had the two did gain two,
  But he that had one hid it 'till his lord come,
     And said, 'there I'll keep safe 'till my lord's due.'

8   So when their lord did come, to account with each one.
     To the man who had five he inclined.
  He then said, " I had five, and have gained five likewise.'
     He said, 'well done, good servant of mine.'

9   Then he that had the two said, ' I've gained two for you.'
     He said, ' well done, heaven is thy reward.'
  Then he that had the one said, 'thou art a hard man,
     Take thy talent, I've kept for the lord.'

10   Then his lord answering, saith, "thou art wicked as death,
     Saying that I reap where I've not sown,
  So thou shouldst have made trade on the talent and made
     That with use I might have had my own.

11   Take the talent from him, give it him that hath ten,
     He who labors, to him shall be giv'n,
  But from him who gains not, shall be took what God brought,
     For the slothful can never gain heaven.

12   When the Son of God comes, on His glorious throne,
     Then before Him all nations shall meet,
  And He shall part them there, as a shepherd with care,
     Doth divide off the goats from the sheep.

13   On His right, sheep he'll set, and the goats on the left,
     And shall say to them on His right hand,
  ' Come ye blest of My Father, in My kingdom gather,
     Prepared ere creation did stand.

14   For when I was an hungered, ye fed Me abundant,
     When thirsty ye gave to me drink,
  When a stranger ye took Me in, naked, ye clothed Me,
     In prison ye blest Me when sick.'

15 Then they said, ' Lord, when saw we, Thee, in those afflictions,
    And ministered there unto Thee?'
  So, He answered and said then, ' as ye blest My brethren,
    Ye there did the same unto Me.'

16 Then the King also saith, unto them on His left,
    ' Unto woe everlasting go ye,
  Long prepared for the devil, and all who do evil,
    Or had not compassion on Me.

17 For when I was a stranger, in hunger and danger,
    In prison and sick, ye shunned Me.'
  Then they said,'Lord, when saw we Thee hungered or thirsty,
    Or sick, and come not unto Thee?'

18 Then He said, ' inasmuch as ye did it not thus
    To My saints, 'twas not done Me by thee.
  So henceforth ye must go, to destruction and woe,
    Nought but righteous have right to life's tree.'

19 Then the righteous shall shine in that kingdom divine,
    Which My Father for them hath prepared.
  There they shall see His face, who have sought for His grace,
    As the word of the Lord hath declared."

CHAPTER XXVI.

1 When these sayings did end Jesus said to his friends,
    " In two days is the passover feast,
  When I shall be betrayed and be crucified dead,
    Through the vengeance of scribes and chief priests."

2 At the house of Caiaphas, who was the high priest,
    They conspired subtilly Him to kill,
  Saying, not on feast day, lest it make a bad fray.
    Jesus then was in Bethany still.

3 There a woman came forth, and on Jesus' head poured,
    Precious ointment as He sat at meat,
  His disciples in haste cried. " why make this great waste,
    Which might given the poor much to eat."

4 Then did Jesus say to them, " why trouble the woman?
    She wrought a good work before thee.
  Poor men ye have all days, Me ye have not always,
    For My burial annointed she Me.

5 Where My gospel unfolds this on earth shall be told,
   For memorial of her what she done,
   Then did Judas Iscariot, with chief priests and Pharisees,
   Conspire to betray Christ the Son.

6 Saying, what will ye pay, if I Him will betray?
   " Thirty pieces of silver," they said,
   From that time Judas then sought to lead Him to them,
   'Twas first feast day of unleavened bread.

7 When at even as He with the twelve sat at meat,
   He said one of you shall Me betray.
   They in sorrow began asking Him, every man,
   " Is it I?" "is it I?" each did say.

8 Jesus said, " He that dips now with Me in the dish,
   That same one shall betray Me ere morn.
   " Woe to that man," he said, " by whom I am betrayed.
   It were better he had not been born."

9 Then He blest bread and break it, and to them he gave it,
   And said, " eat this, my body slain."
   Likewise took He the cup and gave thanks, and said, sup
   This, My blood, for to cleanse sinful stains.

10 Know ye this is that blood, of My Testament shed,
    Which God promised Adam of old,
    I will no more incline to drink fruit of the vine,
    'Till with you in the city of gold."

11 When an hymn they had sung, they went out every one,
    From fair Olives' green Mount with their Lord,
    Jesus said, '' Lo this night they your shepherd shall smite,
    And My sheep shall be scattered abroad."

12 Peter said, " I'll stand by, though all else should deny."
    Jesus said, " Peter, hear what I say,
    Ere the cock crow this night thou shalt disown Me thrice,"
    Peter cried, " I'll die for Thee to day.',

13 Jesus cometh again, with them to Gethsemane,
    Saying, '' sit here, while I go and pray."
    Peter with Zebedee's sons forth with Jesus did come.
    Then great sorrows on Him heavy lay.

14 Jesus cried, " I am pressed 'neath man's sins, down to death,
    O stay here and watch with Me, and pray."
    Then He went little farther, and prayed and said, " Father,
    If possible, pass this cup away."

15 Saying, " not as I will, Father, but as Thou wilt,."
   Then He went His disciples to see.
When He found them asleep over them He did weep,
   Saying, " why could ye not with Me,

16 Watch and pray and repent, lest temptation be sent,
   Soul is willing, but flesh it doth shrink."
He again went and prayed, " let this cup pass ?" He said,
   " If Thou wilt, but if not, I will drink."

17 When again they were sleeping, He left them with weeping,
   And third time prayed, " let this cup pass."
Then He cried, " now sleep on, for behold now the Son
   Is betrayed unto sinners at last."

18 As these words He thus spake, came a multitude great,
   Bearing sabres and staves from high priests.
He that had Him betrayed gave them this sign and said,
   " Whom I kiss that is He, hold Him fast."

19 Judas' band came forthwith, he hailed Jesus and kissed.
   " Jesus said, " friend, wherefore art thou come ?"
When they laid hands on Jesus, it insulted Peter,
   And He drew His sword and smote one.

20 Jesus cried, " put again in its place thy sword stained,
   They who take sword shall perish by sword.
Ye should know I could pray to My Father to-day,
   And His angels My person would guard.

21 But I came from on high. for to suffer and die,
   To atone for man's sins on the cross ;
And the scriptures to fill, as the prophets did tell,
   And to seek and save that which was lost."

22 Peter followed afar, to the council and bar,
   Where the high priests condemned Christ to die.
There they spit in His face, smiting Him in disgrace,
   Saying, " Prophecy, who smote the Christ."

23 Then a maid said to Peter, " sure thou wast with Jesus ?"
   He said, " I deny what thou saith."
Then another maid seeth him and said thou wast with Him.
   Then again he denied with an oath.

24 Others said it is true, thou didst once Christ pursue.
   Then began he to swear and to curse,
And the cock then did crow, making Peter to know
   What his Lord said to him at the first.

25 " Ere the cock crow this night, thou shalt disown Me thrice."
    Then he went out and bitterly wept.
    And he cried, " O Lord, God, strengthen me by Thy word,
    And may I by Thy spirit be kept."

CHAPTER XXVII.

1 Next morn scribes and elders and chief priests came thither,
    And counseled 'gainst Jesus to put Him to death :
    And when they had bound Him they led and delivered
    To Governor Pilate, where Jesus they left.

2 When Judas saw Jesus condemned he repented,
    And came to the elders in grief and great pain.
    He cried, I have sinned, and my joys are all ended,
    In that I the innocent Jesus have slain.

3 They said, " what is that to us, see thou unto it ;"
    He cast them the pieces of silver again,
    Then ran to destruction, because he did do it.
    The sting of great torments, his soul did inflame.

4 They said, " it will not do to keep it as treasure,
    For it is the price of the innocents' blood."
    Then held they long counsel, concluding 'twas better
    To use it to buy ground to bury strange dead.

5 " Art thou King of Jews ?" then said Pilate to Jesus.
    He answered and said, " as thou sayest I am."
    When He was accused of high priests most vehement,
    His answering nothing made Pilate think strange.

6 Then Pilate said, " which at this feast shall I give you,
    Barabbus, or Jesus, whom men call the Christ ?"
    For he knew for envy they had Him delivered.
    They said, " free Barabbas, but Christ crucify!"

7 When in judgment seat, Pilate's wife sent beseeching
    Him not to condemn Jesus Christ, that just man,
    Since she suffered much in the night of Him dreaming ;
    But elders and priests caused Him to be condemned.

8 Then when Pilate saw that his words prevailed nothing,
    He scourged Christ and gave Him to be crucified.
    His soldiers then took Him to most cruel mockings,
    And crowned Him with thorns, and with railings did chide.

9 With reed in His hand and a scarlet robe 'bout Him,
    They bowed the vile knee, crying, " Hail King of Jews !"
    They spit on Him, mocked Him, and with the reed smote Him,
    And with impious railings they did Him abuse.

10 They then led our Saviour forth to crucifiction,
    Likewise compelled Simon to bear Jesus' cross.
    They gave Him to drink gall and vinegar mingled,
    When crucified, they for His vesture cast lots.

11 They watched Him and wrote Him his strange accusation,
    Which was, " This is Jesus, the King of the Jews."
    They passed by Him railing with wagged heads menacing,
    Two thieves on His right hand and left suffered too.

12 They cried, " Thou that buildest in three days the temple,
    If Thou art the Christ now come down from the cross !"
    Chief priests, scribes and elders, all mocking Him, telling,
    " He saved others, yet Israel's king is here lost.

13 Let Him leave the cross now and we will believe Him,
    He trusted in God, let His God save Him now.
    If He is God's, let His Father relieve Him."
    The thieves cried, " Lord save, if a Saviour art Thou."

14 From sixth to ninth hour darkness veiled all that region,
    Then at the ninth hour Jesus loudly did cry,
    " Eli, Eli, lama sabachthani," meaning,
    " My God ! O, My God !" why now forsake Me to die ?"

15 Then some who stood there said. " He calls for Elias."
    A sponge filled with vinegar to drink they Him gave.
    Then Jesus' disciples cried, " lo, He is dying."
    Some said, " we will see if Elias will save."

16 Again He cried loud, " why hath God Me forgotten ?"
    And yielded the ghost as all nature did shake.
    The veil of the temple, from top to the bottom
    Was rent far asunder while earth it did quake.

17 Some graves then were opened and saints rose in glory,
    And some in Jerusalem then did appear.
    Then when the centurion and those that watched o'er Him
    Saw earth quake and darkness, they trembled with fear.

18 There came many women to Christ's crucifiction,
    From Galilee, ministering, anxious with care,
    And Magdalene Mary with Christ's mother weeping,
    And mother of Zebedee's children were there.

19   A rich man named Joseph, who was Christ's disciple,
       Obtained Jesus' body of Pilate that day,
     And wrapped it in linen, embalming with spices,
       And in His new tomb Jesus' body did lay.

20   The chief priests and pharisees to Pilate said, "truly,
       Christ said He would rise from the dead the third day,
     Command that His tomb now be guarded securely,
       Lest His own disciples should steal Him away.

21   And say then that Jesus from death is resurrected,
       And make the last error far worse than the first."
     He said, "go with men that Christ's tomb be protected,
       The tomb seal and set guards in whom ye can trust.

22   Then chief priests and pharisees brought forth armed soldiers
       And guarded the sepulcher, sealing the stone,
     To make sure that death there in triumph should hold Him,
       'Till after His third day had vanished and gone.

23   The guards wait in silence, His third day's approaching,
       The moon nightly gleams on their helmets and spear,
     An angel descends on the guard he approaches,
       And rolls that sealed stone from His tomb without fear.

24   His countenance as lightning, his raiment bright flaming,
       The guards fell in fright, then in fear ran away,
     And came in Jerusalem the great news proclaiming,
       The saints heard them telling it on that same day.

25   Christ's foes made best proofs of His grand resurrection,
       By guarding His tomb and by sealing the stone,
     Preventing His saints from all chance of deception,
       By watching three days with a guard of their own.

26   When those guards shewed high priests that Jesus had risen,
       Then they to the soldiers large money did pay,
     To say the saints stole Him from us for this reason,
       That we were all sleeping and did not awake.

CHAPTER XXVIII.

1   At end of the sabbath as day was a dawning,
      First day of the week, Christ's two Marys came mourning
    Unto Jesus' tomb as an earthquake was rending,
      They there saw an angel from heaven descending
          To salute the Lord who for sinners died.

2 He rolled back the stone from the tomb and sat on it,
   His countenance like lightning and snow white his raim't,
For fear of the angel the guards fell all trembling.
   The angel thus spake to the women, commending,
      " Fear not, since ye seek Jesus crucified."

3 Lo, He is not here, He hath risen in triumph,
   Come, see where the Lord lay, go tell His disciples
That He is now risen and gone on before you.
   In Galilee ye shall see Him as He told you,
      The Emanuel all victorious."

4 They ran from the tomb for to tell His disciples,
   When lo, Jesus met them and hailed most delightful.
They bowed at His feet and adored Him reclining.
   He said, " fear ye not, but in Galilee find Me.
      There ye shall Me see in great majesty.

5 While going to Galilee the watch they heard telling
   The chief priests of Christ's resurrection excelling.
Then gave they large money to bribe Pilate's soldiers
   To say while we slept Christ's disciples then stole Him.
      Then bribed witnesses, did themselves belie.

6 " If sleeping on guard should reach Pilate, we'll hide you,
   And also persuade him not to sacrifice you."
So they took the money and lied as directed,
   From whence unbelief hath their story respected,
      Sleeping witnesses thus did testify;

7 Then Jesus disciples sought Galilee's mountain
Where they did Him see as He them had appointed.
As they Him adored He said all power is given
To Me in the Earth likewise all power in Heaven.
      O ! His Majesty most magnificent.

8 Teach all men baptizing in name of the Father,
Son and Holy Ghost and in My harvest labor.
Teach them to obey all things I have commanded
And lo ! I am with you till this world is ended,
      Then My followers shall be glorified.

9 The ancient of days will in judgment be sitting,
Mid heavenly rays at this great worldly meeting.
The swell of His trump then shall gather all nations
And suns shall not shine with their bright consations,
      O, His majesty ever glorious.

JOHN.

1 In the beginning was the Word,
    The Word was with Almighty God,
    And the Word was God only true,
    And with God in beginning too.

2 All things were made at first by Him,
    Without Him was not made a thing.
    In Him was life which lighteneth men,
    Which darkness did not comprehend.

3 There was a man sent from the Lord,
    Whose name was John, to bear record
    That all men might believe aright,
    John witnessed, but was not that light.

4 Christ was the true light, which John taught,
    He made the world, it knew Him not,
    His own received Him not again,
    Those that received, God's sons became.

5 Which were born not of flesh nor blood,
    Nor of the will of man, but God,
    The Word in flesh did dwell with us,
    Begotten Son of God, in truth.

6 John witnessed, saying, " this is He,
    All glorious, coming after me.
    Who is preferred before my face,"
    His fullness we receive for grace.

7 By Moses God gave law devised,
    But Grace and truth by Jesus Christ.
    No man hath seen God any time,
    His Son hath Him to us defined.

8 John's record is, " I am not Christ,
    Nor yet that prophet nor Elias,
    But one who sounds the gospel word,
    To make the way straight of the Lord."

9 "If not Elias nor the Christ,"
They said, "why then dost thou baptize?"
John said, "with water I baptize,
But with you standeth One most wise.

10 Forth coming after me, Whose shoes
I am not worthy to unlose."
Next day as John saw Jesus come,
He saith, behold the Holy Lamb.

11 Though after me, He is before,
Well known to Israel of yore,
I now baptize to manifest
Him unto Israel the best.

12 I saw God's spirit like a dove
Descending on Him from above.
God said, "On Whom My Spirit flies
He doth with Holy Ghost baptize.

13 John said, "I saw and bear record
That this Man is the Son of God."
When Christ came where John's followers stood,
John said, "behold the Lamb of God,"

14 Then they did follow Jesus home,
As He did welcome all to come,
He told them wonders to record,
Of angels coming from the Lord,

15 Unto repentance I baptize,
That man might gain the paradise,
The land of rest beyond the grave,
Eternal o'er death's Jordan wave.

1 CORINTHIANS.

CHAPTER XIII.

1   "Though I proclaim with tongues of men,
    Or in angelic strains abound,
  And have not charity, I then
    Am as the brass or cymbal's sound.

2   Have I all knowledge, gifts and faith,
    And with them have not charity,
  I am undone without that grace,
    Nought but that Love can profit me.

3   Though I give all to feed the poor,
    And yield my body to be burned,
  And have not charity most pure,
    I am of God and angels spurned.

4   It envieth not, it suffereth long,
    Is kind, not puffed up in self-will,
  Nor acts unfit, nor seeks her own,
    Nor soon provoked, nor thinketh ill.

5   Nor vaunteth, nor delights in sin,
    But ever joyous in the truth,
  It bears all things, believes all things,
    Hopes all, nor fails, but, all endures.

6   Prophecies fail, and tongues shall cease,
    And knowledge vanish and decay,
  For we but know in part of these,
    Which perfect Love shall do away.

7   I when a child did speak as one,
    And understand, and act, and think,
  But when I had a man become
    I put away the childish things.

8   Though now through glass we darkly see,
    We then see face to face each one,
  For only now in part know we,
    Then shall I know as I am known.

9   Faith, hope and charity, blest three,
      Abideth now for man to gain.
    Most great of these is charity,
      The love that ever shall remain.

10   Above all, put on charity,
      Which is the bond of perfectness.
    It sets the soul forever free.
      It is the bliss of righteousness.

THE REVELATION

OF ST. JOHN THE DIVINE.

CHAPTER I.

1   This is the revelation God gave Christ at last,
    To shew to His servants what must come to pass,
    And He sent His angel with it unto John,
    Who wrote what he saw, and of God and His Son.

2   Blest is he that readeth, and they that do hear
    The words of this prophecy, and it revere,
    And keep things there written, for time is at hand,
    To Asia's seven churches, John writes by command.

3   To you grace and peace, from Him which was to come,
    Which was, is, and from seven spirits 'round His throne
    From Christ the true witness, first-born from the dead,
    And Prince of earth's kings, since for all men He bled.

4   And loved us and washed us from sins in His blood,
    Made us kings and priests to His Father and God.
    To Him be great glory, dominion and power,
    Who once died for sinners, Amen evermore.

5   He cometh with clouds, every eye shall Him see,
    They also which pierced Him shall wail and shall flee;
    Because of Him fearing, even so, Amen;
    I'm Alpha, Omega, beginning and end.

6 The Lord now, which is, and which was, and to come,
Almighty Redeemer, the crucified One.
I, John, who am brother, companion and one,
In kingdom and patience of Jesus, God's son.

7 Was in isle of Patmos, for words which God spake,
And for testimony of Jesus to make,
I was in the Spirit there on the Lord's day,
And heard a great voice, as a trumpet then say,

8 I'm Alpha, Omega, the first and the last,
What seest thou write in a book, and it pass
Unto seven churches in Asia, which are,
Ephesus, Smyrna, Pergamos, Thyatira,

9 Sardis, Philadelphia, Laodicea.
I turned to the voice, that thus to me did say,
When turned I saw seven gold candle-sticks there,
Amidst them saw one like the Son of Man fair.

10 Clothed down to the foot with a garment without,
Likewise a gold girdle his breast girt about ;
His head and His hairs were like wool white as snow,
His eyes as a fire-flame most brilliant did glow.

11 His feet like fine brass, burned as furnace, shown round,
His voice as the great many waters did sound ;
His right hand held seven stars, while from His mouth went
A sword, and His face shone as sunlight in strength.

12 I saw Him and fell at His feet as one dead ;
He then laid His right hand upon me and said,
" Fear not, I am first and the last—lived of yore,
I live, and was dead, but I live evermore.

13 Amen, I have keys both of hell and of death,
Write things thou has seen, and the things to come yet,
The mystery of seven stars seen in my right hand,
And seven gold candle-sticks brilliant and grand ;

14 The stars are God's angels of seven churches given,
The gold candle-sticks represent churches seven ;"
The church of the Lord is the best gold of earth,
Who follows God's spirit, in it hath great worth.

CHAPTER II.

1   " Now unto the angel of Ephesus write,"
Saith he with the stars 'mid gold candlesticks bright,
" I know thy works, patience and labor, and how
Thou canst not bear them which are evil, but thou

2   Hast tried them who come as apostles when not,
And hast proved them liars, and My goodness taught,
But yet I have somewhat against thee, because
Thou hast left thy first love, and not watched, but paused.

3   Remember from whence thou didst fall and repent,
And do the first works to which thou wast first sent,
Or I will come quickly and thy light remove,
Unless thou repent and attain thy first love.

4   'Tis good thou dost hate deeds of Nicolaitanes,
Which I also hate, since they much ill contain ;
God's spirit now saith to the churches and thee,
He that overcometh shall eat of life's tree,

5   Which stands in the blest paradise of the Lord,
Where all those who keep His commands shall see God.
To angel of church now in Smyrna this write,"
Saith he which was dead, and who is ever alive.

6   " I know thy works, poverty, (but thou art rich,)
And blasphemous Jews who revile thee, all which
Are of Satan's synagogue, and in his seat ;
Be faithful and thou shalt o'ercome their deceit.

7   Thy sufferings, fear not, although Satan shall cast
Some of you in prison, to tempt you to wrath ;
In earth's tribulations be faithful to death,
And I will give thee a bright crown with the blest.

8   Hear ye what the Spirit to churches now saith,
He that overcomes feeleth not second death.
To angel of church of Pergamos this write,"
Saith He who with sword of two edges doth fight.

9   I know thy works ; though thou art in Satan's seat,
Yet holdest My name, and My faith most discreet.
Thou My martyr Antipas near thee was slain,
Where Satan doth dwell, yet ye held fast My name.

10 But I have these few things 'gainst thee which are naught,
Thou hast them that hold Balam's doctrine, who taught
To cast stumbling blocks to put Israel to shame,
And approbate idols and deeds of ill fame.

11 And Nicolaitanes too, thou hast them about,
Repent, or I'll fight thee with sword of My mouth,
Hear ye what the spirit to churches doth say,
He that overcomes shall eat hidden manna,

12 I'll give him a stone, with new name, who believes,
Which no man can know saving he that receives.
To angel of church of Thyatira this write,"
Saith He Who hath eyes like a flame of fire bright,

13 " I know thy faith, charity, service and works,
Thy patience and last works to be more than first,
Yet I have a few things against thee withall,
That thou sufferest Jezebel to teach, who is called

14 A prophetess, who doth My servants incline,
To deeds of ill fame and idolatrous shrines;
And I gave her space, yet repented she not,
Now great tribulation on them shall be brought.

15 Except they repent, greatest plagues shall them kill,
The churches and all men shall know my just will;
That I try the reins and all hearts do I search,
And give to each of them according to works.

16 To others in Thyatira be it known,
Who hold not this doctrine nor Satan's way's own,
That I other burdens on you will put none,
But that which ye have, now hold fast till I come.

17 He who keeps My works to the end and o'ercomes,
I'll give power o'er nations as God gave His Son,
And He shall rule them as with iron rod,
With great power and mercy, as I rule from God.

18 Who followeth Me, hath the true light of life,
That leadeth to peace, far from sin and from strife.
The morning star I will give him on his way,
Hear ye what the Spirit to churches doth say.

CHAPTER III.

1 To angel of church in Sardis, write these things there,
Saith He who hath God's blest seven spirits and stars.
Thy works are, thy name doth live, while thou dead doth lie,
Be watchful and strengthen things now ready to die.

2 Before God I find thy works not perfect as yet,
Think what thou received, and heard, hold fast and repent,
If therefore, thou shalt not watch, I'll come unawares,
And find thee in sin and then no ransom can spare.

3 Thou hast a few names in Sardis yet undefiled,
They shall walk with Me in white, for they have no guile.
He that overcometh I will clothe him in white,
And not blot his name out of the Lamb's book of life.

4 To angel of church in Philadelphia write thus,
Saith he that hath David's key, both holy and just ;
I know thy works, and a door I open to thee,
And no man can shut it for thy strength is in Me.

5 Since thou kept My Word, and hast not disowned My name,
I'll cast out to Satan liars who hath thee blamed ;
Behold, I will make them come and bow at thy feet,
And know that I love thee, who kept My word discreet.

6 I also will keep thee from temptations to come,
To try all mankind that dwell on earth every one.
For lo, I come quick ; hold fast, let none take thy crown,
O'ercome, and a pillar in God's temple be found.

7 And I will write on thee then, the name of My God,
And name of the city of My God, His abode,
Which is New Jerusalem coming down out of heaven ;
He that hath an ear to hear, repent, be forgiven.

8 To angel of church of the Laodiceans write,
These things saith God's faithful and true witness most bright,
Who is the beginning of creation of God ;
I know thy works, that thou art not cold, neither hot.

9 Because thou art lukewarm, and thy first love kept not,
I'll spue thee out of My mouth, since not cold nor hot,
Because thou saith ' I am rich and nothing do need,'
When wretched and poor, and blind and naked, indeed.

10 I counsel thee buy of Me gold tried in the fire,
    And white raiment thee to clothe, lest shame should appear,
    And eye salve that thou might's see thy sins and relent,
    I chastise those whom I love, so haste and repent.

11 I stand at the door and knock, he that hears My voice
    And opens to Me, I'll come and make him rejoice.
    He that overcomes shall sit with Me in My throne,
    As I in My Father's throne with Him am sit down.

12 He who shall confess My name before men of earth,
    Him will I confess to God, 'mong angels of worth ;
    He that hath an ear to hear, let him not delay
    To hear what the spirit of the churches doth say."

CHAPTER IV.

1 I saw then a door in heaven was opened to me,
    One said, " come. I'll show thee what must hereafter be."
    I then in the Spirit saw one sit on a throne,
    That one looked like ja-per or a bright sardine stone.

2 A rainbow like emerald 'round that throne shone in sight,
    Where twenty-four elders sat on seats clothed in white.
    They wore crowns of gold and lightnings came from the throne
    And thunderings, while seven lamps of fire brightly shone.

3 Before it a sea of glass like crystal did shine ;
    'Round it were four beasts with eyes before and behind.
    The first like a lion, the next like a calf,
    The third as a man, and like an eagle the last.

4 These four had six wings and rest they not day and night,
    But cried Holy, Holy, Holy Lord God of might,
    Which was, is, and is to come, and when they thus cried,
    The twenty-four elders fell, adored and replied,

5 " O Lord, Thou art worthy to receive glorious praise,
    And honor and power, for Thou art righteous always,
    For 'tis for Thy pleasure that Thou hast all things made,
    And man Thee to glorify, that God be obeyed."

CHAPTER V.

1   In the right hand of one I saw sit on the throne,
      Was a book witten, sealed with seven seals.
    Then an angel exclaimed with loud voice to all men,
      " Who is worthy that book to reveal ?'

2   Not in heaven or in earth, was a man of such worth,
      As to open or read that sealed book,
    And I wept much that no one was found worthy to come
    And to read it, or on it to look.

3   One said, " weep not, behold Juda's lion most bold,
      Hath appeared for to open that book ;
    David's root hath prevailed to unloose all the seals
    And is worthy upon it to look."

4   I then saw in the midst of the throne and four beasts,
      'Mong the elders, a Lamb that was slain,
    Having seven horns and eyes, which are God's spirits wise,
    Sent to light men of earth in His name.

5   From the right hand of One, Who then sat on the throne,
      He did take the book closed with seven seals,
    And when He had so done, beasts and elders fell down,
    With their harps 'round the Lamb, Who revealed,

6   Pouring vials of gold, filled with prayers of saints old.
      They all worshipped the Lamb that was slain,
    And they sung this new song, through the heavenly throng,
     ' Worthy, worthy, the Lamb,' they exclaimed,

7   Who redeemed us to God by Thy most precious blood,
      From each nation, and people and tongue,
    Making us kings and priests to the blest God of peace,
    And we'll reign on the earth sung each one.

8   And the angels that sung had a number that comes
      To ten thousand times ten thousand tongues.
    With a loud voice they cried, " worthy Lamb Who hath died,
    To all power, glory, blessing to come.

9   Every creature in heaven, on earth and sea even.
      Heard I all these praises exclaim,
    Blessing, honor, power glory, with these we adore Thee,
    Who sits on the throne and the Lamb.

10 The four beasts said " Amen," and the elders all then,
      Did fall down and adore Him who lives
  Now, forever and ever, who brought us a Saviour,
      Who will praying sinners forgive.

CHAPTER VI.

1 When the Lamb ope'd first seal, then I heard thunder peals,
      And the four beasts bade me " come and see,"
  On a white horse sat one with a bow and crown,
      And forth conquering to conquer went he.

2 When He ope'd second seal, second beast cried, " come see ;"
      Then one rode on a red horse, with power,
  Taking peace from earth 'till they each other should kill,
      And they gave him a great sword that hour.

3 When He opened third seal, third beast said, " come and see."
      On a black horse, with scales, one then came,
  Crying, " measures of wheat each a penny shall be,
      And three measures of barley the same."

4 When He opened fourth seal,fourth beast said "come and see."
      Then a pale horse brought forth death and hell ;
  They had power on the earth for to slay in one-fourth,
      With its beasts, sword and hunger to kill.

5 Then the opening fifth seal, 'neath the altar revealed
      Souls of those slain for witness they held,
  And they cried," how long, Lord,wilt avenge Thou our blood,
      On those sinners that on the earth dwell ?"

6 Pure white robes then were given, to each one from heaven,
      And told that they joyful should rest
  Onward yet for a season, 'till their brethren even,
      Be killed and took home with the blest.

7 When the sixth seal did break, then the earth it did quake,
      With its sun black as sack-cloth of hair,
  And the stars fell from heaven, as fig trees doth even
      Cast figs when the winds mighty are.

8 Then the heavens as a scroll, all together did roll,
      And each island and mountain moved then;   [bondmen
  Captains, kings, great men, strong men, rich freemen and
      Did hide in the mountains and dens.

9 Crying,"O, rocks and mountains, hide us 'neath your foundings,
    From God, and the wrath of the Lamb,
  For the great day is come, of their wrath 'neath the sun,
    Who of us shall be able to stand?"

CHAPTER VII.

1 Then four angels stood forth on four corners of earth,
    Holding four winds that they should be still,
  And blow not on the sea, nor on earth nor on tree,
    When an angel came forth with God's seal.

2 With loud voice cried he out, to the angels about,
    " Hurt not earth, nor the trees, nor the sea,
  'Till God's servants me seal, as the Lord hath revealed,
    To that sealing appointed He me."

3 And them which He sealed unto me was revealed
    Hundred forty-four thousand, of all,
  Of true Israel's blest tribes, who become the Lamb's bride,
    And who on the Lord God meekly call.

4 Juda, Reuben, Gad, Aser, Nephthalim, Manasses,
    Simeon, each twelve thousand revealed,
  Levi, Issachar, Zebulon, Joseph and Benjamin,
    Twelve thousand each tribe has sealed.

5 Then I saw with great wonder, a host none could number,
    Of people, and tongues of all lands
  Stood before God's great throne, and the Lamb, every one
    Clothed with white robes, and palms in their hands.

6 And they cried with voice loud, great salvation to God,
    Him who sits on the throne, and the Lamb;
  And the angels devout, beasts and elders, did shout
    Falling down worshiped God, Great I Am.

7 Saying, "Amen! blessing, wisdom, power, honor, thanksgiving,
    And glory and might be to God."
  Then forever and ever, they shouted together,
    Amen! hallelujah, aloud.

8 Then one saith unto me, " who are these that ye see
    In white robes, whence came they, tell I pray?"
  Thou dost know sir, said I, then he made this reply,
    " Out of great tribulation came they."

9 And their robes washed in blood of the blest Lamb of God,
    Now the song of redemption they swell,
  Serving Him with delight, in His house day and night,
    He who sits on the throne 'mong them dwells.

10 They shall hunger no more, neither thirst as of yore.
    Nor the sun shine on them with its heat
  For the blest Lamb shall feed, and most tenderly lead
    Them to fountains of water most sweet.

11 God shall wipe off all tears from their eyes shall cheer,
    Sorrow, crying, shall be done away,
  They shall feast in His love, in bright mansions above,
    Where the light of the Lord makes the day."

CHAPTER VIII.

1 When seventh seal opened, then silence in heaven
    Prevailed a half hour, when I saw
  Seven angels then stood before God and were given
    Seven trumpets for sounding afar.

2 An angel with censer of gold there did wait
    With incense, for man to atone,
  And offer it up with the prayers of all saints,
    On altars of gold at God's throne.

3 The smoke of the incense, with prayers of the saints,
    Came up from the angel's blest hand,
  To God, to atone for man's sins and complaints,
    Imploring God's grace through the Lamb.

4 Then he filled the censer with God's altar fire,
    And cast holy flame to the earth,
  Then voices and thunderings and all things inspired
    Mankind to seek heavenly worth.

5 First trump of seven angels, with seven trumps did sound,
    Then came hail and fire mixed with blood.
  The grass and the third part of earth's trees were burned,
    Great judgments for sin, sent of God.

6 At next angel's sound a great mountain on fire,
    Was cast in the sea, which turned blood.
  The third of all creatures within it then died ;
    The third part of ships were destroyed.

7   At third angel's sound fell a great burning star,
      On third part of waters 'neath heaven,
    And made them so bitter that men died afar;
      Name "worm-wood" to that star was given.

8   The fourth angel's sound smote third part of the sun,
      The moon and third part of the stars,
    So, likewise the day, one-third darker become,
      The night too, was darker by far.

9   I saw a strong angel fly through midst of heaven,
      With loud voice he cried, woe, woe, woe
    To men on the earth, for the cause of sin, given,
      By three angels' trumps yet to blow.

CHAPTER IX.

1   When fifth angel sounded, from heaven fell a star
      With key of the bottomless pit,
    When opened, a great furnace smoke rolled so far
      That sunlight was darkened by it.

2   Then out of that smoke, locusts came on the earth,
      And had power as scorpions to sting,
    And they were commanded the grass not to hurt,
      Of earth, neither any green thing;

3   But only the men who have not the Lord's seal,
      Them they should torment for five months;
    But it was not given that they should them kill,
      But strike them as scorpions torment.

4   Then men shall seek death when it is yet afar,
      And grieve when it fleeth from them.
    The locusts had shapes like to horses of war,
      With gold crowns and faces like men,

5   They had hair as women, like lions had teeth,
      And breast-plates of iron each one;
    Their wings made a sound like the chariots and feet,
      When war horses battle-ward run.

6   Their tails stung like scorpions, and hurt men five months;
      Their king is Apollyon in Greek,
    His name is Abaddon in the Hebrew tongue;
      From this yet two more shall speak.

7 At sixth angel's sound, one before God did say,
      " Loose angels in Euphrates bound,"
    When loosed, were prepared for an hour, month, year, day,
      To slay the third part of men 'round.

8 The number of th' army of horsemen I rate
      Two hundred thousand thousand known.*
    In vision I saw horses, men and breast plates
      Of Jacinth, and fire, and brimstone.

9 Their horses' heads looked like the lions without,
      Their mouths belching fire and brimstone ;
    By these were the third of mankind killed about,
      By fire from their mouths every one.

10 Their power in their mouths, and their tails was like snakes,
      That have heads with which they do hurt ;
    The rest of the men then not killed by these plagues,
      Repented not of evil works ;

11 Of worship of devils, and idols of stone,
      Of silver, of brass and of gold,
    They neither reported ill deeds they had done,
      Their murders and sorceries of old.

12 The ills and the plagues so afflicting mankind,
      God sendeth to make men repent,
    And seek the loved Spirit of Christ so divine,
      That Lamb whom the Father hath sent.

CHAPTER X.

1 An angel from heaven came clothed with a cloud,
      On whose head a rain-bow shone brilliant and proud,
    His face as the sun light, and also his feet,
      As pillars of fire, shone with radiance complete.

2 A little book open, he held in his hand,
      With one foot on sea, and the other on land ;
    He cried with loud voice, as when lions do roar,
      Then out seven thunders their voices did pour.

3 And I went to write, when a voice said to me,
      " Seal up and write not what the thunders told thee."
    The angel I saw on the sea and on land,
      Did swear by that God Who made all things at hand.

4 That there should be time yet no longer here found;
God's mystery shall finish when seventh angel sounds.
Then that voice I heard first from heaven, did command
Me take of the angel the book from his hand.

5 I said to the angel, give me the small book?
He said unto me, "take it, and eat it up.
In thy belly, then, it shall bitterness be,
But in thy mouth, sweet as honey to thee."

6 I then took the book from his hand and did eat,
And it in my mouth was as honey most sweet,
'Twas bitterness then in my belly when ate;
He said thou "on more kings and people must wait.

7 He who hath God's word, and shall shut it within,
That word shall be bitterness in him as sin;
He who hath God's word and doth speak it without,
It shall be as honey, most sweet in his mouth."

CHAPTER XI.

1 One gave me a reed that was like to a rod,
The angel said, "measure the temple of God,
The altar, and them that do worship in heaven,
The court there without, measure not, for 'tis given

2 To Gentiles, and they shall tread forty-two months
On God's holy city, where goodness reigned once;
And I will give power to my two witnesses,
A thousand and two hundred and three score days.

3 In which they shall prophecy, clothed in sack-cloth,
As two olive trees before God of the earth.
If any will hurt them, fire doth them devour,
Their power can shut heaven to give rain no more.

4 They have power o'er waters to turn them to blood,
And smite earth with all plagues as oft as they would.
When their testimony is finished 'mong men,
The beast of the bottomless pit shall kill them.

5 Within the great city, their bodies shall lie,
Called spiritual Sodom, where Jesus did die;
The people, and kindreds, and nations shall laugh
To see their dead bodies three days and a half;

6 Not suffering them to be put in their graves,
   Since they oft admonished them of wicked ways,
   Then after three days and a half, life from God
   Did enter in them, and they on their feet stood.

7 Then great fear fell on them which saw them arise,
   As they heard a great voice call them from the skies,
   " Come hither," as they rose to heaven in a cloud
   Their foes saw, while thundered a great earthquake loud.

8 A tenth of that city was hurled 'neath the sod,
   Which slew seven thousand, the rest worshipped God.
   The third woe comes quickly, the second is past,
   The seventh angel sounded his high trumpet blast.

9 Great voices in heaven then loud did proclaim,
   The kingdoms of earth have Christ's kingdoms became,
   And He shall hence reign, who for man spilt His blood,
   Then twenty-four elders fell down before God.

10 And said, " we give thanks to Thee, Lord God of might,
   Which art, was and shall be, Thou true God of right,
   Because Thou hast taken Thy great power and reigned,
   Rewarding Thy servants, and prophets and saints.

11 The nations were angry, and Thy wrath is come,
   And time of the dead, that they be judged each one,
   And shouldst destroy them, which destroy'd good in earth,
   Who hate Thy salvation, and scorn heavenly worth."

12 The temple of God then was opened in heaven,
   The ark was then seen, of His testament given,
   And lightnings, and voices, and thunderings, and hail,
   As God in His goodness and strength did prevail.

CHAPTER XII.

1 And then a great wonder in heaven appeared,
   A woman all clothed with the sun, so revered,
   That under her feet the full moon shone afar,
   While bright on her head, blazed a crown of twelve stars.

2 She with embryo offspring cried traveling in birth,
   And pained to deliver a son of great worth,
   Who was to rule nations with an iron rod,
   The Saviour of promise, begotten of God.

3   Another great wonder in heaven appeared,
    A great dragon, red, with ten horns and seven heads,
    His tail drew and cast third of heaven's stars to earth,
    And he stood to kill that blest child at his birth.

4   She brought forth a man-child, who was to atone
    For man, and was caught up to God and His throne,
    In wilds God made place for the woman to flee,
    A thousand two hundred three score days to feed.

5   Great war raged in heaven, the dragon then fought
    Against Michael's angels, but did prevail not.
    But he was cast out, that old serpent, and hurled,
    Called Devil and Satan, that curseth the world.

6   A loud voice then heard I, through all heaven proclaim,
    Now is man's salvation and strength in Christ's name.
    The reign of our God and the power of His Son,
    For Satan, accuser of saints, is cast down.

7   They overcame him through the blood of the Lamb,
    By their word of testimony they did stand,
    They loved not their lives to the death though they fell,
    Rejoice heaven and earth, and ye in them who dwell.

8   But woe to the earth for the devil is come down
    With great wrath, since he by a short time was bound.
    The dragon, when he was cast out to the earth,
    Did persecute her who to Jesus gave birth.

9   With eagles' wings fled she in wilds to her place,
    For time, times and half, from the vile serpent's face.
    The serpent cast floods from his mouth her to stop,
    The earth helped the woman and swallowed them up.

10 The dragon was wroth with the woman indeed,
    And waged endless war 'gainst her remnant of seed
    Which keep God's commandments as he hath devised
    And bear testimony of His Jesus Christ.

CHAPTER XIII.

1   A beast from the sea came with seven heads and ten horns,
    With blasphemy on his head, his horns had ten crowns,
    A leopard, yet having lion's mouth and bear's feet
    The dragon gave him his power, authority and seat.

2 On one of his heads I saw a healed deathly wound,
And all men did wonder after him all around,
And worshipped the dragon which gave to him this power,
And cried, " who is like the beast, who with him can war ?"

3 A mouth had he, speaking blasphemies and great things,
And forty-two months this power was given to him.
He opened his mouth in blasphemy against God,
And blasphemed His name, and them in heaven His abode.

4 It was given him to war with saints and o'ercome,
To him power was given o'er all nations and tongues,
And all men shall worship him, if so that their names
Are not in the blest Lamb's Book of Life that was slain.

5 Hear ye, he that leadeth captive, captive shall go,
Who kills with the sword, he must be killed by its blow ;
Now here is the patience and the faith of the saints,
A beast with lamb's horns came as a dragon and spoke.

6 He exercised powers of the first beast before him,
He causeth all people which are dwelling in sin
To worship the first beast whose death wound had been healed,
He doeth great wonders ; fire from heaven he reveals ;

7 Deceives them who dwell on earth, by power first beast gives,
Bade them imitate the beast with death wound that lives.
He had power to give life to the beast's image then,
That it should both speak and cause as many of men,

8 As would not the image worship, they killed should be,
And caused bond and free, and small and great to receive
A mark in their right hands, or their forheads the same,
That none trade without his mark or number of name.

9 Let wisdom, the number of the beast, count and fix,
And understanding record it, three hundred, three score, six.
Lo! here now is wisdom, O ye wise, understand,
Who takes Satan's mark, can never reach heaven's land.

CHAPTER XIV.

1 I then saw a Lamb on mount Sion did stand,
With Him hundred forty-four thousand at hand.
With His Father's name in their foreheads, wrote there.
Then heard I a loud voice from heaven thus declare.

2 A sound of vast floods; as great thunders impart,
 And great voice of harpers all harping with harps.
 They sung with great joy a new song 'round the throne,
 'Mid elders and seraphs; that song none could learn,

3 But that hundred forty-four thousand, redeemed
 From earth, which were not sin defiled but was clean.
 These are they which follow the Lamb where He goes,
 These blest were redeemed from among men below.

4 They, being the first fruits to God and the Lamb,
 Their mouth spake no guile, without fault they did stand.
 Then saw I an angel fly through midst of heaven,
 With gospel, to preach on the earth, to him given.

5 To all nations, kindreds, and people and tongues,
 With loud voice he cried, " now fear God, every one,
 And give to him glory and honor most free,
 Who made heaven and earth, waters, fountains and seas·"

6 An angel cried, " Babylon is fallen, and still,
 Since nations drank wine of the wrath of her ill."
 A third angel cried with a loud voice and said,
 " If any man worship the beast's image made,

7 Or shall have his mark in his forehead or hand,
 Shall drink of the wine of God's wrath, every man,
 Without mixture, from indignation's dread cup,
 Who hath Satan's mark, must its bitterness sup.

8 He shall be tormented with fire and brimstone,
 Before holy angels, and God's belov'd Son.
 The smoke of their torment forever remains,
 Who worship the beast, or receiveth his name.

9 Here now is the patience of saints, here are they
 Who keep God's commands, and his faith, day by day.
 A voice said from heaven, " write, blest are the dead
 Which die in the Lord, yea from henceforth, God said,

10 " They rest from their toils, and their work follow on ;"
 Then on a white cloud I saw one like God's Son,
 I saw on his head a bright golden crown stand,
 A flaming sharp sickle he waved in his hand.

11 An angel's voice then from the temple cried loud,
 To him with the sickle, who sat on the cloud,
 Thrust in now thy sickle, and reap, time is come
 To reap, for earth's harvest is ripe, cried that one.

12 Then he on the cloud, with his sickle reaped earth,
    Then one with sharp sickle came from heaven, as first,
    One came from the altar, who o'er fire presides,
    To him with the sickle then loudly he cried.

13 " Thrust in thy sharp sickle, reap clusters of vines
    Of earth, for her grapes to their ripening incline.
    The angel then thrust in his sickle to earth
    And gathered the vine of the earth to be cursed.

14 And cast in the wine-press of wrath of our God,
    Which in depth of blood by the war-horse was trod,
    In emblem bespeaking the great judgment day,
    When all the ungodly shall desolate lay.

CHAPTER XV.

1 I saw another sign in heaven,
       Both great, and marvelous, and odd,
   Seven angels with the last plagues seven,
       Which filleth up the wrath of God.

2 I saw a sea of glass with fire,
       And them who vict'ry had obtained
   Against the beast and image dire,
       O'er mark and number of his name.

3 Upon that sea of glass they stood,
       With help of God they sing the song
   Of Moses, servant of our God,
       And song of the redeeming Lamb.

4 Most great and marvelous are Thy ways,
       Lord God Almighty, just and true,
   And all Thy works, Thou King of Saints,
       Who shall not fear Thee, O Lord, too?

5 And glorify Thy name, for Thou
       Art only holy Lord most high,
   All nations shall before Thee bow,
       Thy judgments are made known, and nigh.

6 Angels, with seven last plagues, were seen,
       All clothed in linen pure and white,
   Their breasts with golden girdles gleamed,
       From open temple, fair and bright.

7   Then seven golden vials full
      Of wrath, one gave those angels seven,
    The temple then with smoke did fill
      From glory of the God of heaven.

8   The temple no man could approach
      'Till those seven plagues were all fulfilled,
    And those seven vials outward poured
      On earth for the reward of ill.

CHAPTER XVI.

1   A voice from the temple bade angels pour forth
    Seven vials of wrath of our God on the earth.
    At first vial, fell there a most grievous sore
    On those who the beast or his image adore.

2   Next vial, the sea was as blood of dead men,
    All living souls died, that had life in it then.
    At third vial, fountains of waters were blood;
    "O Lord, Thou art righteous," their angel then said,

3   "Which art, wast and shall be since Thou hast thus judged
    Of thy saints and prophets, they have shed much blood.
    So now Thou hast given Thine blood for to drink,
    Because they are worthy thy angels do think.

4   And then from the altar an angel said thus,
    "God's judgments are all true and righteous and just;"
    When fourth vial poured out, the sun did scorch men,
    Who blasphemed the God who brought these plagues on them.

5   Nor did they repent to give glory to Him,
    Nor cease from their blasphemous sorceries and sins.
    The fifth vial poured on the seat of the beast,
    His kingdom was darkness, great pain, and no ease.

6   They then blasphemed God yet, because of their pain,
    But did not repent their vile deeds to their shame;
    On Euphrates' river the sixth angel poured,
    And dried up; that ways of east kings be prepared.

7   Then three unclean spirits like frogs came from out
    The dragon, the beast, and the false prophet's mouth,
    These are devil's spirits, to kings going forth
    By working their miracles through the whole earth.

8 To bring them to battle, God's great day to come,
   They gathered them all unto Armageddon.
   Behold, as a thief come I, blest he shall be,
   That watcheth and keepeth his garments, lest he

9 Be naked and fearful in that dreadful day,
   When cometh God's judgments without a delay.
   When seventh angel's vial did pour, there did come
   From out heaven's temple this great voice, "'tis done."

10 Then voices, and thunderings, lightnings and earthquakes,
   As men hath not seen on the earth, yet so great,
   The great city rent in three parts, others fell ;
   Great Babylon came in God's remembrance as well ;

11 To give unto her of the cup of the wine
   Of fierceness of wrath, as he now was inclined.
   Great hail fell from heaven, of a talent's weight, 'round,
   Then isles fled away, mountains too were not found.

12 Then men blasphemed God yet, because of ill fate.
   For both plague and hails were exceedingly great.
   In wisdom hath God plagues of punishment sent,
   That man should be mindful to Him and repent.

13 Conforming their minds to the mind of His Son,
   As He purposed first, when creation begun,
   All who have Christ's image, God turns not away;
   By Christ he shall judge all men at the last day.

CHAPTER XVII.

1 An angel said, "Come here and I will shew thee
   The judgment of Babylon, that sits on the sea,
   With whom kings of earth have done infamy, till
   All nations were drunk with the wine of her ill.

2 So carried he me to the wilds, where there came
   A woman who sat on a beast, full of names
   Of blasphemy, having seven heads and ten horns,
   The finest gay colors her person adorned.

3 With a golden cross in her hand, which within,
   Had abominations, and filth of her sin,
   She rode, decked with gold, precious stones and with pearls,
   In high scarlet colors, with purple unfurled.

4 The name on her was, Mystery, Babylon the great,
 The mother of infamous ones of great hate;
 When I saw her drunk with the blood of the saints,
 And blood of the martyrs of Christ, I did faint.

5 The angel then said, " Why dost thou marvel so ?
 I'll tell thee of her, and the beast she rides too,
 This beast was and is not, and shall rise also
 From bottomless pit, to perdition to go.

6 They that dwell on earth, shall wonder, whose names
 Were not in the blest book of life, of the Lamb,
 When they see the beast that was not, and yet is.
 Now here is the mind that has wisdom that sees

7 Those seven heads are mounts, which the woman sits on,
 There are seven, five have fallen, now is one,
 The other is not come, but when he appears,
 He shall but continue a short space of years.

8 The beast that was and is not is eighth, also,
 And is of the seven, to perdition he goes,
 The ten horns are kings, with no kingdoms as yet,
 But their power as kings, with the beast they do get.

9 Those all have one mind, giving strength to the beast,
 All these shall make war with the saints and break peace,
 But he shall o'ercome them who is Lord of lords,
 And is King of kings, and those with him are called,

10 And chosen and faithful, who love not their lives,
 But unto their death for his righteousness strive,
 He saith that the waters the woman sits on,
 Are multitudes, peoples, and nations, and tongues.

11 The ten horns thou sawest on the beast, these shall hate
 The woman, and burn her, and make desolate,
 For God hath it put in their hearts to fulfill,
 And unto the beast give their kingdom, until

12 God's words be fulfilled, and the righteous sustained,
 And Babylon's wickedness cease to remain ;
 The woman thou sawest was that great city, when
 She reigned over kings of the earth, and cursed men.

CHAPTER XVIII.

1 Then saw I an angel come down with great power,
 And all earth was light with his glory that hour,
 He cried with a mighty strong cry unto all,
 Great Babylon is fallen, hath fell its last fall.

2 And is become devils' abode, he averred,
 And home of foul spirits, and cage of vile birds,
 All nations drank wine off the wealth of her ill,
 While kings of the earth joined her infamy still.

3 And merchants waxed rich through her delicate goods ;
 A voice cried, " Come from her, ye people of God,
 For her sins have reached unto heaven most high,
 And God hath remembered her iniquity.

4 Reward her now, even as she dealt with you,
 And give to her double, for that is her due ;
 In cup she filled to you, give double indeed,
 Since she herself glorified out of your need.

5 As she lived deliciously, so much torment
 And sorrow give her, since she would not repent.
 She saith in her heart, " I am queen over thee,
 And I am no widow, no sorrow I'll see.

6 Therefore shall her plagues come in one day, and death,
 And mourning and famine and she be bereft,
 And utterly burned up with fire, for the Lord
 Is strong who doth judge her, and give her reward.

7 Earth's kings, who deliciously once lived with her,
 Shall wail and lament when they shall see her burn.
 For fear of her torment they stand afar off,
 And cry, " Oh ! alas ! mighty Babylon is lost !"

8 Behold in one hour is thy judgment now come,
 All merchants of earth shall weep o'er her and mourn,
 None buyeth their merchandise now any more.
 Of gold, precious stones, silver, pearls, linen stores,

9 Of purple, silk, scarlet, and all Thyine wood,
 All vessels of ivory, most precious and good,
 Of brass, and of iron, and marble immense,
 And cinnamon, odors, ointments, frankincense,

10 Wine, oil and fine flour, wheat and beasts, horses, sheep,
  And chariots, and slaves, souls of men that they keep,
  And all fruits thy soul lusted after are gone,
  All things which were dainty, and goodly, have flown.

11 And thou shalt find them no more hence since her fall,
  For merchants made rich by her shall stand far off,
  For fear of her torment they weeping shall wail,
  And cry, O, alas! that great city hath failed;

12 Whose costliness made all men rich on the sea,
  In one hour, her great desolation we see.
  Ye holy apostles and prophets, rejoice,
  For God hath avenged you on her in His choice."

13 An angel of might took a millstone in hand,
  And hurled in the sea, all majestic and grand,
  And cried "thus shall Babylon for sin be thrown down,
  And no more at all shall it ever be found.

14 The musician, harpers and trumpeter's sound,
  And piper, shall be heard in thee no more round;
  No craftsman, of whatever craft he may be
  Shall ever be found any more hence in thee.

15 No millstone shall sound, nor a candle light thee,
  From voice of the bridegroom and bride thou art free,
  For thy merchants were the great men of the earth;
  Thy sorceries all nations deceived, and have cursed.

16 In her was found blood of the prophets and saints,
  And martyrs of Jesus, and all good men slain;
  So God upon her hath avenged prophets' blood,
  And blood of the saints who for Jesus hath stood.

CHAPTER XIX.

1 I heard a great voice of much people in heaven,
  Who said, " Alleluia, salvation be given,
  And glory, and honor, and power, to our God,
  For righteous and true are His judgments, who judged

2 Great Babylon, which did corrupt earth with her ill,
  God hath avenged her of His prophets she killed."
  The twenty-four elders and four beasts praised God,
  And cried, " Alleluia, Amen, bless the Lord."

3 A voice from the throne cried, " praise Him all ye saints,
And all ye that fear Him, both small and the great."
I heard the great voice of a multitude sound
As of many waters and loud thunders 'round.

4 Which said, " the Lord, God, the Omnipotent, reigns;
Be glad and rejoice, honor give to His name;
Because the Lamb's marriage is come, and His wife
Hath made herself ready in garments of white;

5 Arrayed in fine linen, both pure, white and clean;
(White linen doth righteousness of His saints mean,)
He saith to me, " write ever blessed are they
Who are called to Christ's marriage supper that day."

6 He saith to Me, " these are true sayings of God,"
When I at his feet fell to worship, He said,
" See thou do it not, for Thy servant I am,
Of thy brethren, worship thou God, and not man."

7 At opening of heaven I a white horse did view,
And one sitting on him, called Faithful and True,
His eyes flamed as fire, from his head crowns forth shone,
A name had he written, to none but him known;

8 There clothed him a vesture dipped in his own blood,
The name on Him written is " The Word of God."
Heaven's armies Him followed, in white linen clean,
On white horses, him with His vesture blood stained;

9 And out of his mouth went a sharp two-edged sword,
To smite nations ruling with an iron rod,
He treadeth the wine-press of fierceness and wrath
Of Almighty God, for the sins of the past.

10 A name on his vesture, and thigh did record,
" I am King of Kings, and I am Lord of Lords."
I then saw an angel who stood in the sun,
He cried with loud voice to the fowls every one,

11 " Come gather yourselves to the supper of God,
To eat king's and captain's flesh, drinking their blood,
Then saw I the beast, with earth's kings, from afar
Were gathering their armies together, to war

12 'Gainst him on the horse and his army in white,
Which then took the beast and false prophet in fight;
He that deceived them that took mark of the beast,
And them that had worshiped his image, both these

13 Were both cast alive in the fiery lake's flame,
  Which burneth with brimstone, the remnant were slain
  With sword of his mouth, who sat on the white horse,
  And all fowls of heaven then were filled with their flesh.

CHAPTER XX.

1 An angel I saw come from heaven again,
  With key of the bottomless pit, and great chain,
  And seizing the dragon, that serpent called devil,
  And bound him a thousand years from doing evil,

2 And did cast him into the bottomless pit,
  And seal him, that he deceive nations not yet,
  'Till thousand years should be fulfilled when he must
  Be loosed for a season, the nations to curse.

3 On thrones saw I them, to whom judgment was given,
  And souls once beheaded for Christ's witness, even,
  Who worshiped not beast, nor his image, nor had
  His mark in their hands, nor on their foreheads.

4 And they lived with Christ, and a thousand years reigned,
  The rest of the dead lived not that time again,
  'Till the thousand years of the saints' reign were past,
  This is first resurrection, great woe hath the last.

5 Who hath part in the first resurrection, are blest,
  And holy, and shall not die the second death,
  But they shall be priests both of God and Christ, when
  They shall reign with Him, a full thousand years, then.

6 When the thousand years are expired, Satan then
  Shall go from his prison forth to receive men,
  And gather to war, Gog and Magog, shall he,
  The number of whom is as sound of the sea.

7 They went on the breadth of the earth and compassed
  The camp of the saints, and loved city all fast;
  Then fire, cast from God out of heaven, them devoured,
  The devil, that deceived them, was therefore cast out

8 In the lake of fire and brimstone, where the beast
  And false prophet shall have torment without cease.
  A great white throne saw I, and one sat thereon,
  From whom earth and heaven fled away and were gone.

9 The dead I saw stand, small and great, before God,
   And judged out of books, by their works and His word.
   The sea gave the dead which were in it and death
   And hell gave up dead which in them had been left.

10 And they judged each man there according to works,
   And cast death and hell in the lake of fire first,
   Which is second death, and he who had not there
   His name, in life's book, he was cast in that fire.

CHAPTER XXI.

1 I saw a new heaven and new earth, for first heaven
      And first earth were past, and there was no more sea.
   I saw New Jerusalem come down from God even,
      Prepared as a bride for her husband should be.

2 I heard a great voice out of heaven thus speaking
      The true God now tabernacles here with men,
   And will dwell with them, and they shall be his people,
      And he be their God evermore without end.

3 And God shall wipe off all the tears of their weeping,
      There shall be no death, sorrow, crying nor pain ;
   Their former afflictions shall never more reach them.
      God said, " Behold, I make all things new again."

4 He said unto me, " write these true words I mention,
      Most faithful, for lo, it is done ; for I am
   Alpha and Omega, beginning and ending.
      I'll give him who thirsts, of life's founts from my hand.

5 He that overcometh shall all things inherit,
      I will be his God, and he shall be My son ;
   But liars and murderers, and men of demerit,
      Shall be cast in fire when the second death comes."

6 One of the seven angels of plagues said, " come hither.
      And I will shew the pure bride, the Lamb's wife."
   He carried me up a high mountain in spirit,
      And shewed me the holy Jerusalem, in light

7 Descending from heaven with God's glory filling.
      Her light was like unto a most precious stone,
   Like unto a jasper stone, clear as the crystal,
      With walls great and high, where twelve pearly gates shone.

8 Those gates had twelve angels, likewise had names written,
   Which were names of twelve of good Israel's sons.
   On east, west, north, south, each, these pearl gates had glitt'ring,
   Each gate of one pearl, ever brilliantly shone.

9 The walls of that city had twelve bright foundations,
   With names of apostles that followed the Lamb;
   An angel a golden reed had, for to measure
   The city and gates, with its bright walls so grand.

10 Four square lay the city, its length and breadth even,
   He measured the city twelve thousand furlongs;
   The length, and the breadth, and the height measured equal,
   Hundred forty-four cubits height of its wall.

11 Its wall was of jasper, as pure gold that city,
   As crystaline glass fitly mingled with fire.
   Its wall with all precious stones garnished most fitly,
   First foundation jasper, the second sapphire;

12 The third chalcedony, the fourth was an emerald,
   The fifth was sardonyx, the sixth sardius,
   The seventh was chrysolite, and the eighth beryl,
   The ninth a topaz, tenth a chrysophasus,

13 Eleventh a jacinth, the twelfth was an amethyst,
   Twelve gates were twelve pearls, and each gate of one pearl,
   The city's street pure gold. as transparent glass is,
   The glory of God and the Lamb lights that world.

14 And I saw no temple therein, for the Lord God
   Almighty, and Lamb, are its temple above.
   The city had no need of moon, or the sun-light,
   For God lighteth it with His glory and love.

15 The nations of them which are saved shall walk in it,
   And kings bring in glory and honor, likewise.
   Its gates shall not be shut by day, for a minute,
   No night shall be there, neither darkness surprise.

16 There shall in no wise enter anything in it
   That worketh defilement, or maketh a lie,
   But they who have names in the book of life written,
   And havelaid up treasure with God in the sky.

CHAPTER XXII.

1   An angel shewed me a pure river of water
    Of life, clear as crystal, from God and the Lamb,
  Where fair trees of life, on its banks, ever cluster
    With twelve kinds of fruit, and leaves healing for man.

2   There shall be no more curse, as hath been aforesaid,
    But God and the Lamb shall be there for to bless;
  They shall see His face, with His name in their foreheads;
    His servants shall serve Him and enter His rest;

3   There shall be no night there, and they need no candle,
    Nor light of the sun, for their God gives them light;
  They shall reign forever with Him, free from scandal,
    " These sayings," he said, " are true, faithful and right."

4   The Lord God of prophets, sent his angel shewing
    His servants the things which must shortly be done,
  " Behold I come quickly, blest is he found doing
    The words of this prophecy, until I come."

5   When I John saw these things, and heard them, I fell down
    To worship the angel, he said, " do it not,
  I am of thy brethren the prophets, thy fellow
    Which keepth these sayings, so worship thou God."

6   He saith unto me, "seal ye not these last sayings
    Of this prophecy, for the time is at hand,
  He that is unjust, let him be so remaining,
    And him that is filthy, let him filthy stand.

7   And he that is righteous, let him be still righteous,
    And he that is holy, be holy hence still,
  Behold I come quickly to each man dividing
    Reward, as his work shall be which is God's will;

8   For I am the Alpha and also Omega,
    Beginning and end, and the first and the last,"
  Blest are they who do his commandments obedient,
    That they through the gates of God's city may pass.

9   Outside are dogs, sorcerers, lewd ones, and murderers,
    Idolaters, and those who love, and make lies,
  I Jesus have sent out mine angel to churches
    To testify to you these things lest ye die.

10   For I am the root and the offspring of David,
     And Israel's Shepherd and bright morning star,
   The Spirit and bride say, come without delaying,
     And let him that heareth say come near and far.

11   O let him that thirsts come, and who will draw near it,
     And drink of life's waters from fountain or brook,
   For I testify, unto all men that heareth
     The words of the prophecy of this last book.

12   If any man add to these things what is opposite,
     To him God shall add its plagues written, likewise,
   If any man take from the words of this prophecy,
     God shall take his part from that book of life.

13   He who testifieth these things, saith, " I surely
     Come quickly, to give every man his reward.
   The grace of our Lord Jesus Christ now be with you,
     Amen! and Amen! evermore with you all.

ROMANS.

CHAPTER V.

1   Ye being justified by faith,
     Have peace with God through Jesus Christ,
   By whom we have through faith that grace,
     In which we joy in hope of life.

2   Our tribulations glorious prove;
     They work experience, patience, hope,
   And hope makes not ashamed for love,
     God sends us by the Holy Ghost.

3   Scarce for a good man would one die,
     Christ died for us when we had sin;
   What love for us He shewed thereby,
     That we might pass from wrath, through Him.

4 If when in sin, God sought us so,
   That He for us sent Christ to die,
   Much more if we serve Him below,
   We shall be saved by Jesus' life.

5 And now we also joy in God,
   Through Christ by Whom we have received
   The blest atonement of His blood,
   In every heart that hath believed.

6 By one man sin came in this world,
   Death came by sin and passed on all,
   For that all sinned and down were hurled,
   To death, lest one redeem their fall.

7 Before law came sin did begin,
   But not imputed without law,
   Yet death slew them that had not sinned,
   As Adam sinned first at the fall.

8 They were a type of Christ to come,
   Who suffered death for others' sin,
   But God's free gift hath not so done
   The work of grace man's soul within.

9 For if one's sin made many dead,
   Much more God's gift through grace abounds,
   Which was by one man Christ, who bled,
   And to obedience more abounds.

10 As one man's sin hath reigned to death,
   This free gift God for all prepared,
   That through it man gain righteousness
   And endless life by Christ our Lord.

11 Not as by one's sin is the gift,
   For by one's sin the whole did die,
   God's gift through grace, more sins doth lift,
   And many offenses justify.

12 If death reigned by one man's offence,
   Much more they who do grace receive,
   Through the free gift of righteousness,
   Shall reign in life by Christ believed.

13 As one's offence produced man's fall,
   'Neath condemnation all alike,
   So one's obedience raised them all,
   To justification of life.

14 If one man's disobedience made
    A world of sinners 'neath a curse,
One greater Man's obedience paid
    And made them righteous as at first.

15 God's law appeared to make sin known,
    Man without law no sin had found,
And when that law man's sin had shown
    He wept, but grace did more abound.

16 That at first sin hath reigned to death,
    So might grace reign for man's reward,
That he through righteousness might get,
    Eternal life through Christ our Lord.

CHAPTER VIII.

1 There's no condemnation to them who in Christ
    Are walking not after the flesh,
But after the law of God's Spirit of life,
    Which free'd me from sin and from death.

2 For what law could not do so weak through the flesh
    God sent Christ to do with good will,
Who for sin condemned sin in flesh and saints blest,
    That righteousness they might fulfill.

3 Those after the flesh mind the things of the flesh,
    Those after the Spirit seek grace,
The mind of the flesh feeleth guilt, fear and death,
    The spiritual mind life and peace.

4 The carnal mind enmity is against God,
    In no way made subject to law,
Who follows the flesh then cannot please the Lord,
    Who followeth God fills His call.

5 If any man have not Christ's Spirit within,
    That man is not Christ's, nor hath rest,
If Christ is in you, flesh is dead cause of sin
    Thy soul's life is in righteousness.

6 If spirit of Him Who raised Christ from the dead,
    Dwell in you, then God shall you raise,
And quicken your bodies of death, since Christ bled
    To ransom His saints from the grave.

7 We are debtors then not to live after flesh,
      For if we so live we shall die.
   If we through the Spirit do vile deeds suppress,
      We shall reign with God in the sky.

8 For all who are led by God's Spirit most dear,
      Are truly the sons of the Lord.
   Ye feel not the spirit of bondage to fear,
      But of sons adopted of God.

9 Which, Spirit, bears witness with ours that we in
      Him are sons of God, sanctified,
   And joint heirs with Christ, if we suffer with Him
      We shall be with Him glorified.

10 The sufferings of this life compare not, nor rate
      · With glory of God's belov'd sons,
    Whose earnest expectation patiently waits,
      His manifestation of sons.

11 For God made man subject to death for sin's stain,
      Not willing, but so in hope left,
    That he, through obedience, might come in again
      To freedom of God's children blest.

12 The world groans in pain, and in travail they go,
      We wait our vile body redeemed,
    The Spirit groans for our redemption also,
      And for us, with God intercedes.

13 Who searcheth all hearts, knows their spirit and mind,
      And makes intercession for saints,
    Who after His will, to obedience inclines,
      He hears all their prayers and complaints.

14 We know that all things work together for good
      To them who love God, as He called,
    According to purpose which was that men should
      Obediently worship Him, all.

15 Whom God willed to save, He did predestinate
      That they should conform to Christ's mind,
    That He might become the first-born at that rate
      Among many brethren inclined.

16 Whom God pledged to love, He did predestinate,
      That they have the mind of His son,
    For God loves the image of Christ at that rate,
      That all in that image may come.

17 Who shall get Christ's mind, God did predestinate
   That they heir all things with His Son,
That through such obedience Christ might at that rate
   Be first-born 'mong brethren to come.

18 To put on Christ's mind, God at first all men called,
   Obedient ones He justified,
Of those justified ones He glorified all,
   For that to His will they complied.

19 If God be for us, who against us can be,
   Since He gave His Son for us all,
How shall He not with Him, give us all things free,
   Who keepeth God's word cannot fall.

20 Who shall separate us from Christ's love in God?
   Not war, persecution, distress,
Nor famine, nor nakedness. peril nor sword,
   For Christ's sake we're killed, yet are blest.

21 We are more than conquerers through Christ, Who died,
   For death, life, principalities, nor powers,
Nor things present, nor things to come, depth nor hight,
   Can part us from Christ's love and power.

THE END

THE PIONEER AND HIS DAUGHTER.

BY MRS. A. J. FERGUSON.

CLARENCE DALE LEAVES HIS HOME IN VERMONT FOR THE WEST.

The lofty mount was capped with snow
  On rock and cliff, while evergreens,
With whitened branches bending low
  Upon the mountain's side were seen,
And cold and dreary was that scene
  Until the sun rose clear and bright,
When all those piles of drifts did gleam
  Like sparkling gems of living light.

Beside this lovely mount of gems
  Was seen a quiet farmer's home,
Quite full of youth and beauty then,
  Immortal gems, round his hearthstone.
From morn till night, the farmer toiled,
  To feed his little children dear ;
For small the farm and hard the soil,
  While storms or drouth, did haunt each year.

But swift the busy years flew by,
  And their first-born was twenty-one,
When quietly, yet with many sighs,
  He left them for to seek a home,
Away, far in the distant West,
  Where forests dark o'erspread the land,
On foot, alone, with scanty purse,
  A little pack, and gun in hand.

When from his home he went away,
  And many tears for him were shed,
His parents silently did pray
  For him, as farewell words were said,
That God would keep from every harm,
  Their boy, their darling, Clarence Dale,
And bring him back unto the farm,
  Both pure and good, hearty and hale.

And as he went his weary way,
  He oft looked back the mount to view,
Where he had play'd in childhood's days ;
  To all he now must bid adieu.
He thought of all the happy hours
  Once passed upon that mountain side,
Picking wild berries, and wild flowers,
  As he did wander far and wide.

And as he passed the pebbly brook,
  Where speckled beauties glided by,
He thought of his old fishing hook,
  And strings of trout once caught to fry.
Also of his dear mother's smile,
  When he did have some extra luck,
Which well repaid for weary miles
  Of travel, up and down the brook.

And as he passed the steep hill-side,
  He saw old remnants of his sled,
And thought of schoolmates who did glide
  Down to the brooklets icy bed.
And some were sleeping 'neath the snow,
  In the old church-yard on the hill,
No more of joy or grief to know.
  The place was quiet, hushed and still.

Their merry shouts he heard no more,
  Or boisterous mirth in sport and play,
Their game of ball, or strife in love,
  Had passed, forever passed away.
The brook, the grove, the old stone church,
  The pastor and the old square pew,
Where he did sit to hear him preach,
  To all he now must bid adieu !

He watched the spire 'till naught was seen,
  (As he walked up the winding way,)
But towering trees of evergreen,
  Whose tops the mountain breezes swayed.
Then far upon the winding road,
  He stopped to bid a maid good-bye,
Of love he ne'er had said a word,
  Except with language of the eye.

Although he longed to know his fate,
  And call her his own darling dear,
Yet when her lovely form he met,
  His heart was filled with chilling fear,
That she, so good and beautiful,
  Would ne'er accept his heart, and hand,
And poverty, for she full well
  Knew he had neither house or land.

And when he reached her father's door
  (Beside it stood a lofty tree,)
His fair one stood upon the floor,
  As white as ghosts are said to be,
For she had seen his pack and gun,
  And knew that he for western wilds
Was bound, sad truth to her did come,
  And banish all her cheerful smiles.

He pressed her hand within his own,
  And longed to hold it there for life,
Then quickly said, " my darling one,
  O, wilt thou sometime be my wife,
And I will earn a home for thee,
  Away, in the great fertile West,
And through untiring industry,
  Our home with plenty shall be blest."

And as he spoke her lovely face
  With blushes did the rose outvie,
Then as she faintly whispered " yes,"
  The tears stood in her downcast eye,
For well she knew that they must part,
  Perhaps on earth to meet no more.
This thought with anguish filled her heart,
  To mar the pleasure of this hour.

Then both knelt down and unto heaven
  They lifted up their hearts in pray'r,
That faith and wisdom might be given
  To guide them through this world of care;
He shook her hand, which he soon kissed,
  Then rose and quickly left her side,
And said, " you must remember this,
  I'm true to you what'er betide."

Although his eyes were wet with tears,
   To see her sadly weep for him,
Yet his fond heart was free from fears,
   As on her hand he placed his ring,
And light of heart he speeds away,
   Through swamp, and brake, and forest wild,
To find a home without delay,
   Where land was cheap and climate mild.

For tired of blustering winter storms
   Which swept o'er his New England home,
Making the fields bleak and forlorn,
   Though hiding many stumps and stones ;
And as he passed through forests green,
   The early birds did for him sing,
While his beloved Matilda Dean,
   Did daily weep and pray for him.

She feared the many savage tribes,
   Who hunted on those fertile plains,
Which did abound in deer, besides
   Wild turkey, bear and other game.
She also feared the howling wolf,
   As many times her old grandsire
Told of a fight with one in youth,
   When his old flint-lock missed its fire.

She also feared the dismal swamps,
   Around which poisonous serpents glide,
As they were pestilential spots,
   Which scatter fevers far and wide.
But undismayed did Clarence Dale,
   Press onward toward the setting sun,
Until he found a pleasant vale,
   Where a few settlers had begun,

To cut down trees, and clear the land
   Of tangled piles of logs and brush,
And with stout hearts and stronger hands,
   They built log houses 'mong the stumps,
And covered them with sticks and bark,
   To make a shelter from the storm,
No needless work, or needless art,
   Was wasted on those forest homes.

Then our young hero, Clarence Dale,
  Bought him a farm a mile or more
From those log huts, far up the vale,—
  With lofty trees 'twas covered o'er ;
And then he toiled early and late,
  To cut those lofty monarchs down.
When one did fall the earth did quake,
  And all the woods echoed the sound.

He built a cabin for his home,
  And every day e'er rise of sun,
He went off in the woods alone.
  With fishing tackle, knife and gun;
To hunt for game, for daily food
  Came from the forest, or the lake,
A lovely lake, where fish were good,
  And plenty soon his bait would take.

His fireplace was built up of stone,
  Its chimney made of mud and sticks.
By it he cooked and ate alone,
  And from a spring he took his " drink,"
He made a bunk, dry leaves and brake
  He filled it with to make a bed,
And then a bear skin he did take,
  And tan quite soft, to make a spread.

In dark and silent hours of night
  He thought of his Matilda Dean,
For she was his own heart's delight,
  And of her he did often dream ;
When sleep closed up all earthly views,
  He dreamed he saw her lovely face,
And modest eyes of heavenly blue,
  Her slender form, her graceful ways.

He also saw his mother dear,
  As once she knelt beside his bed,
And prayed that God, in future years,
  Might shower blessings on his head.
And when he rose to clasp her hand,
  Her form did vanish with his dream.
Naught met his view but the fire brand,
  Which on the hearth did faintly gleam.

And naught was heard but distant howls
    Of hungry wolves, in search of food,
And dismal hooting of the owls,
    Upon their perches in the woods.
Homesick and lonely he arose,
    And with pitch-pine he made a light,
To read his Bible, cure for woes,
    To those who trust in God aright.

And as the day began to dawn,
    And stars of heaven to disappear,
The birds began their early songs,
    Which soon his lonely heart did cheer.
Then pen and paper he did take,
    And wrote to his Matilda Dean,
About the beauties of the lake,
    And all the wonders he had seen.

When fields were cleared, and wheat all sown,
    He fastened strong his cabin door,
Then started for his childhood's home
    To see his friends so dear, once more.
Though blest thus far with health and peace,
    The dreaded dangers yet to come ;
For Indian warriors, savage chiefs,
    Were scouting round with knives and guns.

But on he traveled, homeward bound,
    Dried venison from his pack, his food.
At night he slept upon the ground,
    As inns were scarce upon the road.
His health was good, and all went well
    Until one dark and rainy night,
When savage wolves began to yell
    Around him, on both left and right.

On him they rushed with hideous bark,
    When he climbed quickly up a tree,
And through that rainy night and dark
    They fought and howled quite constantly.
Then at the dawning of the day
    Young Clarence Dale prepared his gun,
And when he fired, without delay,
    One fell, the rest did quickly run.

He waited 'till the sun arose,
　Then quickly climbed down from the tree,
And built a fire to dry his clothes,
　Which he obtained from flint and steel.
When dry, he walked through brush and brake
　Until an empty hut he found,
In it he slept, but did not wake
　Until the sun was almost down.

He waited 'till the stars did shine
　Like diamonds on the brow of night,
Then to their Author, the Divine,
　He pray'd, then traveled by their light.
The red man's huts he quickly pass'd,
　In peace and safety, on that night,
And home and friends he reached at last,
　And was received with great delight.

Though old Green mountains of Vermont
　Did frown above his humble home,
Yet dearer far was that lov'd spot,
　Than all he'd seen, while he did roam;
And as he climbed the winding road,
　That led to his Matilda dear.
He rendered thanks unto the Lord,
　For all His wondrous mercies here.

And with light heart, and buoyant step,
　He met her at the cottage door,
Then on her cheek a kiss impressed,
　With joy, to see her face once more,—
Then to his father's house they went,
　Matilda walking by his side,
For they could not be parted yet,
　As she was soon to be his bride.

His parents saw him at the gate,
　When all ran out to welcome him,
No longer could his mother wait,
　Her cup of joy filled to the brim;
And then the stormy winter flew,
　Upon the wings of northern winds.
For Clarence said he never knew
　A winter pass so quick to him.

And now his wedding day was set,
  He must prepare for moving West,
And still he loved to linger yet,
  In that old home he loved the best.
Although the place was bleak and cold,
  Yet dear to him was childhood's home,
When free from care, in times of old,
  Ere he in distant lands did roam.

And when the wedding day did come,
  His friends repaired unto the church,
To see him and Miss Dean made one,
  So to remain while here on earth.
The ceremony was soon o'er,
  When all repaired unto the feast,
Which was prepared the day before,
  Enough for each and all the guests.

Their presents were not fancy things,
  But flannel sheets made thick and warm,
And home-made linen, white and clean,
  And needed things, on a new farm.
Their goods were packed in wagon strong,
  And piled up high, whereon they sat,
The docile cattle were hitched on,
  And all the last farewells were said.

They sat upon a box of goods,
  And started on their wedding tour,
To their log cabin in the woods,
  Perhaps three hundred miles or more.—
For many days and weeks they toil'd
  Along the rough and crooked roads,
To their new farm, whose fertile soil
  Was sheltered by the ancient woods.

Then Clarence led his little wife ¦
  Into the cot he called his home,
And said, " thou darling of my life,
  Fear not oftimes to stay alone."
They bought provision on the way
  Enough to last 'till harvest time,
And when they put their things away,
  They brought their table out to dine.

While Clarence chopped, his wife did spin,
  When from her household duties free,
Of wool and flax which he brought in,
  She made clothes for her family.
And Sundays they would wend their way
  To the log school house in the vale,
For there the neighbors went to pray,
  For God to bless them without fail.

Large crops grew from the fertile soil,
  And peace and plenty did abound,
Although their hands were hard with toil,
  Yet happiness his home did crown.
Then time flew by on downy wings,
  When a young cherub did appear,
And to the parents' hearts did bring.
  Extatic joy, she was so dear.

They called her darling " Lillie Dale,"
  She was so lovely and so fair,
Yet constantly and without fail,
  She brought her mother many cares ;
And ere two happy years had flown,
  They knew she was no common child !
More like an angel she had grown,
  Or lovely flower of forest wild !

As if by instinct, knowledge came,
  And wisdom, far beyond her years;
Letters, and art, were all the same,
  Instead of tasks, they seemed to cheer ;
Her little golden sunny head,
  Was daily seen among the flowers,
Which grew beside the garden bed,
  Where woodbines made a shady bower.

A stranger came to them one day,
  And opened wide the garden gate,
And when he went another way,
  He left that little gate unshut,
And ere the mother knew 'twas done,
  Far off among the thickets wild,
Freely did roam her little one,
  A happy, 'though a poor lost child !

She played among the leaves and ferns,
   And threw small pebbles in the creek,
Until she was so tired and worn,
   That she sat down and fell asleep.
And while she's sweetly sleeping there,
   With nature's curtains round her bed,
Parents are looking everywhere,
   To find her little golden head.

When they had looked an hour or more,
   Among the brush and brambles wild,
Young Dale went to each farmer's door,
   And called for help to find his child.
Then, as the shades of night came on,
   The mother's eyes were wet with tears,
For ere another morning's dawn,
   Wild beasts might kill her child, she fear'd.

At night a torch was given to each,
   Also a small supply of food ;
Then all began a thorough search
   O'er hill and vale of the " big woods."
Before the men, went a huge dog,
   Off in the darkness, coursing round,
Until he came to a large log,
   Where he did bark, and scratch the ground.

Then Clarence said, " I'll go and see,
   Perhaps the dog has found my child."
Then from that fallen hollow tree,
   The father drew her forth and smil'd.
She said, "my pa, I was afraid
   The Indians had come after me,
You know you said you fear'd a raid
   Would be made on the whole country.

They fired three guns and blew the horn,
   That all might know that she was safe,
And by the dawning of the morn
   The mother did her child embrace.
For joy she wept, and then she smiled,
   When she her daughter did obtain,
Then said her darling little child
   Should never wander off again.

Then to her husband she did say,
  "Suppose her precious soul was lost,
Then let us teach her how to pray,
  And keep her eyes upon the cross."
The years sped on, and she became
  The wonder of the country 'round,
Her beauty, knowledge, and her form,
  A constant theme on every tongue.

And stories, mathematics, rhymes,
  The laws of nature and of grace,
Fill'd her young brain most of the time,
  And folly there could find no place.
While music, poetry and art,
  Were naught with her but common themes,
To help refine and bless her heart,
  More than earth's simple, vulgar things.

The spring with tiny buds and flowers,
  And birds, with all their varied song,
Enticed her to their shady bowers,
  Away from all this world's gay throng,
For dear to her the brooklets thread,
  Which wound along the meadow's vale,
Where modest violets hung their heads,
  While shedding fragrance on the gale.

She was dame Nature's lovely child;—
  The dearest spot to her on earth,
Her father's house, and forest wild,
  A daily source of joy and mirth—
She knew naught of the city's arts,
  Where pride, and fashion and deceit
Lay waste so many human hearts,
  And leave them sad and desolate.

She lov'd the forest wilds so well,
  That oft her parents had to go,
With her, the name of plants to tell,
  Though scores of them they did not know.
A cluster of young pines did grow,
  Not far from her dear father's cot,
And daily to that bower she'd go,
  (It was a quiet sacred spot),

To read her Bible and to pray,
  And with the birds sing happy songs ;
She longed to walk in wisdom's ways,
  With God to guide her from all wrong ;—
Her life passed like a summer dream,
  No care or sorrow did she know,
'Till Clarence said, " she's most fifteen,
  To some high school she now must go."

The cares of life must now begin,
  For she must leave the old home nest,
Learning and fame, she now must win,
  And nevermore on earth find rest.
The trunk was packed, and farewells said,
  To parents, brothers, sisters, all,
The bower of pray'r, and green wildwood,
  She left for Academic halls.

The scholars were all strange to her,
  Also their ways and foppish airs,
Homesick as death, she did aver,
  She felt while she was staying there.
Her talents, beauty, quiet grace,
  Soon waked to envy, wicked souls,
Her innocence and artless ways
  They soon began to ridicule.

Her modest speech they turned to jest,
  Which sent the blushes to her cheek,
For she'd been taught truth to respect,
  And not use slang, or vulgar speech.
Her compositions ran to ryhmes,
  The poem which she first did read,
Was a few sad and truthful lines,
  Upon the fate of Alice Mead.

LINES ON THE DEATH OF ALICE MEAD.

The Lady Alice was quite fair,
Her long thick curls of golden hair,
Hung 'round her neck of swan-like grace,
And partly veiled her lovely face.

Her eyes were of the heavenly blue,
Of violets wet with morning dew,
Her teeth like pearls from ocean's wave,
And kind and lovely all her ways.

The young and gallant Captain Wade,
Oft went to see his charming maid,
And he had won her heart, and she,
His loving bride was soon to be.

Unto her home, one snowy day,
His steeds he drove in grand array,
To take her to a New Year's ball,
On her with pride he quickly called.

That night he drank two bowls of punch,
Which proved to be two bowls too much;
He was the gayest of the gay,
And drank, and danced, 'till break of day!

His cup of pleasure did run o'er,
He never was so gay before;
The lady Alice saw his plight,
Her face was sad and pale with fright;

A drunken man did hold the reins,
To guide those steeds back home again;
And how those fiery steeds did go
Their drunken master did not know !

They soon were running fast away,
And off a bridge upset the sleigh,
There cold and dead, young Wade was found,
His dying bed the snowy ground,

The lady Alice did not know
That he was dead, for in the snow
Her frozen senseless form did lay,
Her spirit there had passed away !

—L. D.

Next composition day she read
  A wonderful strange dialogue,
Between a maiden and a bird,
  That many wondered at the song.

DIALOGUE BETWEEN A MAIDEN AND A NIGHTINGALE.

Maid—"O, nightingale, please always stay,
 Within my bower, and sing thy lay,
 I ne'er would tire of thy sweet song,
 Though it should last my whole life long.

 When winter comes, please go with me
 Unto my home, I will feed thee,
 Thy choicest food I will prepare,
 And watch thee with untiring care!"

Bird—"Dear maid I'll not deceive thee
  When I do tell thee true,
 That you'd soon tire and leave me
  To seek for something new!

 For man is but a shadow,
  That vanisheth away,
 And he'd be tired of beauty
  That changed not every day.

 Of stars, he'd soon be weary,
  If constantly they shone,
 Through clouds and storms most dreary,
  Ceaseless by night and noon!

 But stars are lost in light of day,
  Quickly do fade the flowers,
 And soon I'll cease to sing my lay
  Far in these lonely bowers.

 For when the winter storms do come,
  And drive me far away,
 In fairer climes I'll chant my song,
  Until another May."

Maid—"Farewell, dear bird, I now will say,
  I hope no fatal accident
 Will hinder your return next May,
  'Till then I'll try to be content.

     —L. Dale.

TRUE FRIENDSHIP.

●

LINES ON THE DEATH OF A FRIEND.

True friendship, solace of the soul,
Is scarcely found from pole to pole,
   In man's deceitful heart.
But when 'tis found, her cheerful light
Will help to guide us in our flight
   From sorrow's poisoned dart.

Yes, purest friendship has the power
To cheer and calm each troubled hour,
   With happiness and love,—
Sweet foretaste of the joys sublime
In yonder bright and peaceful clime,
   The bright, bright world above.

But mortals all are naught but clay,
And friends on earth will soon decay,
   Alas! how quick they're gone!
Then may we place our hopes above,
Where all the friends we dearly love,
   We'll meet beyond the tomb.

There no false friendship e'er will come,
Or dare invade the soul's sweet home,
   The happy home on high;
Where saints in sweetest friendship sing,
Loud songs to their great Friend and King,
   That echo o'er the sky.

            —L. DALE.

THE CHILDREN.

LINES TO HER MOTHER.

See the children's happy faces,
   Why are they not always so
Free from care, and sorrow's traces?
   As through life they onward go.

O the path is steep and stony,
 Which the little ones must tread,
And life's rose proves rough and thorny,
 As they pluck it from its bed !

Treat them patiently and gently,
 Make them happy while you can,
For the world will use them harshly,
 Ere they reach three score and ten ;

Young immortals in our keeping,
 As we wander here below,
And dependant on our teaching,
 For whatever they should know.

Teach them all the laws of nature,
 Temperance, and industry,
Which will make them strong and healthy,
 And through life look cheerfully.

Teach them science, truth and mercy,
 Virtue, kindness, honor bright,
For the world will try to worry
 Them off from the path of right !

Teach them good and gentle manners,
 As the Saviour once did do,
And to kindly treat all others,
 As you'd have them do by you.

Teach them to look up to heaven,
 And to keep a conscience clear,
Naught of earth to man is given,
 To sustain through every fear.

Teach the prayer the Saviour taught us,
 Lead not in temptation's way,
He who hath salvation brought us,
 Learned us thus to watch and pray.

When the last good night is spoken,
 May we meet them on that shore,
Where no ties can e'er be broken,
 Praising God forever more.
       —L. D.

THE SOLDIER'S FAREWELL.

Farewell, O, farewell to thee dear loving mother,
　Farewell, for my country is calling for me,
Farewell, dearest sister and dear loving brother,
　Stern duty now calls me from home and from thee.

That home where I passed the bright hours of my childhood,
　And gathered the wild flowers that bloomed in the vale,
Or sought for the berries that grew in the wildwood,
　Or mimicked the song of the lov'd nightingale.

Farewell, all my schoolmates, with whom I have studied,
　Through many a winter and warm summer day,
Or over the evergreen hillside have wandered,
　Or joined in some innocent sport all for play.

Now duties of camp-life and war's dreadful carnage
　Must fill all my time 'till we conquer or die,
When peace crowns our efforts, then to my home cottage,
　And dear loving friends again quickly I'll fly.

But if I should fall 'neath our star spangled banner,
　And my body upon the dread battle ground lie,
May I through God's grace meet in heaven my father,
　And all my dear friends in that home bye and bye.

　　　　　　　　　　　　　　　　　　—L. D.

CHAPTER II.

THE CONSPIRACY TO RUIN LILLIE DALE.

A certain club of gay young men
　Were talking of young Lillie Dale,
" I'll bet my watch," said one of them,
　" That she can ne'er be led astray."
I'll bet my watch," said Harry Gay,
　(A self-sufficient, wealthy youth,)
" That I can lead that girl astray
　From virtue, innocence and truth."

And nearly all of that gay throng
  Bet on the side of Harry Gay,
Watches and money were laid down,
  While obscene jokes some one would say.
Young Harry had three months of time
  To finish up his dreadful game ;
Those on his side did soon combine
  To ruin gentle Lillie Dale.

On Sabbath eve, to church he'd go,
Because Miss Lillie went there too,
Almost a saint, he did appear
To her lone heart, and without fear,
She walked with him safe home each night,
As if he was her heart's delight.
At last his time was almost gone,
And still his bet he had not won.

But the last night he soon did tell
How he did love her very well,
She slily looked up to his eyes
And to her sad and great surprise,
She saw a serpent glitter there !
Which filled her heart with sad despair,
And then he long and vainly tried
To steal her virtue, woman's pride.

She looked to heaven, and then did pray,
" Lord, keep me safe in virtue's way."
Then she was blest with faith and strength,
And courage to reject his wealth,
And offers base, in friendship's guise,
And all arts he could devise ;
Then she arose and ope'd the door,
And said to him, " please nevermore

Insult me by your presence here,—
And now I pray soon disappear
Out of my sight, I long to be
Free from your baleful company."
Dumb with amazement, there he stood !
At last he said he hoped she would
Forgive his folly and revoke
His sentence.   Then she quickly spoke,

"I can forgive, perhaps forget,
But now you must remember yet,
'Tis not as bad to rob of gold,
As innocence from artless souls.
So confidence, when once 'tis lost,
Is hard to gain at any cost,
And now look up to God and live
Man penitent, He will forgive."

Then Harry said, " to win your heart,
I used all vile and wicked arts,
Instead, I now have lost my own,
My bet I also have not won."
He said, " good night," then went his way,
Wiser and better from that day.
From this, let all a warning take,
And live henceforth for virtue's sake.

CHAPTER III.

MISS DALE LEAVES SCHOOL AND RETURNS HOME.

Miss Dale learned all the books required,
    On science, music, and fine art,
And when her days of school expired,
    She sped for home with happy heart,—
No spot on earth like that dear home,
    Where parents, sisters, brothers dear,
Ran out to meet her when she came,
    And on her neck shed happy tears.

The grand old woods, where once she stray'd
    In childhood, now she sought once more,
And each lov'd spot, where once she play'd
    Was viewed with pleasure o'er and o'er.
But dearer than all other spots,
    That shady place, her bower of pray'r,
Here all things earthly were forgot,
    For none but God was present there.

CHAUTAUQUA LAKE IN SUMMER.

LINES TO A FRIEND ON THE BEAUTIES OF THE LAKE, NEAR HER FATHER'S

RESIDENCE, BY LILLIE DALE.

"No splendors of a gorgeous East,"
　Can with Chautauqua Lake compare,
When on each little billow's crest
　Reflected suns are sparkling there!

If you would dream of Paradise,
　Get in a boat, and swiftly glide
Over the waves, which gently rise,
　When the pale moon, and stars beside

Are shining down above your head,
　And also from beneath your feet, .
Reflected from that watery bed,
　As in a mirror most complete.

No brilliant, or enchanted scene,
　Can with this charming lake compare,
Surrounded with rich meadows green,
　Whose flowers with fragrance fill the air.

And splendid parks of native trees,
　Whose lofty tops, with verdure crown'd,
Sway gently in the summer breeze,
　A cool retreat where birds abound;

To rear their young, and sing their songs,
　Through all the long warm summer days,
Ere winter, with its snow and storms,
　Drive them from this lov'd spot away.

Here bees and humming birds abound,
　And sip the honey from the flowers,
Which with the ferns cover the ground,
　Nature's great carpet for her bowers.

This lake has lovely, quiet bays,
  Springled with water-lillies white,
Whose creamy petals softly lay,
  And bask in the warm sunshine bright.

And shining fish sport in its waves,
  Or through its crystal waters glide.
Or sleep within its rocky caves,
  Or 'neath the weeds and lillies hide.

And when the sun sets in the west,
  A view of brightest vision take,
Thousands of broken rainbows rest
  Upon the bosom of the lake!

And then look up unto the heavens.
  And see God's finger writing there,
These things unto mankind are given,
  To prove that God is everywhere.

Who sits amid the rainbow's light,
  On heaven's great and dazzling throne,
While sun and stars, and waters bright,
  Reflect from Heaven the Eternal One;
                              —L. D.

An artist from the city came
  To fish and sail upon this lake,
And through the forest hunt for game.
  And lovely views and landscapes paint.
This artist early started out,
  One morning with his line and hook.
For he had heard that speckled trout
  Were plenty up the forest brook.

Then quietly he walked along,
  So still the fish he would not scare,
And nought was heard but gayest song
  Of bird, or brooklet's murmur there.
A long and weary walk he had,
  Before he reached the forest wide,
Then he sat down in cooling shade
  Of evergreens, the brook beside.

He listened to the nightingale,
  Whose plaintive melancholy notes
Did echo o'er the shady vale,
  And silence of the woodland broke,
But soon he heard another song
  Come floating on the perfumed air.
It was no bird, but mortal tongue,
  The music of a lady fair ;

He caught a glimpse of her sweet face,
  As she stooped low to pluck a flower,
Which she placed in a tiny vase,
  Held by a child, as through the bower
She walked close by the lady's side;—
  All unobserved the artist gazed
Upon their forms, till they did glide
  Out of his sight, among the trees.

He caught a few more fish that day,
  And then returned, but not a word
Did he to any person say,
  About the lady of the woods,—
Day after day he fished for trout,
  Beneath the trees of evergreen,
The forest lady 'twas he sought,
  Yet she was nowhere to be seen.

At last a hunting he did go
  For rabbits, so he faintly said,
All through the forest sure and slow,
  'Till he saw one, which quickly fled
Into a thicket of young pines,
  Which grew out in a farmer's field,
He thought it shook the weeds and vines
  Which grew beneath those shady trees.

And with unerring aim he shot
  Among those lovely trailing plants,
And when he ran unto the spot,
  He saw a sight which chilled his heart.
The lady of the forest lay,
  Wounded and fainting on the ground ;—
This was her bower where she did pray
  In secret, which he now had found;

The artist saw what he had done,
    And begged forgiveness on his knees,
Which she did grant in a low tone,
    As she could hardly speak or breathe.
The ball had passed quite through her foot,
    Which had nought but a slipper on,
That he removed, then bound it up,
    With strips off from her apron torn.

She sent him to her humble home,
    Which stood not many rods away,
To tell her father he must come,
    And take her home without delay.
" My father's name is Clarence Dale,
    And mine is Lillie," she did say,
" Now what is yours?" " Tis Merlin Hale,
    My home is near the deep blue sea."

Then to her friends he quickly went,
    When called, all ran to take her home,
He told them 'twas an accident,
    Hereafter he'd let game alone.
Instead of hunting every day,
    He came to see the forest maid,
His hook and lines were put away,
    And undisturbed the fishes played.

He carried books, and fruit, and flowers,
    And pictures of some foreign scenes,
To help beguile the weary hours,
    And make the time much shorter seem.
Ah ! quickly passed those golden hours,
    For love's young dream, and beauty's bloom,
Like zephyrs bland o'er morning flowers,
    Shed all around a faint perfume.

After the summer's heat was past,
    Young Merlin Hale did linger yet,
And Lillie's wound was well at last
    Yet she had stole away his heart.
At last his parents sent for him,
    And he could now no longer stay,
He said, " good bye," but ne'er a hint
    Of his lost heart to her did say.

And when he reached his parents home
  He found they had a match in view,
A wealthy lady they had found,
  Who had both wit and beauty too :
He told his parents of his love
  For that sweet flower, young Lillie Dale,
And that no power on earth could move
  His heart from her, though friends assailed

And drove him forth into the world,
  To toil and labor for his bread ;—
His master, in the days of old,
  Had scarce a place to lay his head ;—
Then he resolved to earn a home,
  To offer with his hand and heart,
From place to place afar he roamed,
  And sold his pictures, gems of art.

About this time war was declared
  Against some savage western tribes,
Who on the settlements did raid,
  Where thinly scattered far and wide.
Heartsick and sore, young Merlin Hale,
  Enlisted with a little band,
Whose orders were to never fail,
  And drive those Indians from the land.

Then long they marched through forests damp,
  At night they slept upon the ground,
Without a fire to cheer the camp,
  For it might guide the foe around,
The captain sent off cunning scouts,
  To find the savage, or his trail,
But they returned, and without doubt,
  They said, he'd left that wooded vale.

Gay autumn leaves were scattered 'round
  Chestnuts and game were plenty there,
And fish, in numbers did abound
  In the cool waters bright and clear.
And they marched on from place to place.
  No signs of savage foe appeared,
Until one day, with hurried pace,
  The scouts returned, and said they feared

The Indians were a numerous host,
  And on the war path now had come,
And surely all would now be lost,
  Unless all quickly marched for home.
The captain said, "I came to fight,
  I've looked a long time for a foe,
And now that they have come in sight,
  I'll not return, but quickly go,

And with a trusty, faithful spy,
  Find out their strength and numbers too,
I'll win the battle, or I'll die,
  And hope my soldiers will prove true."
He chose a tall and stately youth,
  To go with him unto their camp,
'Twas Merlin Hale, a man of truth,
  And courage bold, nothing could daunt,

When darkness veiled them from the sight
  Of friends or foe, they sallied forth,
And traveled 'till they saw the light
  Of many camp fires in the North.
Behind thick trees of evergreen
  They walked around the camp that night,
And by those blazing fires were seen
  Soldiers, whose uniforms looked like

The frontier settlers; of all kinds
  And shapes and colors, they were made,
And spun and wove by female hands,
  Where fashion's power had never stray'd.
Some of the men quite busy seemed,
  Around the fires, loading their guns,
And as they gazed upon that scene,
  Young Merlin said, "I know that one

Who looks so sad with grief and woe;
  Great God, what can the matter be?
To him I now will quickly go,
  I'm sure he will remember me."
Then to the sentinel they went,
  And said, a friend, one Clarence Dale,
They wished would unto them be sent,
  For they must see him without fail.

Then as they spoke, their blankets fell,
　　And thus disclosed their soldiers' dress,
Which so o'erjoyed the sentinel,
　　His cheers rang through the wilderness,
And roused the sleepers in the camp,
　　Then all did shout the glad refrain,
" The army's come, it's come at last,
　　Now we'll resume our march again !"

When Clarence saw young Merlin Hale,
　　The dreadful news he feared to tell.
But then he looked so deadly pale,
　　Young Merlin knew all was not well,—
And with a sinking heart he said,
　　" My friend, how is your folks at home ?"
Clarence replied, " An Indian raid
　　Ravaged those parts, and Lillie's gone.

She taught the school down at the town,
　　And Friday night started for home,
None knew the savages were 'round,
　　Therefore she walked the road alone ;
You know far down the forest glade,
　　A thicket stands beside the road,
A purple ribbon tied her braid,
　　And there we found it in the mud !

A dreadful struggle she did make,
　　As pieces, from her apron torn,
Were trampled down, with bush and brake,
　　Along the trail they traveled on ;
We thought she'd staid to town that night,
　　And did not miss her 'till next day,
Then all these men said they would fight,
　　And rescue her without delay."

Then Merlin said, " dear Mr. Dale,
　　I love her better than my life,
And if we find her, I'll not fail
　　To ask her to become my wife."
The captain said, " I'll bring my troops,
　　And we'll go on without delay,
If you will find within these woods,
　　Some one to lead." Dale did say,

" An Indian maid, once in our woods,
 Came where our Lillie gathered flowers,
And said to her, ' bring me some food,
 I'm starving now within these bowers.'
Then Lillie ran unto her home,
 And carried her both bread and meat,
Then on a log she did sit down
 To see the dusky maiden eat.

When she arose, she said. ' farewell,
 This kindness I'll remember long,
A trapper lived with us awhile,
 Of him I learned the English tongue.'
Dear Lillie's face she ne'er forgot,
 And now she is within this place,
To guide us to that distant spot,
 Where they have carried her in haste.

She says we must protect her now,
 Her tribe, and country, she must leave,
If they hear she's a traitor squaw,
 She dare not face her nation's chief."
The captain's army then appear'd
 With weapon's burnished for the fight,
The brave backwoods-men loudly cheered,
 And all marched on, just at daylight.

The Indian maiden led the way,
 Her trusty footsteps never fail'd,
Day after day without delay,
 She kept them on the Indian's trail.
At last the Indian maiden stopped,
 And said, " halt here behind this hill,
I'm going to the chieftain's cot,
 Sly as a panther, and as still,

Be silent, let no sound disturb,
 Or echo on the silent night,
By midnight if I don't return,
 March down this brook prepared to fight."
Then through the darkness she went forth,
 Nought but the stars her steps to guide,
But she knew every winding path
 Which led up on that steep hillside !

The Indian warriors slept in peace
   Within their lodges, on that hill,
And " Eagle Eye," their daring chief,
   Saw not the foe behind the hill.
Secure within his lodge, was made
   A couch of moss, and skins of bear,
For Lillie Dale, the " forest maid,"
   On which she knelt in silent pray'r !

Curtains of skins hung round her bed,
   To shield her from the warrior's gaze,
Who guarded her, the Chief then said,
   " She'll be my bride ere many days !
I'll wash me white, and I'll put on
   My Yankee soldier's suit of blue,
I'll prove to her that I'm the son
   Of one of Spain's great Nobles, too !

My father's marriage was unknown
   To all, except three trusty friends,
My mother sent me from her home,
   With two good priests unto this land ;—
They taught me many kinds of lore,
   According to my father's plan,
To fit me for my native shore,
   When he should call me home again.

Upon a farm in one small house,
   In peace we lived until they died,
I traveled then both north and south,
   'Till taken by a savage tribe !
In English, Spanish, then in Dutch,
   Unto the Chief I did lament,
And of the last, he had heard much,
   As he'd lived near their settlement.

He then adopted me as son,
   To act as his interpreter,
When traders from the east did come,
   I talked with them and sold our fur.
The papers which my teachers left,
   To prove my noble origin,
I hid within the wilderness,
   Beneath a rock, in box of tin.

And when the tribe went out that way,
  Their furs and baskets for to sell,'
Slily from them I'd steal away,
  To read those papers in the dell.
Then white men shot my chief, who died,
  And I swore vengeance I would take,
They'd broken treaties, and had lied,
  And robbed us of our best estate!

For deeds of daring I have done,
  I soon was made their chosen chief,
The rights of each, and every one,
  I will maintain through life 'till death.
As luck would help me, I had been
  To read those papers in the wood,
When 'long the road this maiden came,
  Singing as gaily as a bird.

Love conquered me, I thought of Spain,
  And all my noble ancestry,
If she would be my bride, again
  I would return to my country,—
That lovely farm, (you don't forget
  Where once I lived,) has long been sold,
That money's drawing interest yet,
  And when I wish, I get the gold."

He said this to those standing near,
  His trusty guard, while he did rest,
The captive maiden all did hear,
  Who wakeful pray'd in her distress.
When Lillie heard the chieftain's speech,
  Her heart with quiet joy was filled,
A learned white man not long would keep
  A lady there against her will.

She sweetly slept until next morn,
  Then came to her an aged squaw,
And said, " you are a lady born,
  What will you have for breakfast now?"
She led her to another room,
  And helped her to arrange her dress,
And then her silken hair she comb'd,
  And placed wild flowers on her breast.

The chief came in and took her hand,
  And led her to a table spread
With richest food in all the land,
  "Now eat enough," to her he said,
"For after breakfast you must sing
  The tune you sang ere you were caught,
You made the woods and valleys ring
With angel music there, I thought."

"You know I cannot sing," said she,
  My heart is weary, sad and lone,
And friends are mourning now for me,
  In that dear spot, my childhood's home."
"O say not thus," the chief replied,
  "Your life and honor I'll protect,
After one month, if you decide
  My heart and hand both to reject,

I'll guide you safely to your home,
  And now, I'll sing and play my harp,
I hope your smiles, instead of frowns,
  Will cheer my lonely, loving heart."
A door he opened by his side,
  And from a shelf he took a harp,
With gold and jewels 'twas inlaid,
  And polished with superior art.

He play'd and sang old songs of Spain,
  And Scotch and English songs of love.
Like sweet and melancholy strains
  Of nightingales within a grove;
When he stopped singing, Lillie's eyes
  Were wet with tears, like morning dew,
Sparkling on flowers, ere sun doth rise,
  And snatch the pearl drops from your view.

The chief's adopted mother led
  Fair Lillie to her private room,
And lifted up a feather bed,
  And thus disclosed a large flat stone.
The chief then moved that stone away,
  Beneath it there, a hole was found,
Down some rough steps he led the way,
  To some large rooms beneath the ground!

The woman old, then touched a spring
  Beside the wall, when open flew
A door, through which they entered in
  A room, where splendor met their view !
Upon a table stood a lamp,
  Which lighted up the wondrous room,
Its chairs and sofas, carpet, mats,
  Were such as Lillie ne'er had seen !

The chief's adopted mother said,
  " My husband was a mighty chief,
Out in that other room we hid
  Dried meat and corn away from thieves.
Much gold and silver from afar
  We did obtain, I hid it here,
This treasure I to you transfer,
  Since all are dead, my children dear.

If war should come, and you should need,
  You'll find in here a safe retreat,
For on the brooklet's side, the weeds
  Conceal an entrance quite complete !
And then to each she gave a purse
  Of gold, and then she quickly flung
'Round Lillie's neck a chain of pearls,
  And gold, inlaid with costly gems !

The chief went out, but soon returned,
  (He was a white man, dressed in style,)
Then came to Lillie, shook her hand,
  And said, " I hope to see you smile."
His paint washed off, his blanket dress
    Exchanged for such as white men wore,
He looked unlike the savage chief,
  Which she had seen an hour before.

" You need not look amazed," said he,
  " I am a Spanish noble's son,
A missionary I'm to be,
  Therefore I've learned the Indian tongue.
The Indians call me ' Eagle Eye,'
  My real name, Leon St. Clair,
I've watched you long, though in disguise,
  At home, at school, most everywhere."

They looked around, then up the stairs,
   All went some pictures for to see,
The chieftain's servant, old Navare,
   Met him, and said, " come quick with me."
They went into a room alone,
   When Navare said unto the chief,
" You know the daughter of old Cone?
   Well, she has gone, 'tis my belief

To guide an army to this camp,
   She's mad because you brought Miss Dale,
She wanted you herself, and that
   Is why she'll lead them on your trail."
St. Clair then unto him replied,
   " Please go yourself, and quickly, too ;
If they are near our steep hillside,
   Then soon return, and let me know.

I'll call a council, while you're gone,
   The best, and wisest of the tribe,
And be prepared, when you return,
   To do whatever they decide.

If not, send forth an agile scout
   To see if they are on our trail,
Tell him to find their numbers out,
   And if their Captain's Clarence Dale."
He called a council and explained,
   The power, and greatness of the whites,
And said, " if we our camp defend,
   And whip them now, in a fair fight,

A larger army soon will come,
   And starve us here upon this hill,
Which will soon be your final doom,
   Although you fight hard as you will,
I'd sell this land, and find a home,
   Far in the West, where you'll be free,
On all the land for game to roam,
   Where the Great Spirit leadeth thee."

The chief sat down, another rose
   And said, "our father's bones lie here,
Through summer's heat, and winter's snows,
   We've lived in safety many years ;
The Spirit Great, his will be done,
   Extermination is our fate,
Unless toward the setting sun
   We hastily do emigrate."

When he sat down, the chief arose,
   And said, "all who agree with him,
To sell this land unto your foes,
   Your wives and children quickly bring
Unto my lodge, I'll show the way,
   Where none will ever follow you ;
At sunset come without delay,
   And I will tell you what to do."

At sundown nearly all the tribe
   Stood 'round their chieftain, " Eagle Eye."
He looked at them, then said with pride,
   " Your graves, I will defend or die !
Now one by one, all follow me,"
   And down he went into the cave ;
When all were safe beneath, said he,
   " Dried meat and corn, for you I've saved,

In case of siege or famine here.
   Now each of you just take one sack,
'Twill last 'till you can hunt the deer,
   Then follow close upon my track."
He moved the stones which closed the cave,
   On the cliff's side, close to the brook,
Then traveled in its winding way,
   For to evade all foe's pursuit.

When all arrived to a safe spot,
   The chieftain said to all, "farewell,
Your future chief will be, " Black Hawk,"
   A warrior whom your foes will dread,"
Then he returned into the cave,
   And closed the entrance up secure,—
His foster mother and Miss Dale,
   Stood waiting there beside the door:

He said to them, " now go to rest,
　While I will wait my scouts' return,"
And ere the moon set in the west,
　He heard their signal bugle horn ;
He quickly ope'd the secret door,
　To let his trusty scouts come in ;—
They all sat down and eat, before
　He asked them all what they had seen.

The oldest scout did then reply,
　And said, " we've seen enough to-night,
To make you wish your eagle eye,
　Looked from some other mountain's hight ;
An army's camped behind the hill,
　Ready to fight at break of day ;
Those painted pale-faced thieves who kill'd
　The farmer's stock ; then ran away

And said, " the Indian was the thief,
　Then straightway for an army sent,
Are there beside the white man's chief,
　Describing this, our settlement ;
Now where are all our warriors brave ?
　We'll kill those twenty lying knaves,
But Lillie's father we must spare,
　For with those thieves he has no share."

St. Clair replied, " our warriors brave,
　Have left us five to fight alone ;
And if by cunning, we can't save
　Our homes, we also must be gone,
Or stand within our hollow tree ;
　And pick off every thief we can ;
Then ere they reach us, quickly flee
　Into this cave, to them unknown.

Our women we will hide in here,
　A vault secure 'tis made of stone,
And if the fight ends my career,
　Some one can show Miss Dale back home."
Then all did rest till break of day,
　The chief then all his household call'd,
And said, " come, let us kneel and pray,
　We know not who ere night may fall ;"—

When all were ready to depart,
  (The scouts looked like brave warriors bold ;—)
The chief then said, " you've got my heart
  Miss Dale, now take my purse of gold,
And if you see my face no more,
  Return unto your father's home,
My foster-mother'll ope' the door,
    And show the way, don't go alone,"—

All said, "good-bye," then quick did go,
  To watch the pathway up the hight,
And then they saw a numerous foe,
  With banners waving in the light.
The chieftain said unto his men,
  " Waste not a single shot to-day,
Those twenty thieves now cross the glen,
  Leading the army on the way."

Then to each scout he gave his glass,
  And each did single out his man,
Then as the army reached the pass,
  Five leaders fell down in the glen ;
They made a halt, and none so bold,
  But feared to cross that narrow place ;
The other fifteen said, " behold
    There's danger here for us to face !

Those Indians must have sent a spy,
  And seen that we were coming here,
They've hid behind that tree close by
  The rocky hight, where none I fear
Will ever pass without a fall.
  Let's call a council now of war,
And see who wish, among them all,
    To walk the narrow pass up there."

Among them all, none dare ascend
  The hight, except one Merlin Hale,
And Lillie's father, his dear friend,
  Who were in search of Lillie Dale.
The captain said. " 'tis certain death,
  To climb that fearful pass alone,
We'll pitch our tents here on the earth,
  Until we starve out every one,

Place sentinels around the hill,
  Let not a red man e'er escape,
We've hunters here enough to kill,
  What game we need here in the camp."—
A busy scene was in the vale,
  While some were marching round the hill,
'Twas sport for all, but Clarence Dale,
  He feared his daughter would be killed.—

The chief then said to his brave men,
  " They're fixing now to starve us quite,
But they may try the pass again,
  When darkness hides them from our sight,
And they may find some other way
  To climb the cliff, the other side,
We must watch close both night and day,
  And all our toil we must divide."

As each went 'round he stopped for food
  At the chief's lodge, above the cave,
All night one traveled through the woods
  As still and cheerless as the grave;
The hill and pass, from morn till night,
  Were watched and guarded by St. Clair,
And his old servant, who would fight
  A foe, whether a man or bear.

From night till morn the other three
  Did guard the pass, night after night,
But yet no foeman could they see
  Attempt to climb upon the hight,
'Till one whole week in quiet passed,
  Then something moved like evergreens,
Slowly along the hillside path,
  And up the hill the movement seemed.

They waited till a cloud swept past,
  Which veiled the stars and light of moon
And when they reached it, 'neath the mask,
  They found the daughter of old Cone;
Around her form branches of pine
  Were lashed, to hide her from the view,
Miss Lillie Dale she came to find,
  And said she should to her prove true,

One of the guard had lov'd this girl,
  But she was bound to have the chief,
This man then said, " I now will tell
  What has took place, so now believe,
Our honored chieftain, " Eagle Eye "
  Is not an Indian, but a white ;
And if Miss Dale his suit denies,
  He'll never take you for a wife ;

If you should see him now, you'd say
  That he's a Spanish noble true,
His Indian suit he's put away,
  And wears a soldier's suit of blue" ;—
She looked up to the other guard,
  And said, " is all that story true ?
" It is " the guardsman then replied,
  And also, I must say to you,

That you are sent here as a spy,
  I must confine you in a lodge,
In all our secrets you will pry,
  Then from us you will quickly dodge,
We'll keep you safe, in there," said he,
  Until a peace will be declared,
Then marry this fine fellow here
  And be henceforth a happy pair."

Meanwhile St. Clair on conquest bent,
  The forest lady's heart to win,
The powers which art and nature lent,
  Were faithfully improved by him ;
And when each hard day's toil was o'er
  At night, he sung, or play'd the harp,
Or read the tales of ancient love,
  Or showed his pictures of fine art.

He had a picture of her home,
  The fields, the forest, and the lake,
He painted it when oft he roamed
  Unto that spot, for her dear sake.
He said, " our tribe oft-passed your home,
  Their baskets and such things to sell,
I went with them and watched you close,
  Yet did not dare my love to tell !

The night on which they caught the spy,
  St. Clair came in and looked quite sad,
When Lillie asked the reason why,
  He said, " a vision I have had.
I think my father has been lost
  Upon the stormy ocean wide ;
He oft has said that he would cross,
  And see his son before he died.

If my grandfather had have known
  My mother was a protestant,
My father would have been undone ;
  Therefore, to this new world I was sent,
Where I'd be free to teach mankind,
  The freedom of God's holy word,
Which doth no person's conscience bind,
  But bless all who love the Lord."

" Please tell your dream," said Lillie Dale,
  " Its cause perhaps a restless mind,
Or work, perhance your health has fail'd,
  No omen bad I hope you'll find."
" I never shall forget," said he,
  " The vision was 'graved on my soul,
All night it seemed to flash to me,
  Like northern lights around the pole !

Discouraged oft with doubts and fears,
  My mind has worried much of late,
I wished to know my duty here,
  And also what my future state.
When but a child, my parents dear
  Did sacrifice me to the Lord,
And I've been taught for many years
  To teach mankind God's holy word.

Last night when stars did brightly shine,
  Like diamonds on the brow of night,
Then to their Maker the Divine,
  I pray'd that He would send me light,
And courage, for to do His will,
  Through all the changes of this life,
Through persecution, or good will,
  To ever battle for the right."

CHAPTER IV.

ST. CLAIR RELATES HIS DREAM OR VISION TO MISS DALE.

" I dreamed I saw the Son of God
Descend like lightning from a cloud,
And in a moment I was slain,
As if by lightning, without pain ;—
His chariot shone with many suns,
Which were set 'round it like bright gems,
And all the streets seemed paved with gold
On which his flaming chariot roll'd !

And on his head He wore a crown,
Which shone like thousand suns around ;
His crown of thorns no more had place,
And darkness fled before his face ;
And sun and moon were vanquished quite,
For of all heaven He was the light,
All earthly splendor was forgot,
All earthly grandeur seemed as naught.

The crowns of kings and diamonds bright,
Were scattered now far out of sight,
He stretched His wand o'er land and sea,
And said, " ye faithful come to Me."
When vast the multitude that rose
From southern climes and northern snows,
From ocean's deep, and desert's sand,
They heard the Saviour's great command !

Then as they rose from bended knee,
Each shouted, " glory, glory be
To God," who rules in heaven above,
The God of wisdom, truth, and love."—
Then angel's wings to all were given,
That each might soar unto high heav'n,
And endless glories there behold,
As onward endless ages roll.

Then as they passed before God's throne,
He gave to each a shining crown,
And said, " My kingdom is reward
Of those who trusted in My word,
And lov'd me when vile scoffers raged,
And faithful proved in every age,
Were not ashamed to own my cause,
And live obedient to my laws."

And as I passed among the throng,
He placed upon my head a crown,
And said, " rejoice forevermore,
For all your sorrows now are o'er."
Then instantly on angel's wings,
I rose above all earthly things,
And sped my way to planets far,
Which from the earth seemed but small stars.

I traveled as on beams of light
Until I reached a planet bright,
'Twas one on which I'd often gazed,
In wonder at its crimson blaze !
I did alight upon a hill,
And from its side there flowed a rill
Of nectar sweet, of which I drank,
As I reclined upon its bank.

Tall trees were waving o'er my head,
Their leaves and fruit were rosy red,
And scarlet flowers hung on each tree
Beside ripe fruit, which tempted me
To pluck and taste the mellow pulp,
Which grew within a crimson cup,
All fitted for a paradise
Of angels, free from sin and vice.

Perhaps like Eden, once on earth,
Ere sin brought woe, and pain and death.—
I made a couch of rosy flowers,
Which grew beneath those shady bowers,
Their fragrance scented cooling breeze
Of zephyrs bland, among the trees.
Then as I on my couch reclined,
I heard sweet music most sublime.

Nought on the earth could e'er compare
With this, which came from upper air,
And soon the singers came in sight,
Clad in rich robes of dazzling white,
Their words which I could understand,
Were " hallelujah to the lamb,
Who on mount Calvary was slain,
To save my soul from woe and pain."

I raised my voice, and joined the choir,
When all descended to my bower.
Then from the nectared rill each drank,
And ate ripe fruit upon it's bank,
Then we all slept till morning light,
Though darkness never veiled the night,
One or the other of her moons,
Upon the planet nightly shone.

Then I proposed a voyage to make
Around the planet, and to take
A view of all her surface grand,
If rocks, or mountains, sea or land,
Then we all walked, our wings closed down,
Like beings of the human form,
Examined plants, and rocks, and ore,
As we had done on Earth before.

We came unto a rocky glen,
Sparkling with rubies, gold and gems,
Beside the rocks there grew small trees,
Their fruit like honey of the bees.
Between the cliffs, a sparkling rill,
Came tumbling from the upper hill,
There slowly on its banks we walked,
And of the Maker's greatness talked,

Until we found a wondrous cave,
One side of it the brooklet laved,
No cave on earth did e'er compare
With this, whose diamonds, rich and rare,
Among the rocks, did shine so bright,
That we did need no other light!
It seemed a house not made with hands,
For the redeemed of other lands !

The floor was made of rubies red,
Inlaid with pearls from Ocean's bed,
And looked as if ere it was cold,
They had been dropt in molten gold,
And when we left that charming place,
No pearl or diamond did we take,
As of such things we had no need,
For all could see them when they pleased,

There all of us were dressed alike,
No envy, jealousy, or spite,
Did in a soul of us abide,
But all were free from foolish pride ;
And love did all our actions guide,
No foolish crimes had we to hide ;—
Each other's views we did respect,
No smiles, or sneers, or cruel jests

Were made of those whose ignorance,
Or teaching, had always been false ;
There all did strive to learn aright,
Old views and errors fled from sight,
And many petted faiths there fell
(Which on the earth were lov'd full well,)
To an abyss of dark despair,—
False doctrines all lay shattered there.

No troubles past, or horrid fear
Of what would be in future years,
Did e'er disturb our happiness,
Or friendships false the heart distress ;
No one did judge the other there,
Misunderstandings had no share
In that calm peace which filled each soul,
And ne'er would cease while ages roll'd,

We rested in the diamond cave,
Until the dawning of the day,
When all did go new scenes to seek
Upon a distant mountain's peak.
And from the bushes by the brook,
We picked the scarlet colored fruit,
And walked on beds of lovely flowers,
No such on earth e'er graced a bower.

Of sovereign prince, or orient king,
None e'er beheld such splendid things,
All colors, forms, and sizes, too,
To suit all tastes, there wildly grew.
We traveled on until we came
Unto a hill beside a plain,
On top there stood a temple great,
King Solomon's was nought to it !

No palaces on earth could show
Such form, and size as this, also
'Twas made of many kinds of stone,
Such on the earth there ne'er was known,
The light shone through them faint and dim,
But just enough to see within;
All shades of colors brightly shone,
And were reflected from each stone,

Brighter than any rainbow's hue,
Which on the earth mankind doth view.
Transfixed almost, we stood and gazed,
And then all sung a song of praise;
Which those within the temple heard,
Then all came forth with welcome words,
To guide us through the temple's halls,
And show the pictures on the walls.

I followed on, with many more,
Until we came to a closed door,
A word was said, then open wide,
The door was swung unto one side,
A noble couple greeted me,
Then turned and looked again to see,
When both exclaimed, "My son I view,
Thank God that you've reached glory too."

My parents dear I did embrace,
As I gazed on each happy face;
They said my portrait was received
Before they died, and both were pleased,
I had so much like father grown,
They said they knew I was their own.
My mother looked on me with joy,
And said, "My dear, my darling boy,

Now persecution we'll not fear,
For naught can e'er molest us here;
As we think best we worship God,
And none molests or makes afraid."
Then I was led with them away,
To one vast room, without delay,
Where thousands sung and praised the Lord,
Who had redeemed them with his blood.

O blessed vision, in that crowd,
A saint did sing so sweet and loud,
To see his face, I looked around,
"Twas my old tutor I had found;
With joy and love he greeted me,
And said, "I'm glad you now are free
From sin, and sorrow, doubt and care,
And all the world's delusive snares;

I preached God's word, and now rejoice,
That I once bore the Saviour's cross."
And as we talked a shout arose,
Which echoed through the space enclosed,
A soul on earth had been forgiven,
Therefore a shout arose in heaven;—
No envy there, or discontent,
Because a soul on earth repents.

I wished to view the landscape o'er,
And visit with my friends once more,
Parents and teacher with me went,
To view that wondrous continent.—
We came unto a sea of glass,
Our forms reflected, as we passed,
From its smooth surface clear and bright,
Like some vast mirror in the light.

About its wonders we did talk,
As on the surface we all walked,
Until we reached the farther shore;
A mountain vast there stood before
Our wondering eyes, it was so high,
To reach the top we had to fly;
It rose full twenty miles in height,
Yet we all reached the top that night.

And as we forward did advance,
A level plain of vast expanse,
Was spread before us, and the view
Filled us with joy and wonder too !
We looked to earth, it shone as bright
As any planet in our sight,
I longed to view its surface o'er,
Through telescopes of extra power.

We reached a lofty tower at last,
Of lenses made, all polished glass,
A space there was to walk between,
And through that glass, vast sights were seen,
They magnified like telescopes,
And brought the stars and planets close,
Unto our view, majestic sight,
Which struck us speechless with delight !

Around our sun, bright meteors roll'd,
Their numbers vast, could not be told,
No telescope made on the earth,
Would e'er to man their light bring forth.
I watched them till my eyes grew dim;
My heart was fill'd with love to Him,
Who made that vast stupendous light,
To bless vast worlds with day and night.

The " milky way" I turned to view,
And wonders great I saw there too,
Thousands of suns appeared in sight,
Which had before seemed but faint light,
And all that " milky way" so white,
Resolved to suns as dazzling bright,
As that which shines on man by day,
With sparkling and effulgent rays ;

And as I looked an angel came
And stood by me, his eyes like flame,
He said, "What more you wish to know ?
I'll lead you where you wish to go."
I did reply, I wish to see
A man who once lived near to me
Upon the earth, who cursing died
While he was drunk, lost in the tide ;

Ere he had sense to lift a pray'r
For pardon, death o'ertook him there.
"Then follow me," he said, and flew,
His flashing wings I kept in view,
Until we reached the mounts and vales
Of the earth's moon, where rocks prevail'd,
And hurricanes, and dreadful storms
Swept o'er its face from night till morn.

There red hot lava ceaseless flowed
From craters, where deep thunders roar'd,
And darkness overhead was cast,
By clouds of lava, smoke, and dust,
While ceaseless earthquake's rumbling sound,
Fill'd all with fear, that the whole ground
Might rise or sink, no one knew where,
And quarrels rose about it there !

All hearts were fill'd with dread and care,
And rocks and mountains, in despair
Were call'd, to hide them from the face
Of God, whose mercy and whose grave,
Had been despised, rejected, scorn'd,
With self-conceit, which needed none
To pardon, or forgive their sins,
The Saviour therefore not their King.

We travel'd on, until at last,
We came unto a cavern vast,
Disputes and cursing from it rose,
Which ended oft in fearful blows;
Sufferings of guilt, and dark despair,
Fill'd every soul who dwelt in there !
We pushed our way among the crowd,
Until we came to one who bowed,

And said, "on earth I did abuse
God's servants, and did harshly use
All those who warn'd me of my crimes,
And bade me flee God's wrath in time ;
I then despised God's holy word,
And laughed to scorn His servants good,
I was to proud then too repent,
And now I have my punishment."

This was the man I wished to see,
As he looked up he then knew me.
"My friend, how came you here," said he;
"On earth you warned me oft to flee
The wrath to come, and to repent,
But your advice I did reject;
I hoped there was no God above,
To whom I owed my life and love."

I said, "I came to visit you,—
This angel led me here to view
The woe, and danger, I've escaped,
Through faith, repentance, and God's grace."
He said, "send angels now in haste,
And warn my brothers of this place,
May they repent ere 'tis too late,
And be forgiv'n for Jesus' sake.

Remorse and anguish, grief and shame,
Will haunt me till the judgment day,
When God, with unquenchable flame,
Will take Eternal Life away.
For in the perfect heav'n above
None will exist who do not love,
And glorify the God of life,
Where peace will reign, unmixed with strife."

Then as he spoke, a crowd rushed past,
With howls like fiercest tempest's blast,
War was declared, and all must fight,
To gratify their rage and spite!
That scene of strife we quickly left,
For one of everlasting rest;
And as we left that frightful shore,
Where envy, strife and malice pour'd

A flood of torment on each soul,
Who'd been through life by them controll'd
We saw a troop of angels bright,
Ascending to our home of light,
Where peace doth reign forevermore,
And as we reached that happy shore,
A shout arose which shook the heavens,
Of praise to God for sins forgiven!"

                        [End of the vision.

CHAPTER V.

" Then I awoke, my vision fled,
  But left a happy memory,
My doubts and fears are all dispell'd,
  For hope has gain'd the victory :—
This savage warfare soon must cease,
  For earthly things are naught but dross,
I've listed with the prince of peace,
  To fight hereafter 'neath His cross !"

Then just before the morning dawned,
  The camps were still and hushed below,
The chief's main guard then marched along,
  When he advised them what to do,
" The Indians all gave their consent,
  The night before they went away,
To sell this land to government,
  And guns and blankets take for pay.

I'll dress myself as ' Eagle Eye,'
  Well known as chief among this tribe,
What land belongs to you and I,
  We will not sell, but we'll divide.
I'll make a bargain, 'twill be strong,
  Three thousand acres of this land,
To us and heirs it will belong,
  And no one dare molest us, then.

Leave off your savage names and dress,
  To live like whites, we must prepare,
A Christain name you must possess,
  My real one is Leon St. Clair."
He then went down into a cave,
  His Indian suit was in a pack,
Which he took up, and then he came,
  Through the low door into the creek.

Naught but the stars shone o'er his head,
　And 'neath the trees 'twas dark and still,
And no one heard his stealthy tread,
　As he passed by the sentinel!
The scouts then watched the narrow pass
　Quite patiently, both day and night,
Until the army, tired at last,
　Declared they would go home, or fight.

With stones they threw some ropes around
　Some trees, which stood upon the cliff,
Then Clarence Dale they safely bound,
　And quickly drew him up the hill.
He loosed himself, let down the ropes,
　And Martin Hale they soon drew up,
And as they saw no one, they hoped
　That all might safely reach the top,

Then as one of those fifteen thieves
　Were swinging high up by the rock,
A scout came 'round behind the trees,
　And sent to him a fatal shot.
Just then he heard the signal sound,
　But ere he ran, he struck young Hale,
And left him bleeding on the ground,—
　Then loudly echoed through the vale,

The sound of guns, close by the pass,
　He hurried on, and soon did see
The army rushing up quite fast,
　Just as he reached the hollow tree,—
The scouts had loaded twenty guns,
　And their flint-locks were all prepared,
Which they soon fired, then every one
　Of all those troops soon disappeared. '

'The scouts then watched for them some time,
　And loaded all their guns again,
When one of them a tree did climb,
　And saw the army down the glen.
Then two went back unto the place
　Where one had wounded Merlin Hale,
There o'er him with a pale sad face
　Stood Lillie's father, Clarence Dale!

Soon as he saw these Indian scouts,
  He fell down on his bended knee,
And said, "please bring some water out,
  And I your prisoner then will be."
The water soon revived young Hale,
  And he was carried to the lodge,
Beneath which knelt fair Lillie Dale
  In secret pray'r unto her God,

They laid him on a couch of skins,
  And doctored him most faithfully,
When Clarence said unto the men,
  "I wish I could my daughter see."
The scouts replied, "your daughter's safe
  From harm, and so are both of you,
If you stay here, and keep your place,
  Your lovely daughter soon you'll view."

After a time the chief arrived,
  And quickly to the army went,
Then for the captain he enquired,
  He had a pass from government,
He was all dressed in city style,
  His paint and feathers all removed,—
None dreamed that he was "Eagle Eye,"
  The mighty chieftain of the wood!

He was conducted to the tent,
  When captain, officers, and men,
All stood around, brows sternly bent,
  Consulting what to do, and when,
To drive the Indians from their post,
  Their friends to rescue, ere they died
Of hunger, with the savage host,
  Or torture might on them be tried!

Then to the captain he did say,
  "I wish you would these papers read,
This land is mine, please move away,
  And this is my good title deed,"
The captain then read quickly there,
  Three thousand acres, hill and vale,
Belonged to one Leon St. Clair ;—
  The Indians had made a great sale!

Of all these lands, for to go West,
  And were to move without delay,
And let the buyer peaceful rest,
  After the date made on that day.
The captain then to St. Clair said,
  " Three of our friends are on that hill,
And they must to our camp be led,
  Or we will fight those Indians still."

" Be calm," St. Clair to him replied,
  " I will escort your friends safe home,
To-morrow morning be prepared
  To leave this vale to me alone."
With splendid form, both strong and tall,
  He bowed, and said to all, " good night,"
Then like a prince, their council hall
  He left and vanished from their sight.

The narrow pass he did ascend,
  And gave the signal to his scouts,
All rushed to meet their trusty friends,
  The forests echoed their glad shouts.
" What prisoners have you on the hill?
  The captain said that you had three."
" 'Tis Lillie's father and one Hale,
  A city chap, in love must be

With your fair maid, within the cave,
  The words he said when he could speak
Were, " how can I dear Lillie save?
  I am so helpless, faint and weak."
Then pale as death, turned brave St. Clair,
  He heaved a sigh, and then a groan,
Then said, " did you hear him declare
  That darling Lillie was his own !

For if he did, I'll leave this place,
  And go unto the distant West,
And pass my life teaching God's grace
  To savage tribes, and no more rest."
His servant said, " fear not, dear chief,
  Her heart was free when she came here,
If it was not, 'tis my belief,
  You'd hear more sighs, and see more tears."

" You cheer my heart," the chief replied,
 And soon I'll see her lovely face,
For her own lips must soon decide
 The color of my future fate."
He then went down into the cave,
 And met Miss Dale, who quickly smiled,
A joyful greeting also gave
 To him, which seemed quite free from guile.

He told her all that he had done,
 And that her father and one Hale
Were now confined in his own room,
 Caught by his scouts upon the hill.
" To-morrow morning I shall go
 With you and them unto your home,
And ere I leave you, I must know
 From you, what is my final doom !"

She answered not, her downcast eyes,
 Looked like blue violets wet with dew,
And on her cheek a blush did rise,
 Like roses red, we sometimes view.
The chief then said, " I now must see
 The prisoners," when she caught his hand,
And said, " please send papa to me,
 I'm longing so to see a friend."

" I'll lead you now up to his room,
 And you may stay long as you please,
The Indians have to westward gone,
 Your father and young Hale are free.
Here's a new dress I brought for you,
 You've had no change since you came here,
Please put it on, then bid adieu
 To this lone cave, and every fear."

She hastened to her prison cell,
 And dressed herself with extra care,
The necklace made of gold and pearls
 Hung 'round her graceful neck so fair.
St. Clair gazed on her lovely charms,
 As she did meet him by the stair,
Then led her to her father's arms,
 And when they met, both knelt in pray'r.

The noise awoke young Merlin Hale,
　Who slept behind a screen of furs,
Then he came out to see Miss Dale,
　Quite sure that voice belonged to her.
They both shook hands, then unto all,
　She introduced Leon St. Clair,
Who stood there watching Merlin Hale,
　With jealous look of sad despair.

St. Clair then said, "I was the chief
　Of all the Indians round this hill,
But white men coming from the east,
　Began to build their ' whiskey stills,"
And sell them whiskey for their fur,
　Which soon reduced the tribe to want,
My Bible teaching and my work,
　I feared on them would all be lost.

I bought them out and sent them West,
　And now this land belongs to me,
And here's my deed from government,
　Three thousand acres you can see.
Now all be ready at the dawn,
　And I will see you all safe home,
The army then will soon be gone,
　And leave me here in peace alone."

Then with amazement, Clarence said,
　" Are you the chieftain, ' Eagle Eye,'
On whom the whites have looked with dread,
　And talked of much by all our spies ? "
" The Indians gave that name to me,
　My real one, you just have heard,
For I was born across the sea,
　My father was of noble blood.

I was sent here with two good priests,
　To teach the heathen is my trade,
I'm needed now here in the East,
　And for God's help I long have pray'd !"
Then Clarence Dale devoutly said,
　" May God your pray'r in mercy hear,
And future glory will reward
　Your labors, if you persevere.

The army will not leave this place,
  Where they have marched, and fought, and toil'd,
Until they see the lady's face,
  And are rewarded with her smile."
Then Clarence looked far down the vale,
  The army stood prepared to march,
Waiting to see fair Lillie Dale,
  The lost, for whom they long had searched.

Then leaning on her father's arm,
  Along the ranks she walked and smiled,
And shook each soldier's toil-worn hand,
  And thanked him for his care and toil.
And when she bade them all farewell,
  She said, " please meet me on that shore,
Where we shall never cease to tell
  Of God's great goodness o'er and o'er."

Then all the hills and valleys rung
  With cheers for her, as all marched on,
Except two soldiers who did come
  And say, " they must see her safe home,"
Then each took turns beside young Hale,
  And helped him o'er the logs and brush,
And then ere night he had so fail'd
  He could not walk, and was much worse!

They pitched the tent, and made a bed
  Of blankets, and soft forest leaves,
On which to rest his aching head,
  But nought could give the patient ease.
For he called Lillie to his side,
  And said, "I have a fever got,
My senses soon will be denied,
  And death perhaps will be my lot;

Please doctor me the best you can,
  And if I die here on the way,
These papers, I put in your hand,
  Will tell you what I wish to say.
This letter send to parents dear,
  And now my trust is in the Lord,
For He has banished all my fears,
  And Heaven I hope is my reward."

The Indians had taught young St. Clair,
   The uses of each herb and plant,
And medicine he soon prepared
   From herbs, which grew near by the tent.
But ere the morning light did dawn,
   Young Hale knew nothing of his pain,
He was delirious, sense all gone.
   And often spoke Miss Lilhe's name.

The men took turns, and watched with him
   Day after day, night after night;—
While fish, and deer, each one would bring,
   And pitch-wood for to make a light.
One night it was the soldiers' turn
   To watch with Hale and care for him,
The rest were sleepy, tired and worn,
   And soon were in the land of dreams.

The soldiers' names were Jack and Jim,
   And while the rest all peaceful slept,
They went outside, and on the end
   Where Lillie slept, they cut the tent!
Between her and the rest, were hung
   Blankets, which answered for a screen,
Behind which she did sleep alone,
   And nought could wake her from her dreams!

For in her food the night before,
   Unknown to her, they placed a drug;—
Tied in a sheet her form was borne,
   Upon a pole, between them hung.
They walked along the brook awhile,
   To hide the traces of their tracks,
Then through the forest, dark and wild,
   They carried Lillie in the sack!

For moccasins, they changed their shoes,
   And every step they took with care
To not disturb the ground or leaves,
   Or break the bushes anywhere.
The moon and stars all night did shine,
   Until the dawning of the day,
They rested then for a short time,
   And then went on their weary way!

A house of logs they reached next night,
   Between two lofty wooded hills,
When Lillie 'woke pale with affright,
   And said, " where am I ? please do tell."
They told her she was free from harm,
   And that she was their darling maid,
They did adore her lovely charms,
   And that she must not be afraid.

" Two lovers now for you will care,
   Instead of Hale, who soon will die,
Forget him soon, and then prepare
   To be our mistress bye and bye."
A silent prayer to heaven she sent,
   For wisdom to direct her there ;—
Then God in mercy gave her strength,
   And hope, her sorrows all to bear.

Then unto them she did reply,
   " Please wait 'till I forget my home,
And if my lover is to die,
   Please give me time for him to mourn.
If you don't treat me with respect,
   And kindness, as I have been used,
You will forevermore regret,
   That you have brought me here with you.

Please give me now a room alone,
   Free from intruders while I stay,
Where I can weep for friends and home,
   And for my lover's soul can pray."
A door they opened to a room,
   And gave the bolt into her hand,
And said, " please now make this your home,
   We'll wait on you at your command."

They brought her supper on a plate,
   Trout from the creek all nicely broiled,
And nuts and fruits, to suit her taste,
   Which grew around the forest wild.—
She slept but little on that night,
   Part of the time she passed in pray'r,
That God would guide her steps aright,
   And through His grace protect her there.

Next morning all prepared to go,
  And follow St. Clair through the woods,
For he a shorter route did know,
  Where they could shoot wild game for food.
St. Clair assisted Merlin Hale
  Adown the steep and narrow pass,
He was so weak, and faint, and pale,
  He often had to stop and rest.

While Lillie took her father's hand,
  And followed close behind St. Clair,
And his two servants came behind,
  With tent and blankets well prepared ;
And when they reached the vale below,
  Two soldiers sat there on the ground,
Who said, " we waited here to know
  If that lost girl, was surely found.

That night the soldiers slept quite sound,
  Then 'round her room she looked with care,
And in the wall a crack she found,
  As she stood high upon a chair,
And when the morning light arose,
  And she looked out upon the ground,
She saw the thickly falling snow,
  On tree, and plant, come sifting down.

She knew if they had left a trail,
  By St. Clair it would soon be found,
But now her hopes began to fail,
  For snow did cover all the ground.
She listened long with great desire,
  At last she heard Jack say to Jim,
" If you will cook and keep the fire,
  I'll go and hunt, and food bring in.

Enough to last through longest storms,
  Also to dry in case of need,
The deer are fat, but won't be long,
  After the snow gets very deep."
Then Jack locked Lillie in her room,
  And in his pocket placed the key,
Then he was sure while he was gone,
  That she would have no chance to flee.

She pray'd that God would give her faith,
　And change the hearts of Jack and Jim,
That they might take her from that place,
　To her dear friends and home again,
As Jim went out and in for wood,
　He often listened to her pray'r,
And wished himself one-half as good
　As she, who was his prisoner there.

That night young Jack had shot a deer,
　And on a hand-sled brought it home,
They skinned it by the log heap fire,
　Then cut the steak all from the bone.
Day after day Jack went to hunt,
　Or fish beside the little stream,
Which was quite full of speckled trout,
　They made a dish fit for a queen.

The day before Jim's turn to hunt,
　He told Miss Dale what he would do,
He'd try to make Jack give her up,
　And take her home and quickly too.
She listened nearly half that night,
　To hear what Jack to Jim would say,
But he was bound that he would fight,
　Ere he would let her get away!

She also heard Jim say to Jack,
　" We've done a mean and wicked thing,
We better carry Lillie back,
　And ask God's pardon for our sins.
All day I've heard her weep and pray,
　That God would help her in distress,
And turn our hearts in wisdom's way,
　And lead her from this wilderness."

Then unto him did Jack reply,
　" To-morrow morning you may hunt,
I care not for her tears and cries,
　My bride she shall be in one month."
Jack was the strongest and Jim said ,
　" Do as you please, I'll say no more,
The curse will not be on my head,
　I am forgiven from this hour."

Next morning Jim took down his gun,
  And said, " I'll hunt on the East hill,
If I fire twice, then quickly come,
  For you may know a deer I've kill'd.
Jim had been gone but a short time,
  When Jack went out but soon came back,
Then Lillie on a chair did climb,
  And saw him with a poisonous plant.

Then in a basin from the shelf
  He steeped it well, before the fire,
Then hid it where none but himself,
  Could find it, which was his desire.
At last resounding through the vale,
  She heard Jim fire his gun off twice ;
Then Jack soon hastened to his aid
  Upon the hill of snow and ice.

Disgust and horror fill'd her mind,
  She feared that he would poison Jim ;
Because he was to good inclined,
  And wished to rescue her from him !
When they came home quite late that day,
  They brought a deer between them there,
But Jack gave her no chance to say,
  To Jim, what she had seen prepared .

All night she watched, to get a chance
  To say a word to Jim alone,
When daylight came she heard Jim ask
  Jack for to bring some water soon.
He also said he was quite sick,
  And was unable to get up,
Jack took the pail and very quick,
  Went after water to the brook.

Miss Dale then told Jim what was done,
  And where the poisonous plant was hid.
He found it there, then seized his gun,
  As Jack came in, and shot him dead !
Then from his pocket snatched the key,
  And quickly opened Lillie's door,
And told her how to make some tea,
  To vomit him, then said no more !

Then a long time, to her dismay,
  Helpless he lay, and very ill,
She nursed and doctored him and pray'd
  To be resigned unto God's will.
This " Lady of the forest," fair,
  Did carry water and saw wood,
And did assume all household cares,
  And built her fires, and cooked her food.

She spread a sheet all over Jack,
  And covered him up deep in snow,
Then to the Lord she did give thanks,
  For all His wondrous mercies shown.
The cold increased, the snow was deep,
  And soon the hungry wolves came 'round,
They howled so loud she could not sleep,
  For Jack's dead body they had found !

They growled and fought until daylight,
  And when she rose up in the morn,
Nothing of Jack was left in sight,
  Except his garments soiled and torn :
Jim was some better by this time,
  But was unable to walk 'round,
He told her then in case he died,
  Which way to go to reach her home.

CHAPTER VI.

CLARENCE DALE GETS UP AND FINDS HIS DAUGHTER GONE.

When Clarence found his daughter gone,
  And stolen by those soldiers two,
His heart was sad, and so forlorn,
  He hardly knew what he should do.
St. Clair said he would find their trail,
  If they had made one anywhere.
Then after two days' search he fail'd
  To find their tracks, then in despair,

He said to Clarence, " I will go
   And take my scouts all with me, too,
And we will search both high and low,
   And all the hills and valleys through.
But first we'll take Hale to your home,
   Where with good care he will get well,
Then through the forest wild I'll roam,
   Until I find young Lillie Dale."

Then with his servant and two scouts,
   Each with a knife and pack and gun,
And compasses they started out
   On the next day, ere rise of sun.
Hale was much better, and could walk
   Slowly with Clarence towards his home.
Then of fair Lillie's worth they talked,
   And hoped and pray'd she might be found.

For weeks St. Clair then traveled on,
   His " Eagle Eye " o'er vale and hill,
He told his men to fire no guns
   When they could catch fish from the rill.
All day they waded through the snow,
   At night they built a hut of poles,
And covered it with pine wood boughs,
   Which did protect them from the cold.

One night they heard the wolves so near,
   They had not time to build a fire,
All climbed a tree, urged up by fear,
   And to the top each did aspire ;
The wolves came on, 'twas a large pack,
   And soon were howling 'round the tree,
They all had followed the men's track,
   As hungry as a wolf could be.

To climb the tree they all did try,
   At length discouraged, down the vale
They went, then soon a plaintive cry,
   Was heard, like some young infants wail !
" Was that a panther," said St. Clair,
   "Or have those wolves there found a child ;
Perhaps some one is hid down there,
   In that secluded spot, and wild !

He then climbed farther up the tree,
　It stood upon a steep hillside,
He told his men that he could see
　A light far down the creek beside!
"What shall we do?" each one did say,
　" Perhaps some one is in distress,
The wolves are howling down that way,
　As if with food they had been blest!

A scout then said, "stay here till morn,
　If we go there, 'twill be too late.
They will devour us then quite soon,
　And none be left to tell our fate."
Hungry and cold, they soon became,
　And from the tree they all climbed down,
And they soon started a big flame
　Of fire, from pitch knots they had found.

All ate, then slept, except St. Clair,
　And he sat up to guard the rest,
He could not sleep, for in despair
　He felt for her he lov'd the best.
Next morn the sun rose clear and bright,
　Then all marched off, far down the vale,
Unto the place they saw the light,
　And when they reached it, all turned pale!

For there upon the trampled snow,
　They found Jack's cap, and tattered clothes,
But where he was they did not know,
　Perhaps he had deen slain by wolves!
Behind a thicket of young pines
　There stood a house, all closed and still,
St. Clair then said, " your guns all prime,
　For we must rescue Lillie Dale."

And then he said unto his scouts,
　" What plan of action shall we take?"
Wait here until some one comes out
　Or try our skill the door to break."
The scouts then said, "out here we'll hide
　Behind these trees, till set of sun,
We then may learn who doth abide
　Within those walls, if any one."

They waited there till almost night.
  Hungry and cold, the door to view,
At last it opened, and in sight
  Came Lillie, almost white as snow !
She looked all round upon the hills,
  A water-pail was in her hand.
And then she came towards the rill
  Which ran close by the little band.

She dipped the water with a cup,
  St. Clair then said " 'tis now our time
To rescue her," then all rushed out,
  And carried her behind the pines !
She almost fainted quite away,
  " Fear not," he said, " you are safe now,
We'll carry you without delay
  Unto your home, as I have vow'd."

" Please stop a moment," then she said,
  " Go in the house, and stay to-night,
No one is there except a friend,
  You will be safe till morning light."
Then to the house all quickly went,
  And there they found Jim sick, in bed,
Then Lillie soon the table set
  With food enough for all of them. .

That evening Lillie told St. Clair
  What Jack had done to poison Jim !
Because he would protect her there,
  And wished to take her home again.
St. Clair then said, " I'll go next day,
  And find a root which will cure him,
And we will all, here with him stay
  "Till he is well, if 'tis till spring."

They hunted 'round the woods for game,
  And shot some rabbits and two deer,
While Jim was getting well again,
  And Lillie had dismissed her fears.
Warm sunny days did melt the snow,
  And left the ground in places bare,
St. Clair said, all can travel now,
  So in the morning be prepared."

Next morning each had filled his sack,
  With venison dried, and blankets too,
And all stood waiting, by the creek,
  For Lillie to prepare to go.
When she came out, she said to Jim,
  " Have you left all your gold in there,"
He said, " I have no gold within,
  All I have got is with me here."

Then she said to him, " I have found
  Beneath my room, a pot of gold !
One night while digging in the ground
  For to escape, I made a hole."
Jim said, that " Jack has robbed for years,
  I thought his gold was hid somewhere,
Keep it as a reward for fears,
  Which you have suffered while in there."

She told all to go back again,
  The gold she would divide around,
A board she pried up, with a cane,
  And there the gold was, in the ground.
She gave some unto every one,
  Then in her sack she put the rest,
And then all quickly marched for home,—
  With happy hearts, they all were blest.

The seventh day, all reached Dale's home,
  And found all well except young Hale,—
Hard toil and labor, was unknown
  To him through life, therefor he failed.
St. Clair stood by, and doctored him,
  'Till health returned, and he was well,
And in their private talks both learned
  That each did love young Lillie Dale.

Young Merlin said, " I will request
  Her to decide which of us two,
If either, she does love the best,
  And trust in God, in all we do."
When she came in, young Merlin said,
  " Dear Lillie, I have loved you long,
And now between us please decide,
  To which of us you will belong."

"I might have lov'd you once, friend Hale,
  But now too late," she then did say,
Pride is the cause, and has not failed
  To separate us here this day.
Until I knew that I was lov'd
  For my own self, and not for gold
Which I had not, and that has prov'd
  My safeguard, and I've not been sold.

" I once did love young Harry Gay,
  'Twas in my childhood, and I knew
But little of man's wiles and ways,
  Or what a girl like me should do.
But when my ruin he did seek,
  My love all turned to steadfast hate,
But since, my heart I've tried to keep
  From doubtful lovers ever safe.

But wounded long my heart did feel,
  When you left me without one word
Of love, (before I thought you true as steel.)
  But daily I pray'd to the Lord,
To keep my heart on heaven above,
  Also my feet in wisdom's way,
But if you had declared your love,
  I should have lov'd you from that day."

She gave her hand then to St. Clair,
  And said, "I hope we shall prove true,
And may our hearts in holy pray'r
  Be joined, 'till heaven our home we view."
Young Hale then to the city went,
  And preached God's word unto the poor,
His wealth and talents were all lent
  Unto the Lord, for many years.

A splendid wedding then was made,
  And to the church all did repair
To see the Lady of the Woods,
  When she was married to St. Clair.
Then to the poor for miles around,
  Fair Lillie sent a wedding cake,
A piece of gold in each was found,
  Which she put in ere it was baked.

St. Clair proposed a voyage to take,
  Across the sea, and visit Spain,
To see his father ere to late,
  As death might soon his spirit claim.
Then to his father he did write,
  And say, "I'm coming with my bride,
In three days from to-morrow's night.
  We start to cross the ocean wide."

But ere the third day had arrived,
  A letter came from Spain to him,
Saying your father has just died,
  And willed to you a box of things,
Which we have sent across the sea,
  And no one knows what it contains,
When it arrives you then will see
  What he desired you should obtain.

St. Clair gave up his voyage to Spain,
  Since his dear parents were no more,
And waited for his box, which came
  All safe and sound to his own door.
He took it up with trembling hand,
  And carried it into his room,
For his dear father once did stand
  Beside that box in his old home.

He opened it, and there on top,
  His father's ancient bible lay,
He kissed it, then he took it up,
  Twas worn with use, and dim with age.
He opened it, and from it fell
  A letter from his mother dear,
'Twas written when she knew full well
  That death to her was very near.

She said, "when toils of life are past,
  Please meet me on that happy shore,
Where Christ will conquer death at last,
  O may we meet to part no more.
Your father's portrait, and my own,
  Also my ring I send to you.
I'll write no more, for very soon
  To you and all, I'll bid adieu."

He found a will, 'twas very old,
  As he looked in the box once more.
And underneath it, sacks of gold,
  And then he counted it all o'er.
Then gold to build a house and barn,
  He gave to each one of his scouts,
He also gave to each a farm,
  Of hill and vale, where once they fought.

He then hired men to clear his land,
  And also some to build a mill,
Beside the creek which swiftly ran
  Below the pass, beside the hill.
Some of the men then went their way,
  Through forests wild to make a road,
The rest did follow the next day,
  To drive the teams which drew their load.

Another route then went St. Clair,
  To buy material for his mill ;
His bride went with him, and Navare,
  Who was his faithful servant still.
They rode on horseback, till near night
  They reached an inn, and called for rooms,
And then St. Clair prepared for fight,
  As robbers might molest him soon.

Till midnight, nought was heard below,
  Then steps were heard upon the stairs,
And suddenly a frightful blow
  Broke in the door, where stood St. Clair.
The first who entered he shot dead,
  The next who came inside the door,
Struck brave St. Clair upon the head,
  And he fell senseless to the floor.

Four robbers more came up the stairs,
  And searched his pockets through and through.
Some gold they found, but all declared
  His bride had hid the rest from view.
She threw to them her purse of gold,
  And said, " 'Take that, but let me go."
" Ah ! no, " they said, "We'll not be sold,
  We'll have your purse, and also you.".

Navare had slept out in the barn,
   On purpose for to watch their steeds,
When Lillie screamed, he was alarmed,
   And to the house he ran with speed,
But ere he reached the scene of strife,
   Two shots were fired which wounded him,
Then to the woods he ran for life,
   And in a tree top, hid from them.

He waited long, then saw a light
   Come moving down towards the creek,
And soon he saw a horrid sight,
   Which rent his soul, and blanched his cheek.
The robbers were dragging St. Clair,
   And also one of their own men,
And some had hold of their long hair,
   As if all life were out them.

Then through the creek they drew their forms,
   And disappeared beneath the bank.
Navare then waited there quite long,
   And was not seen when they went back.
He hurried then to St. Clair's friends,
   And to his trusted scouts of old,
Then with some officers and men,
   Set out to find those robbers bold.

Next night the inn, they did surround,
   And some went in to search the place,
But St. Clair's bride could not be found,
   Neither the robbers could they trace!
Navare then said, " Let's go and see
   Where they have buried young St. Clair,
We may there find his dead body,—
   His bride perhaps his fate has shar'd."

The men all follow'd on the trail,
   Where he was drawn the night before,
Until they crossed the creek, then pale
   Each one did look, for on the shore
Beneath some vines, they heard a sound,
   Muffled and low, it seemed to be,
Like some one digging in the ground,
   But yet no person could they see!

Careful they searched among the vines,
    Until they found a wall of stone,
Which had been moved within short time,
    And then all heard some person groan !
To work all went to move the wall,
    The noise seemed louder than before,
And soon for help some one did call !—
    Then all was still, they heard no more !

A hole they opened very soon,
    Into a cellar under ground,
Faint with fatigue, there in a swoon,
    Yet still alive, St. Clair was found;
All bruised and swollen, was his head,
    Water they took, and washed his face,
Then he revived, and quickly said,
    " Thank God my friends, I now feel safe.

But where is Lillie, my dear bride ?
    I do not see her here with you ! "
" She's missing," then Navare replied,
    " To look for her we all must go."
They struck a light, then looked around,
    To see what might in there be hid,
The robber chief they quickly found
    In Indian costume cold and dead !

St. Clair look'd on, then spoke at last,
    And said, " I know that cunning chief,
He's one who tried to climb the pass,
    And was one of those twenty thieves !
The night they struck me on the head,
    I knew no more 'till in the creek,
I then pretended to be dead,
    And we were buried very quick ? "

They found a chest of many things,
    Silver, and gold, and costly plate,
Watches and jewels, and gold rings,
    Which had been worn by small and great !
Then all set forth with brave St. Clair,
    To help him find his missing bride,
A great reward, he did declare
    He'd give to him who should her find,

They searched the woods, and every path,
　Which might lead to some hiding place,
Till quite discouraged, they at last
　Declared of her they'd found no trace,—
Weary and sad, with garments torn,
　They broiled their venison steak that night,—
With longing hearts, they thought of home,
　And all its pleasures and delights,

St. Clair went 'round to cheer the men,
　Though almost breaking was his heart,
When suddenly he met friend Jim,
　Who once knew all the robbers' arts,
He said, " I'll help you find your bride,
　I know the robbers' hiding place,
Please keep your men close by my side,
　For we shall have a foe to face."

He led them to a river's bank,
　There in the brush two boats were found,
They all embarked, and rowed quite fast,
　As shades of evening closed around.
The moon rose o'er the lofty trees,
　Whose shadows danced upon the waves,
And heavy laden was the breeze
　With odors, which the wild flowers gave.

Then steadily they plied each oar
　Along the crooked river's bank,
Where rocky cliffs guarded the shore,
　Like battlements beside their track.
They reached a little cove at last,
　Where Jim did safely guide the boats,
As by a tree we glided past,
　He hitched them to it, by some ropes.

Then silently all stepped on land,
　And for their orders looked to Jim,
And while they waited his command,
　They heard four guns the hill within !
Jim ran unto a hollow tree,
　A pile of swords from it he drew,
And said, " now quickly follow me,
　And use these weapons bravely too."

He opened then a secret door,
　Which led into the steep hill-side;
And there upon the bloody floor,
　Some of the robbers had just died!
The rest lay moaning, wild with pain,
　Expecting soon death's awful call,
For by each other they were slain,
　Fit ending of the robbers all!

St. Clair then said, "where is my bride!
　Please tell me quick, your end is near."
One pointed to a door, and sighed,
　"'Twas cursed whisky brought me here!"
St. Clair then searched. and found his bride,
　At prayer upon her bended knees,
She fell upon his neck and cried,
　"The Lord hath now remembered me."

The robbers had but just left me
　In here, when a dispute arose,
About who should their leader be,
　Each to the other was opposed.
They quarreled till their guns discharged,
　I heard no more, except their groans!—
The Lord has saved, and I'm not harmed,
　We'll praise his name as we go home."

Now all those twenty thieves are dead,
　Excepting Jim, who had reformed,
Then blessed peace the border had,
　And he was loved and honored long.
As escort. all went with St. Clair,
　'Till with his bride he was safe home,
A great reward he did prepare,
　And presents he did give each one.

Through life, both toiled to teach mankind
　To walk in wisdom's narrow way,
A friend in Jesus they did find,
　Who never would a soul betray.
Thus virtue triumphs at the last
　O'er all the trials of life's way,
The righteous, when earth's toil· are past
　Shall rise to Heaven's eternal day.

[THE END.]

ELRIC AND EARL.

AN ALLEGORY.

BY MRS. FERGUSON.

1 As I walked out one sunny day,
Unto the woods, not far away,
The cooling shade, and gentle breeze,
Play'd " bide and seek," among the trees.
The leaves, which once those trees adorned,
Were scattered there upon the ground,
A carpet soft they made, between
The moss and plants, of everygreen.

2 And as I slowly passed along,
I heard a lovely wood-bird's song,
Then I did wish the bird to see,
Which could produce such melody ;
I travel'd on, with hurried pace,
Expecting soon to find the place
On some green bough of lofty tree,
Where I this wondrous bird should see.

3 A little path led through these bowers,
(And on each side were lovely flowers,)
And as I on it sped along,
The music seemed to keep beyond !
This path led to a crystal fount,
Which from beneath a rock burst out,
And tired and faint from wandering,
I stopped to rest beside this spring.

4 Then from a cup of leaves I drank,
As I reclined upon the bank,
Still softly up the glen I heard
The music of that unseen bird.
And as I rested calm and still,
Two children came along the rill,
With little pails, and lines, and hooks,
To catch the fishes from the brook.

5 Then from my seat I did arise,
    And they looked up with much surprise,
    And said, they wished to find that bird,
    Whose song far up the glen they heard.
    We traveled on, with joy and glee,
    (The boys chased squirrels up the trees)
    Until a pile of thorns and brush,
    Stopped up the path in front of us.

6 On our right hand we found a path,
    Which led into the forest vast, ·
    But on the left, a road was found,
    Which seemed to lead to some great town.
    Then we debated what to do,
    Which road was best? Where should we go?
    But soon an aged man appeared,
    And said the road to left he feared,

7 Would lead us from the thing we sought,—
    Though many went that way. he thought,
    Because the road was smooth and broad,
    And had an easy downward grade,—
    The boys were called Elric and Earl.
    One said, " I wish to see the world,
    And follow after that gay throng,
    Instead of that lone wild bird's song.

8 Then Earl did say, " The song is best,
    'Twill comfort us when we need rest,
    I want that bird shut in my cage,
    'Twill help to soothe the cares of age."
    Then Elric said, " Hear *me* I pray,
    We've wandered on, for many days,
    That bird of song, we ne'er have seen,
    Among so many leaves of green;—

9 'Tis all imagination's power,
    Which makes you search it in that bower,
    There is a bird of song for all,
    And *mine* I'll seek where pleasure calls."
    " O no, do not," then spoke up Earl,
    " That bird is scarce in this vain world,
    When tired, and worn with age, and lame,
    How can you walk this road again?"

10 Then Elrie said, " See that gay throng,
With them I now shall go along,
And if you wander off alone,
On that straight path you now are on,
And get discouraged, then come back,
I'll welcome you on this broad track !"
Then Earl replied, " you'll find no bird,
Come back to me, and take my word.

11 I'll help you find your bird of song,
So when you wish, just come along."
Then Elrie passed a lady gay,
Who took his arm without delay,
And to the haunts of vice and shame,
They traveled down that road again !—
Then spake the old man unto Earl,
And said, " you've left this sinful world,

12 Think not your trials are all o'er,
For disobedience haunts the door
Of every heart upon this road,
Without a constant trust in God.
And though you try this road to keep,
You'll find rough places for your feet,
And enemies are on each side,
Who in dark corners always hide,

13 To pull or push you from the track,
Or make you wish you had turned back !
But onward press, look up to heaven,
The "bird of Paradise" is given
To those who walk this narrow way
Unto the end; and always pray
For grace and pardon, for each fault,
Which pulls you from this narrow walk.

14 Now take this Book, 'tis ever blest,
"Twill guide you to the land of rest."
Almost discouraged, Earl went on,
But soon he heard that cheerful song
Ring out upon the balmy air,
A talisman from doubt and care !
Encouraged then, he onward prest,
For hope had flown into his breast.

15 The forest which before looked dark,
     He entered now, with happy heart,
     As he looked upward, wrapped in prayer,
     The light of heaven reflected there,
     And as he joyful marched along,
     He saw some other human forms
     Walk hand in hand, along the path,
     To shield each other from the wrath

16 Of wily dragons of the wood,
     Which lay concealed, they understood,
     Among the rocks, and darksome caves,
     Beside the straight and narrow way !
     As he came near the hindmost one,
     Their leader shouted, " brother come,
     We soon shall reach that serpent's den,
     Whose business 'tis to swallow men ;

17 Especially the faint and weak,
     Who linger back beyond our reach.
     Now trust in God, the war's begun !
     I see the serpent's forked tongue,
     I see the glitter of his eye,
     I scent the charm he conquers by,
     I see his sparkling colors bright,
     As he glides o'er the rocky hight !
     This serpent is the wicked one,
     Who once rebelled against God's throne.

18 He wages now unceasing war,
     Against all goodness and God's law.
     Cling to each other, do, and dare,
     Each other's burdens for to bear ;
     And banish every slanderous tongue,
     And help the weak, you, who are strong"—
     Then Earl kept close up to the rest,
     And soon he heard loud arguments,
     And blasphemies against God's name,
     Were boldly uttered, without shame !

19 With cursing and deceitful words !
     The serpent ridiculed the Lord !
     Made sport and laughter of His law,
     (Which is man's perfect guiding star ;)

And as he once did ruin Eve,
By baseless lies, and vile deceit,
So now, each soul born on the earth,
Is tempted, for to try its worth !

20 Then all knelt down, and prayed for grace,
    To help them through that hateful place,
    Except one youth, who could not bear
    The ridicule made of him there !
    For his vain heart was full of pride,
    And soon his feet began to slide
    Down, down the rocks, besides the path,
    Until he reached the mire at last !

21 That serpent old then slimed him o'er
    With doubt, and darkness, by his power,
    And then he whispered in his ear,
    " You'll not be swallowed now, don't fear,
    If you will take these fees and bribes,
    And tempt mankind where power, and pride,
    And wrong, and tyranny, bear sway;—
    For all such work, I'll richly pay !

22 Now here's a garment you must use,
    'Twill change its color when you choose,
    And if you would deceive mankind,
    'Twill make you seem what you incline,
    A politician, or a priest,
    A saint, a sinner, or a thief!
    And now depart without delay,
    And travel on the broad highway ! "

23 Earl sadly watched that dreadful fall,
    And on the youth did loudly call,
    But 'twas too late, that serpent's grasp,
    As in a vice, held him quite fast.—
    Those who escaped, their voices raised
    Unto the Lord, in songs of praise,
    Though some were weak, and shed sad tears,
    Yet Earl said to them, " do not fear;

24 Hark ! now I hear my bird's sweet song,
    To guide us through this waste forlorn,
    Where serpents, dragons, and wild beasts,
    Are watching 'round, to make a feast

Of us, if from the path we slide,
By trusting in ourselves as guide.
Let penitence and prayer incline
Our hearts to trust in God divine."

25 Then he passed by the faint and weak,
With courage bold, the front to seek,
That he might smooth, and make more plain
The path of those who followed him ;—
Sharp thistles in the way tramped down,
And turned aside o'er-hanging thorns,
And jagged rocks, he moved with care,
Lest some weak one should stumble there.

26 Then by the leader he did stand,
And read the Book held in his hand.
It taught him virtue, wisdom, truth,
To love his Maker in his youth,
And yield obedience to his laws,
And battle for His holy cause
With evil spirits, serpents called,
Because they try to poison all !

27 Then as they quiet marched along,
Sometimes in prayer, sometimes in song,
They heard a tumult on one side,
And there they saw a lovely bride,
Who wished to reach the narrow track,
But her own husband held her back !
He said, " you'll take no pleasure there,
My future is not made of prayer,

28 I wish to show the envious world
Your beauty decked with gold and pearls."
She said to him, " no pearl outvies
The one Christ gives, pearl of great price.
He also robes his saints in white,
And crowns them all with glory bright.
All earthly ornaments seem dim,
Compared with those which Heaven brings.

29 I long have slept on beds of down,
My parents' love my life did crown.
Accomplishments of every kind
Of art, and science, filled my mind,

My form was clothed with richest robes
Of silk, and velvet, on this globe !
And song and dance, were brought to cheer
My heart, and keep my thoughts from fear.

30 But happiness cannot be bought
With gold or robes, though richly wrought,
And though your love did crown my life,
Yet I'm not happy as your wife !
For on my life I feel God's frown.
My wasted life, with fashion worn,
My idle life, no soul I bless
With work, or care, in their distress !

31 The poor and needy, I've despised,
Nor on them would I set my eyes,
Nor lift a finger to efface
Their care or sorrow, lest disgrace
Might fall on me, the child of pride ;
Therein the Lord I've crucified,
Don't hold me back, but come with me,
God will forgive both you and me !

32 Please help me to the narrow way,
For God's commands I will obey,"
The leader reached, and took her hand,
And pointed to the heavenly land,
While Earl drew up her husband dear,
Which filled her heart with joy sincere,
Then a great shout arose to heaven,
Two sinners more had been forgiven !—
While all stood firm, and peaceful there,
No enemies did even dare

33 To rush on them, from coverts dark ;
Then each one kept a watchful heart ;—
And o'er the path hung luscious fruit
(Instead of thorns,) of which they took.
The woods, so green on all sides round,
Made some forget the cross and crown,
And walking on sweet-scented flowers,
Made them forget the higher power ;

34 And deem themselves quite strong to save
From enemies, both bold and brave ;—

While resting there, without a fear,
Slily the serpent in one's ear
Did whisper of great wealth and power,
Which could be gained in one short hour ;
" While others sleep, I'll lead the way,
You can be back, ere break of day !

35 Then none will know you have been gone
Off of the track, now come along."
He followed on, and only wrote
Another's name upon a note,
And only hoped another day,
This speculation he could pay,
And in some fear he hurried back,
But could not find the narrow track !

36 He wandered round 'till broad daylight,
The sun then rose in glory bright,
Instead of flowers, and fruit, and shade,
The scorching heat beat on his head.
He found himself upon a road,
Where vile debauch and curses poured
From victims, who had been beguiled
By that old serpent, Satan's wiles !

37 Now every voice would make him start,
For fear was tugging at his heart.
His wealth and power all seemed a sham,
For peace had left this anxious man.
His speculations all had failed,
And with an inward cry he wailed,
He heard the dreaded torrents roar,
Ah fool ! he thought to wish for power.

38 Then other crimes he did commit.
To cover up the first ;—nor yet
Had he been missed upon the way,
Where all did work, and watch, and pray.
To keep the tempter from each heart,
Lest they should feel the serpent's dart ;
That serpent who once tempted Eve,
And did her foolish heart deceive !

39 And *now*, her daughters and her sons
Do hear the whisper of that tongue,

Reviling God, his word, Christ's birth,
By lies, and ridicule, and mirth,
And promises of great rewards
To those who will reject the Lord.—
At last the news did come to all,
Of their dear brother's horrid fall !

40 How officers were on his track,
Ere he had power to hurry back
To that dear path, which he had trod
In peace, and joy, and love to God.
Then all did watch with anxious care,
To keep each other from the snares
Which were set 'round them on all sides,
By that old serpent, who would glide

41 So sly around, and tempt a soul
To leave the narrow way for gold,
Or power, gained by fraud and crime,
Or aught unjust to human kind.—
But soon the tempter came to Earl,
In form, a young and lovely girl,
She sweetly smiled, and said to him,
" Why be so temperate and prim ?

42 Why not enjoy yourself while young ?
You can repent when age comes on."
He might have listened to her words,
Had not a teacher from the Lord,
Just warned him of the sad, sad fate
Of one who had put off too late,
Repentance, and his hopes of heaven,
And death, had found him unforgiven.

43 He did resist the tempter's charms.
By trusting the Almighty's arm,
Who always rescues from a fall,
Those tempted ones who on him call.
Then echoed through the wilderness,
Sweet music, which Earl's soul did bless,—
His friends then sung a song of praise,
Which cheered their soul with hope and grace.

44 And thus they traveled on awhile,
Enjoying peace and heaven's smiles ;—

While many more did join their ranks,
And for Christ's pardon they gave thanks.
But that old serpent could not bear
That peace should long reign with them there !
He sent a spy there in disguise,
Whose pretences most reached the skies !

45 Soon those most faithful felt his wrath,
He meant to hurl them from the path
With leis, and slanders, hatched in hell,
Which soon upon the doomed ones fell !
Then those who trod the great broad-way,
Stood looking towards the narrow way,
To see the righteous quickly driven
Far from the path which leads to heaven !

46 Although the battle lasted long,
And lies were spread by many tongues,
Yet God preserved the righteous there,
Who called upon his name in prayer ;—
But many names, found on church books,
Were then deceived by lies, and looks,
Which caused distrust and fear to rise,
'Gainst many hearts, who once were prized !

47 And some refused to walk along
With those whom they supposed were wrong,
And such were left to walk alone,
Exposed to every slanderous tongue !—
And some were tempted to turn back,
When they saw on the narrow track,
The forked tongue, and glittering eyes
Of that old serpent in disguise !

48 Concealed beneath fine robes of white,
Like those wore by the saints of light !
And he appeared so circumspect,
He did deceive many elect ;
Which, when Earl saw, he hurried on,
To catch the music of that song,
Which always cheered when trouble came,
Or doubts, or fears, or unjust blame.

49 Then for a while he walked alone,
And by rude thorns his flesh was torn,

As without help he pushed them back,
To make his way along the track,
There hideous vipers, self and greed,
On every side hissed in the weeds!
But antidotes for all his wounds,
In the Redeemer's love he found.

50 Then soon he saw a lady fair
Before him walk along the path.
Faith, hope, and charity, the pearls
Which did adorn this lovely girl,
And modesty, like robes of light,
Her chief adornment in his sight.
And love did soon cement their hearts,
And they did wish no more to part.

51 Then marriage made her his for life,
A patient, faithful, happy wife.
Then hand in hand they traveled through
The wilderness, where flowers now bloomed,
Until they came to one high hill,
And at the foot, a gulf was filled
With turbid water, deep and wroth,
Which they were soon obliged to cross.

52 And though both toiled, and prayed, to save,
Yet one dear child sank in the wave
Beneath the bridge, where dark and cold,
The waves of death did o'er it roll!
Their hearts were faint, and sick and sore,
Yet hope did cheer them on once more,
To meet in heaven their little one,
When all the toils of life are done.

53 Then hill on hill did upward rise,
Before their sad and weeping eyes,
Yet they pressed on without delay,
And to the Saviour daily pray'd
For strength to lead the rest to heaven,
Of those dear children God had given,
Then carefully they watched the path,
Lest that old serpent in his wrath

54 Should tempt them from the Saviour's love,
And all his mercies useless prove.—

At last they reached a mansion, where
Soft music floated on the air,
Also the sound of flying feet,
As many dancers there did meet,
It stood one side the narrow track
On which Earl traveled on quite fast.

55 In hopes his children, now quite grown,
Would pass by all without a moan.
But as those parents then did fear,
The serpent whispered in their ears—
That same old story, which was told
In Eden, in the days of old !
"Twas " disobey the Lord's command,
'Twill make you wisest in the land !

56 There's nought in there which can you harm,
If you will follow all my charms !"
In spite of all, one now must see
The folly of what ruined Eve.
For Earl got all his children past,
Except his first-born son, who asked
To stop, and hear the music there,
Then Earl went with him wrapt in pray'r.

57 And when they got among the throng,
His son was pushed from him along,
Then for some time he looked in vain,
Ere he did find his son again.
Then with some youths, about his age,
In a fist fight he was engaged !
Back in a room where those repaired,
Who wished to drink or play at cards !

58 And they were bound that he should drink
Their whisky, though he did not wish.
Then Earl unto his son did say,
" The serpent tells me every day
There is no punishment, no hell,
Where disobedient man can dwell,
But *now* I know there's *one*, I've found
So many of its imps around !

59 And if you take not their advice,
Those imps will soon yourself despise.

And persecute, and harshly use,
Because their works you do refuse !"
There was great joy when they got back
Alive, into the narrow track,
Where they felt satisfied to walk,
And of the Saviour's goodness talk.

60 At last they reached a pleasant town,
Which did invite them to sit down
And rest awhile, ere they went on,
Into the wilderness beyond ;
And as a teacher of great worth,
Was soon to preach within the church,
They all went in to hear God's word,
To strengthen them upon the road.

61 But *there* they saw the Pharisees,
And men of wealth and high degree,
With wives, and daughters, decked in gold,
And costly gems. like queens of old !
Yet many came whose voices raised
In song and pray'r, the Lord to praise,
Yet many poor, 'most tired to death,
Are tortured till their latest breath,

62 By fashion's " thumb-screws," of late years,
Now made of ridicule and sneers !
The great invention of this age,
By which successful war is waged,
By that old serpent, on the poor,
To keep them out of the church door !
Who will account for woes and crimes,
Caused by the fear of fashion's shrine ?

63 But that great preacher, Earl declared,
Established him in faith and pray'r.
His words and arguments proclaimed
That *he* was not of truth ashamed :
For Earl had worried much of late,
With doubts about his future state,
And he was tempted oft to fear
That his poor pray'r God would not hear :

64 But when he heard the preacher say,
" You are walking in the narrow way,

If you love God, his saints, his word,
And trust in the Redeemer's blood."
His joy increased, with courage bold
He did resist that tempter old,
And well he did, for he ere long,
Did need much grace, for like a throng

65 His troubles came, that serpent old
Was after lambs from his own fold!
Those darlings, which the Lord had given
Into his hands, to lead to heaven,
Therefore he'd brought them to the town
To school, that knowledge might them crown,
But that old serpent there did glide
Through narrow lanes, and streets quite wide.

66 He hid in low and lofty places,
And oft was masked by smiling faces!
Deception was his chief intent,
And therefore through the town he went!
He taught the youths lies to believe,
And those of age were oft deceived,
He drugged the consciences of men,
By flatteries of tongue and pen!

67 And ere Earl knew, or did suspect,
Some of his children had been swept
Into the vortex of despair,
By that masked serpent's charming snares!
His daughter had ran on quite fast,
She saw some roses by the path,
To gather them, she stepped one side,—
A viper then to her did glide!

68 To the form of man, he did aspire,
And he was robed in grand attire,
With graceful ways, and subtle art,
He tried to win the maiden's heart!
He whispered flat'ry in her ear,
And praised her beauty, called her dear,
Her cheeks to roses, he compared,
As he did pluck them for her there.

69 Her virtue, innocence, and truth,
Made her believe this guileful youth,

She thought him perfect, just, and good,
A lover fit for womanhood,—
Her father said to her, " beware !
I fear you'll find a serpent there
Concealed beneath that stylish garb,
Although he speaks such flattering words !

70 Keep on the narrow way my child,
Be not like Eve, who was beguiled !
I'll follow back upon his trail,
To find him out, I will not fail."
Earl traced him to a gambler's den,
Where drunkenness, and every sin,
Was practiced there, in such disguise,
None saw but the most watchful eyes.

71 Then to his daughter he did go,
O horror ! with what grief, and woe,
He saw her lover quickly snatch
Her from the straight and narrow path,
To bear her off to his vile den,
Where demons dwelt inside of men,
Whom business 'twas to waylay youth,
And keep them from the path of truth.

72 Earl looked to heaven, then sword in hand,
He followed after that vile man,—
Then long and fierce the battle raged,
(For youth did struggle there with age.)
Until God heard Earl's earnest pray'r,
And filled his foe with sad despair,
When he retreated to his den
Humbled, but yet revengeful, then

73 Earl bore his daughter to the path,
Where penitence and pray'r, at last,
Restored her mind to joy and peace,
And hopes of heaven, where trials cease.

74 Then Earl resolved to move away
Into the wilderness, and stay
Where he could watch his children dear,
And guide them on the path each year,
Unto the music of that song,
Which was not often heard among

The roar and struggle after wealth,
And fame, and fashion, sin and self !

75   When they all reached the wilderness,
His children did their sins confess,
Then flowers did bloom on every hand,
Whose odors, by the zephyrs bland
Were wafted o'er each burning brow,
Then to the Saviour's name all bowed,—
Hark ! listen to those notes so clear,
The " Bird of Paradise " they hear.

76   Then all pressed on with much ado,
Of that sweet bird to get a view,
And as they walked it did recede,
Upward, and onward, it did lead.
On angel's wings the time did fly,
While they were looking to the sky,
And louder was that music sweet,
As they ran on with willing feet,

77   Till worn at last with age and pain,
Earl said he had a view obtained,
A river there did roll before
His eyes, and on the farther shore,
He saw her glittering pinions spread,
To waft him o'er the waves of death !
Then with a shout he left the shore,
And on the path was seen no more.

78   His wife stood looking towards that home,
Where he had gone, and as she mourned,
She prayed that she might follow him
To that blest shore, where no more sin,
Or pain, or death, could e'er again
Disturb their peace, but love would reign
Forever in those mansions fair,
Which their dear father had prepared.

79   And though she tottered on the path,
And dreaded the cold waves of death,
Yet on her Saviour's arm she leans,
While all her children help sustain
Her courage, 'till the angel bore
Her spirit to the " shining shore,"

Where she received a glorious crown,
The just reward of work well done.—

80 Now unto Elric we will turn,
    And see of *him* what we can learn,
    The serpent taught him to use guile,
    By which he profited awhile.
    He was the gayest of the gay,
    As he walked down the great highway,
    And like an ox to slaughter, went
    Quite heedless of the consequence !

81 A lady traveled with him there,
    (Quite gayly dres'd, men's hearts to snare,)
    Until they reached the slaughter pen,
    Where that old serpent murders men !
    His mask removed, with visage bold,
    He crushes them beneath his folds,
    And few escape without a shield
    Of virtue, made as strong as steel.

82 Elric at last escaped alive,
    And then resolved to take a wife,—
    A wealthy one, who would restore
    Him unto fashion's ranks once more!
    At last he found one, though quite old,
    And plain, yet she had " got the gold,"—
    By love his heart was never blest,
    In anguish lone he found no rest.

83 Yet outwardly, he looked quite gay,
    But conscience smote him night and day;
    And desperate he hurried on,
    Among a drunken cursing throng,
    Into a pool called " politics,"
    To cheat the people by his tricks
    And promises to be their friend,
    But to deceive them in the end !

84 That pool was large, and did extend
    From the broad road (where he went in)
    Unto the straight and narrow way,
    Where it was clear, and light as day.
    And he did wade towards that side,
    In hopes the ship of State to guide

In safety, through the storms and shoals,
Which wrecked so many states of old.

85   But soon the mud began to fly,
As towards the center he did hie ;
And near the place where he then stood,
A serpent rose above the flood,
With fiery eyes, and forked tongue,
And unto Elric he did come,
And bade him use some great machines,
(Which went by lightning and by steam.)

86   To throw the mud on every soul,
Who tried to wade into that pool !
The voice of justice was not heard
Within that pool of slime and mud !
And that old serpent did declare,
That nought should drive him out of there,
For 'twas a place of power and might,
Where he could battle with the right.

87   And those upon the narrow way,
Were anxious for their friends away,
Lest they should sink in the abyss.
And always hear the serpent's hiss,
Instead of coming back once more
To that safe spot upon their shore,
As pure and good, as when they went
Into that pool of discontent.

88   Then Elric floundered on awhile,
With anxious heart, but outward smile ;
Then sad and weary, parched with thirst,
He drank the cup presented first,
To stupify his aching brain,
That he might not feel woe and pain !
For drunk, his sons had been brought home,
The sight he looked on with a groan.

89   He saw the serpent's poisoned fangs,
Were clinging to his children's hands,
To drag them to the ditches where,
The drunkard's crown is black despair :

90 Their souls, he knew that he had wrecked,
By his example and neglect !
Then he exclaimed. " I was a fool
To leave the narrow way, and Earl,"
Regret, then filled him with despair,
The *thought* that he had brought them there,
Those little ones which had been given
Into his arms, to lead to heaven.

91 And thousands round him struggled on,
With critic's eyes, and blatant tongues,
And savage hearts, by satan led !
Then in despair he cried, and said,
" I wish that Earl would come to me,
And help me from this place to flee,
Alone I cannot face the scorn
Of all this proud delusive throng !

92 Then with an effort of great strength,
He climb'd a rock, which rose from thence,
Beside it, was a whirlpool vast,
And that old serpent at the last
Crawled up the rocks, and cast him o'er,
Into that gulf, to rise no more !—
Regret, and sorrow, and despair,
The serpent's great reward down there !

93 His wife, in jewels and rich dress,
Stood looking on, in great distress.
Her consience filled her heart with fear,
How vain her jewels all appeared
Beside the souls, which she had lost,
Her children, wandering from the cross
Without a mother's faithful pray'r,
To guide them through this world of care !

94 She bore the name of *mother, wife*,
Yet worshiped fashion all her life,
Loved gold, and earthly mansions fair,
Instead of those which God prepares !
Now weary with her wasted years,
From the broad road she disappears,
And sinks where Elric sank before,
And on the earth is seen no more.

95 For both had walked the road which led
Where souls are filled with fear and dread,
Who have the Son of God despised,
And heeded not His warning cries,
"Straight is the gate, narrow the way,
Which leads to life and endless day ;—
But broad the road, and wide the gate,
Which leadeth to destruction great."

[THE END.]

THE LOST BOY.

BY MRS. FERGUSON.

1   " I want to go home, I want to go home "
        A little lost boy did say,
    For weary and faint, he sadly did moan,
        " O who will show me the way?"

2   " O my son come home, O my son come home,"
        Then he heard his father say,
    " For all through the wilderness I have roamed,
        While searching for you all day!"

3   And many lost boys have wandered from home,
        From the one which is far away,
    In that brightest world from which they now roam,
        And heed not the words, " don't stray."

4   And some poor children who have got no home
        On the earth, where they can stay,
    Yet they have one above, to which they roam,
        In bright mansions far away!

5   And other poor boys, who have got a home,
        Do cast its love far away !
    And know not its worth until it is gone,
        Past hope of recovery !

6   Now, has any one lost a child from home,
        Then go after it I pray,
    And bring it back, for the Holy One
        Will ask, " where's your child which stray'd ?"

7   Then bring them all home, O bring them all home
        From the wicked tempter's sway,
    And follow them up, and help them walk on
        The straight and narrow way.

8   " I want to go home, I want to go home,"
        Every sinful soul should say,
    To my Father's house, for he bids me come,
        And Jesus will show the way."

THE END.

A YOUTH IN PURSUIT OF HAPPINESS.

BY MRS. FERGUSON.

'Twas early morn, and wet with dew,
Were flowers, while opening to my view,
And wafting incense on the breeze,
Where birds were singing in the trees,
And Nature seemed to swell with praise,
And joy, beneath the sun's bright rays.

I met a youth of noble form,
As he sped o'er the dewy lawn,—
His hopes were high and lit his face,
Where disappointment had not traced,
As yet, sad lines of grief and care,
To mar his brow, so smooth and fair.

He scarcely stopped to say " good day,"
But hurried on without delay,
Nor would he heed my kind advice,
To stop awhile, but cold as ice
The look he gave, as he did say,
" I saw an angel pass this way."

And I must find her, ere the trace
Of her I love, has left this place ;
Her name is Pleasure, and I'll find
Her on this road, in a short time.
I shall be happy then ;—farewell,
If you'll not follow where she dwells."

Great sympathy for him I bore,
For I had walked that road before,
And knew the being, who had passed,
Would not an angel prove at last.
But nothing now would ope his eyes,
So perfectly was she disguised.

She wore a robe of rosy hue,
And lovely flowers all gemmed with dew,
And when our youth her form he spied,
He soon was standing at her side ;—
She led him to a gilded hall,
Where pictures graced the massive walls.

And from rare flowers, a faint perfume
Was wafted all around the room,
Where dancers with their flying feet,
Were keeping time to music sweet,
And happiness, without a care,
Did seem to bless each couple there.

The youth then with surpassing grace,
Led his fair partner through the maze
Of dances, waltzes, and the crowd
In silent adoration, bow'd :
Till tired and weary he would rest,
She said, " come take some wine, to test

Its virtue will your strength restore,
And cheer your heart forevermore !"
Still undeceived, her charming speech
Allayed his fears, and he did reach
His hand, and take the poisoned cup,
And drink her health, that was enough

To cheer his heart and fire his brain,
And tempt him oft to drink again ;—
Then in the drunkard's ditch he fell,
Forsaken by false Pleasure there !
I feared she would this youth deceive,
Therefore I went to his relief.

Yet, when he was to health restored,
A pleasure new he did adore,
He thought that this one would prove true,
And with great ardor, he pursued
Her footsteps o'er the winding way,
Which led to wealth, and castles gay,
Where she did dwell, in grand array,

Amid the wond'rous works of art,
On which proud genius set his heart,
And toiled through many weary hours,
To carve a stone, or paint a flower,
For wealth, or power, or else to gain
A niche in that great temple *Fame*.

Where also he had hoped to view
The smiles of Pleasure on him too,

And though I warned this heedless youth,
That this was vanity, not truth;
Yet he swept past with proud disdain;
To look on me he scarcely deigned:

But worked and worried every day,
To gain that castle far away,
Where Pleasure had for him in store
A crown of joy forevermore,
And thought all wisdom and all grace
Did dwell upon that lofty place.

I watched him sadly from afar,
As one would watch a falling star,
Until he reached the castle gate,
(A servant then on him did wait,)
And on his back a load he bore,
Of jewels, and much golden ore;

Which he did put in iron safes,
And many a secret hiding place.—
And with an anxious weary way,
He watched his treasures day by day,
And wandered 'round from room to room,
And hoped that happiness would come!—

And as the fleeting years went past,
He waited, till despair at last
Did on him fall, for happiness
Did never come, his soul to bless;
His gold, and grandeur, at the best,
Had proved to be nought but a jest.

He softly then, said to himself,
"I'll now buy office, with my wealth,
'Twill honor bring, then happiness
Will dwell with me, and I shall rest."
Then years he toiled for power and place,
'Till lines of care were on his face.

Then honors great did crown his brow,
Yet happiness he had not found.
For how could happiness, or peace,
Dwell where vile slanders never cease
To worry those who would be great,
In honor, or great wealth and state?

He came to me, and with a sigh,
He said, "I've searched both low and high,
And still no happiness I find,
To cheer, and calm my troubled mind :
With honors of a gaping crowd,
And things of earth, I soon am cloy'd.

Earth's pleasures are not what they seem,
Of purer joys than those, I dream.
I'll marry now, that is the thing :
A wedded life will comfort bring,
A lovely wife and children dear
Will help my lonely heart to cheer."

Away he went, his hopes were high,
That he an angel soon would find,
Whose beauty, loveliness, and grace,
Would fill his soul with perfect peace.
Then long he looked, at last he found,
A woman, with great beauty crowned.

Who did consent his bride to be,
And bring the hoped felicity,
Which he had looked for long in vain.
But found instead great care and pain,
And disappointment, and much woe,
Concealed beneath Earth's fairest show !—

At length his wedding day arrived.
In splendor like to paradise,
Then youth and beauty graced the day,
With flowers, and presents, grand array,
And good enough for any queen ;—
And happy then the bridegroom seemed.

I saw no more of him till late,
His children, grown to man's estate,
Had worried him almost to death,
Yet he had hoped they'd bring him rest.
Though many years had passed away,
He came to me, and thus did say,

" True happiness I ne'er have found,
'Tis not on earth, or neath the ground.
My hopes are blasted, all is sham.
To harass out the life of man."

I then unto the man replied,
" In selfishness it ne'er abides ;—
Work for the world, the human race,
And trust in Jesus for his grace,

Instead of man, whose will and force,
Oft changes Nature from her course,
To miracles of wonder grand,
Which nought but him can understand,
And fashion from crude ore, machines,
Of which dame Nature never dreamed.

And yet, with all his wond'rous skill,
When one poor insect has been killed,
He can't restore its life again ;
Yet oft he boasts with might quite vain,
Of his great power, and Nature's laws,
And scoffs at God, the Great First Cause.

But Christ says, " come and follow Me,
And keep all my commands, and flee
From sin, and own my holy Name,
Of such I will not be ashamed
Before my Father and His throne,
Where angels dwell in heaven, our home."

Now follow Him and he will bless,
And bring to you true happiness."
" I'll heed your words kind friend," said he,
" And don't forget to pray for me,
I see the follies of my youth,
Now lead me in the way of truth."

His heart was changed from hate to love,
To help and bless mankind he strove,
Then happiness did crown his life
With joy and peace, instead of strife.
And sinful thoughts, revenge and pride,
Which once within him did abide.

Then happily we both walked on
Together, to our heavenly home ;
We trust in Christ, and happiness.
Abides with us, to ever bless ;
His pardoning grace, forever free
Will cheer us through eternity.

THE END.

THE SAVIOUR IS WAITING.

BY MRS. FERGUSON.

The Saviour for sinners is waiting.
　And ready to forgive
All those who repent and obey Him,
　And on Him do believe.

For this Saviour is full of compassion
　For every sin-sick soul,
And he will prepare them bright mansions,
　Before His Father's throne.

There saints of all ages are singing
　Loud praises to the Lamb,
Who did suffer for sin, though sinless,
　To ransom guilty man.

Then follow Him, He will sustain you
　Through all temptations sore.
And lead you safe home to fair Canaan,
　Where trials are no more.

THE END

www.ingramcontent.com/pod-product-compliance
Lightning Source LLC
Chambersburg PA
CBHW021048030726
47496CB00006B/1737